say

what

you

think

HAVE YOU EVER WONDERED HOW BOOKS ARE MADE?

Fox & Ink Books (formerly UCLan Publishing) is an award-winning independent publisher. Based at the University of Lancashire, this Preston-based publisher teaches MA Publishing students how to become industry professionals using the content and resources from its business; students are included at every stage of the publishing process and credited for the work that they contribute.

The business doesn't just help publishing students though. Fox & Ink Books has supported the employability and real-life work skills for the University's Illustration, Acting, Translation, Animation, Photography, Film & TV students and many more. This is the beauty of books and stories; they fuel many other creative industries! The MA Publishing students are able to get involved from day one with the business and they acquire a behind-the-scenes experience of what it is like to work for a such a reputable independent.

The MA course was awarded a Times Higher Award (2018) for Innovation in the Arts, and the business was awarded Best Newcomer at the Independent Publishing Guild (2019) for the ethos of teaching publishing using a commercial publishing house. As the business continues to grow, so too does the student experience upon entering this dynamic master's course.

www.foxandinkbooks.com
www.foxandinkbooks.com/courses/
foxandink@lancashire.ac.uk

ALSO BY RACHAEL FERNANDES

The Mercury in Me

RACHAEL FERNANDES

say what you think

Fox & Ink Books

Say What You Think is a Fox & Ink Books book

First published in Great Britain in 2026 by
Fox & Ink Books
part of the University of Lancashire
Preston, PR1 2HE, UK

978-1-917894-14-2

1 3 5 7 9 10 8 6 4 2

Set in Kingfisher by Becky Chilcott.

A CIP catalogue record for this book is available from the British Library.

Printed and bound in Great Britain by Clays Ltd, Elcograf S.p.A.

Ysabelle – for believing in my writing

since we were teenagers

One

'Call It' from *The In-Between*

'THREE, TWO, ONE,' we chorus in unison, watching the timer on my laptop screen tick down.

Spotify refreshes and there it is, each greyed-out song title changing to shiny tappable white: Rose Conrad's new album, *The In-Between*.

All three of us scream. Kira grabs me. 'What are you waiting for? Let's put it on!'

I immediately press play, listening with heightened senses. It's impressive how awake I feel, considering it's midnight and it feels like I've been up forever at this point. At least Rose

Conrad released this during the summer holidays, so we could listen to it all night.

At this exclusive listening party are Kira, Faye and me. And by exclusive, I mean I didn't invite anyone else because right now are all I need are these two. We've been Rose Conrad fans since Year 7, when her first album came out. In fact, I think it's the reason we're all friends. I had a pin of her signature rose symbol on my blazer and Faye shyly asked me about it, and then Kira loudly asked me about it, and it's been the three of us ever since.

The first listen, we sit in near silence, only quickly speaking during the outros.

'Ooh, that one was good.'

'The chorus is *brutal*.'

'Oh wow, did you see she's announced a tour for this?' This is followed by more screaming.

Then on the second listen, more raptured comments.

'I think this one is about that year she spent in Paris,' says Faye.

'She mentioned it in the Vogue interview,' says Kira.

'*Your words are sharp as diamonds, but as dark as coal* is a line.'

'"Call It" as a single doesn't describe the complexity of this whole album.'

Around the fourth listen, we're all getting sleepy. I turn off the music, and we all clamber into my bed. Only-child privileges means my king-size bed can safely fit all three of us.

'You know why I love Rose Conrad?' I say. I catch a glimpse of us in the mirror next to my bed. We are certainly an ethnically diverse British collection: myself, Indian; Faye, Irish; and Kira, Ghanaian. Kira likes to call us the Neapolitan.

'Is Selena Pia, the world's biggest Rose Conrad fan, only going to give us one reason?' says Kira, yawning and nearly smacking me in the face. Okay, maybe this king-size bed doesn't work for three.

'Yeah, can you say anything about Rose Conrad without bursting into a speech?' says Faye.

I roll my eyes and continue. 'It's because every time she releases a new album, I feel like something pivotal is going to happen in my life. The last time she did, it was our GCSE year, remember? Faye, you had that thing with Eric—'

'We shall not mention his name,' says Faye, holding up her hand.

'And Mum's arthritis had just got worse, and the album really helped me through it.'

'Ahem,' says Kira.

'Oh, and Kira was really worried about not having the top GCSE result in our year,' I say, deadly seriously, and this time she hits me on purpose.

'The point,' I continue, 'is that Rose Conrad always releases an album at the moment something new is happening. And we're going into upper sixth this year. It is a big year. And this album is going to be the soundtrack to the year.'

I feel inspired and moved by my speech.

'Or you might be taking your English A level too seriously and reading into symbols that aren't there,' says Kira.

I shove her and she falls out of the bed laughing.

— ★ —

The next day, Faye leaves early as she's working in her parents' shop, so Kira and I have breakfast together.

'I've got to go around lunchtime. No binge-watching TV,' says Kira. 'There's a summer Young New Left party meet up that I want to make in London.'

'I can't believe it's nearly the end of the summer holidays and you want to spend it talking about politics. You'll be back to studying it in a couple of weeks,' I say.

'I need all of this for my uni applications,' says Kira. 'I want to be as prepared as possible. This girl ain't going to make it to Prime Minister by slacking!'

Kira is obsessed with becoming Prime Minister. Considering she's Black and a woman, the statistics aren't in her favour, but good for her. But rather than a pipe dream at eighteen, she's making it her life mission to do everything possible to get there as soon as she can. It's either genius or delusional, I can't say. Either way, it's a drive that I don't have.

'You need to start thinking about what you're going to put on your application,' says Kira. 'You don't have any extracurriculars.'

'I do cross country,' I say. 'Occasionally.' When the weather looks okay and I feel like turning up to practice. Which, with the weather in England, isn't that frequently.

'Yeah, but nothing subject-related. How are you going to show you care about what you want to study?'

'I don't even know what I want to study yet,' I say, picking at my cereal with my spoon.

'You need to sort that out too, Selena,' says Kira, pointing her spoon at me. 'Time is running out. You've got until January to do your application.'

I sigh and put my bowl in the dishwasher. I know for Kira the deadline is motivational, but for me it brings a torrent of anxiety.

'How was your listening party?' says Mum, saving us from the argument. She walks into the kitchen with a slight hobble. Everyone can tell Mum and I are related: we're both tall, slight, and have the same long faces and wide eyes. When I learnt about cloning in Year 8 Biology, I joked to Mum that it had basically happened with me because we look the same. Plus, I have no idea who my dad is, so for all I know I could have one set of genetics. Mum assured me I definitely have two.

'It is unreal,' says Kira, just as I say—

'Phenomenal, outstanding, the album is another lyrical masterpiece,' I say.

'Good to see that English A level is coming into use with your vocabulary,' says Mum, moving towards the kettle.

I get ahead of her and start making her a cup of tea. She shakes her head but goes and sits down at the dining table.

This is her first tea of the day. Of about fifteen. I don't know how she's never jittery, the amount of caffeine she consumes in tea form.

'You know we study books and write essays, not learn the thesaurus?' I say, handing her the mug.

'I know, I know.' She laughs. 'I've done my time with essays.'

Mum used to be a museum curator, back in the day, despite not going to university. She went around the world, as an archeologist's assistant, then got pregnant and moved back here and became an art dealer and sat on the board of some museums. While she was there, she long-distanced her degree and graduated when I was twelve. Then she got some joint problems, and couldn't commute into Central London any more, so now she is a programme manager for the Croydon museum. She went from working in some of the most prestigious artistic places in the world, to our hometown museum, which barely anyone visits. Even the people who work there mostly work from home.

'How's it going, Kira?' says Mum. 'What are you doing today?'

'I'm going to a Young New Left meet up,' says Kira. 'For my uni application.' She looks at me pointedly.

'And have you thought any more about your uni application?' says Mum, turning to me.

I look away. 'No.'

She sighs. 'Okay, well think about it? You can talk to me.'

And normally I do talk to Mum about everything. I know

both of us want me to go to university, but as I watch her shuffle out of the door, I wonder: how can I leave her alone here by herself, while I go away?

Two

He's so beautiful
I can't stop starin'
The boy wonder
Is this heaven?

'Boy Wonder' from
The Brink of Teenage Freedom

KIRA AND I are binge-watching *Hollingworth*. Or at least trying to – Kira keeps looking at her phone to check the time every twenty minutes.

'You know it's not suddenly going to be twelve?' I say. 'You're like Cinderella waiting for the pumpkin to come.'

'It is now basically twelve,' she says.

'Time moves at one speed.'

'Well, why do they say "time flies while you're having fun" then?'

We make eye contact and both start cackling, just as Ollie walks through the door.

People wandering in is a big no for most people, but Ollie isn't most people. One, he's been my closest friend and next-door-neighbour for the past seventeen years. I bet he's come in through the backdoor, which is usually unlocked, via the gap in our garden fence.

'How's it going?' he says.

The other thing to know about Ollie Pointer is . . . I have fallen irrevocably in love with him.

The problem is, Ollie has always been hot, as my friends have been telling me since puberty. His thick brown hair, his green eyes, a lanky body that had filled out over the summer. But because we were raised next door, almost like siblings, I never saw it.

Until six months ago, when I realised: how could I have *not* seen it before? It was like a light switch had been flipped on inside of me. My hands get clammy and it's pure electricity when we touch.

And I'm starting to hope he feels the same way too.

'Ah, Pointer,' says Kira, standing up with a bit of a swagger. 'I'm about to go to a Young New Left meet up, you know.'

'Getting it for that ol' UCAS form, Kira?' says Ollie, with a smirk.

'It's because I support the party,' says Kira, even though she literally told me she was going because of her UCAS form about two hours ago. I don't take sides here though; this is Kira and

Ollie's endless dance. They want to study similar things: Ollie, Law, Kira, Politics; and are both wildly competitive with each other, despite going to different schools. Ollie is at the boys' private school, myself and Kira at the state all-girls' grammar school.

'Have you decided where you want to apply to?' says Ollie. 'Early deadline is October.'

'I'm aware of the calendar,' says Kira. 'And I haven't made my final choices yet.' She points at me. 'Don't tell him what I'm thinking.'

'I'm not going to apply to the same places to spite you . . . where I'd undoubtedly get in,' says Ollie.

'And I am not engaging with this conversation,' says Kira, clicking her fingers. 'I'm out of here. See you later, Selena.'

Ollie laughs and sits down next to me. I shake my head, then lean against his shoulder.

'Why do you two fight so much?' I say.

'Because we're competitive.' He shrugs. 'How was the listening party?'

'Great,' I say. 'I wish you liked Rose Conrad, you could have come too.'

He shakes his head. 'It's not that I dislike her, she's not my vibe, you know? Also I'd cramp your style. Who wants a *boy* there?' he says, playfully shrugging and pushing me off his shoulder.

'Fair point, you wouldn't be there for all the pillow fights and dance routines.'

'Is that what you all do?'

'No!' I laugh. 'I'm messing with you. We just sat down and listened to the album.'

He stands up. 'Kidding aside, shall we get going?'

— ★ —

Ollie and I have started a new tradition this summer. Annie Banannie Bananas Ice Cream on the high street is doing a different flavour every week. And if you try every flavour you get a stamp on your card, and with a full card you can enter into a prize draw to win a year's supply of free ice cream.

And because Annie Banannie doesn't have a huge weekly clientele, Ollie and I have a good shot of winning. We've promised to share the ice cream between us if one of us wins.

'Welcome to Annie Bannanie.' Kristy, the dirty-blonde cashier, smiles. She does this every time, greets us as if she's never met us, even though we're in here every week. I have the feeling she doesn't want to engage with us, so it's easier pretending she doesn't remember us. She's only working here during her uni summer break, after all.

'Flavour of the week,' I say, slapping down my stamp card, like I'm a cowboy at a saloon paying for a drink.

'Make it two,' says Ollie, putting his card down next to mine.

'Only one more week to go,' says Kristy, scooping us two cones of a lilac-coloured ice cream. 'Here you are, two scoops of Lavender Dream.'

We pay up, and then leave, walking down the street, eating our ice creams.

'I can't believe we're halfway through now,' I say wistfully. 'It feels like a countdown to the end of summer . . .'

'I really want a full stamp card,' says Ollie. 'I hate things being incomplete.'

'It's only a few weeks away,' I tell him. 'You'll get the full collection soon enough. I told you before, obsessing over the stamps isn't going to make it go much faster. What do you think of this flavour?'

'Not convinced about flowers in ice cream,' says Ollie. 'I think there's a reason it's not been done before.'

'That's the point of the Annie Banannie invented flavours. Remember when they did Stilton Summer? Gross. This one I can get behind.'

Ollie laughs. 'True, I don't think I like any of these out-there flavours. Classics are classics for a reason.'

'So you're just doing this for stamps?' I tease.

'Well, also to hang out with you,' he says, looking over at me with a smile that melts me way faster than my ice cream in the sun. 'But mostly for stamps.' He grabs my arm, tugs me towards him. 'Here,' he says, rubbing his thumb on the side of my mouth. 'You've got some on your face.'

I freeze under his touch, under his spell. I have to tell him how I feel. Surely he feels the same way too?

Three

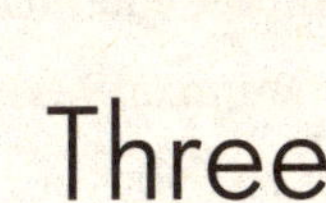

Sea-green eyes, drown me
Let me taste the salt, before it washes away
That's the memory of when
I loved you like that

'I Loved You Like That' from *Dreamers*

Selena Says: We are halfway through our last school summer. Only three weeks to go until upper sixth begins! After school it'll be uni, then it'll be the real world. No more summer holidays! This is the best time of year, but are those days numbered?

THE RESPONSE TO my Selena Says is immediate.

Bleak, messages back Kira.

Don't you normally wait until term starts before you send

these out? messages Faye. *I don't need this negative energy right now.*

I've been sending 'Selena Says' since Year 9 when I saw Briar McDonald's mum storm into school to argue with a Chemistry teacher about her child's B grade. My hot take then was you shouldn't get your parents to fight your battles for you, even if they look like they could wield a battle axe.

Kira and Faye enjoyed it so much that I've been sending them ever since.

Ollie and I are hanging out again today. I look at myself in the mirror, brushing down my sundress. I've made more of an effort than usual, wearing some light make-up, curling my hair. Ollie has seen me in all states over the years, but today there's only one way I want him to see me: romantically.

Because today, I *will* tell him how I feel.

I meet Ollie out front. Looking at our houses side by side, it is bizarre we are next-door neighbours. Half of our street is a string of semi-detached, suburban homes, of which mine is one. Then it suddenly becomes a string of, well, mansion-esque detached houses. Of which Ollie's is one.

Ollie has told me before that his house isn't a mansion, and 'it's all relative', as multiple friends of his from his fancy private school have way bigger homes than him. I guess he's got a point.

He holds up a picnic basket, the contents no doubt raided from his mum's well-stocked fridge. I swear I once saw caviar there. I've brought a blanket and garden chairs and we head off to the park around the corner.

'Can't believe we're halfway through summer,' I say, sinking into the garden chair.

'Final year of sixth form coming up,' he says, sitting down next to me and taking out the food.

'Are you looking forward to going back to Benson's? Surely they'll have some ritual sacrifice or something to round off your final year,' I tease. I take a crisp and scoop up some fancy garlic dip.

'It's a summer solstice festival at the end of the year, not a ritual sacrifice,' he says, a bit strained. 'And it's a good tradition.'

'At least you only have to do it once more now,' I say lightly. Ollie gets a bit defensive about his school. In general, he doesn't enjoy being teased.

He nods, saying nothing, and we sit in silence for a bit. I continue making my way through the crisps and garlic dip, but in my head I'm doing cartwheels about how to bring up my feelings. Do I say: *Hey, I think I like you . . .?*

No. I can't do that.

Maybe: *This feels like a date . . . because maybe it is one?*

Bad again.

If Ollie notices my internal turmoil, he doesn't say anything. He just seems to be staring out across the park; but then suddenly he turns to me. . .

'What are you most looking forward to this year?' he asks me.

I sigh inwardly, but then my answer comes immediately.

'Going to Rose Conrad's tour,' I say. 'I can't believe she's coming before Christmas! She said she wanted to tour this album as quickly as possible.'

'Of all the things that can happen in this year, and you're most looking forward to Rose Conrad's tour?' says Ollie disbelievingly.

'Her music is pure escapism. I'm in the moment, I'm there. And to experience it live – I can't imagine it.'

Ollie laughs. 'You're starting to sound like a Rose Conrad song yourself. Overly nostalgic.'

'Hey! I know you're not her biggest fan, but you're going to help me get tickets, right? There's some complicated online queuing system, and I need all the help I can get.'

'Absolutely,' says Ollie. 'Anything for you, Selena Pia.' He touches my arm, and I look at him, and our eyes meet. I feel caught in them, like they're tugging me forwards.

'There's something I have to tell you,' says Ollie.

This is it. I don't need to confess my love to Ollie, because he's about to do it to me! The greatest turn of events that could happen.

'I'm moving next week,' he says.

'What?' I feel winded. 'As in, moving house?'

He nods.

'So you can get closer to your sixth form?' I say, a sinking feeling starting in my stomach.

'To Manchester,' says Ollie, looking away.

'Manchester? As in—'

'The North of England Manchester,' says Ollie, now looking up to the sky.

'But why?' The words escape me in a near howl. 'We were just hanging out yesterday. It was normal. You were normal.'

'Dad got a job there,' says Ollie, finally looking at me. 'I've known for a month now, but I didn't know how to tell you. I didn't want to ruin summer.'

'So you waited until the week before you move to tell me?'

'I'm sorry,' says Ollie. 'But I don't have a choice. It's a big opportunity for him.'

I hear the bitterness in Ollie's voice, and realise I haven't even thought of how he feels.

'You still have school. Your A levels.'

Ollie shrugs. 'September is in a couple of weeks, I'll be in Year 13, and then it's university, right? I'll have had to leave everyone behind at that point anyway.'

I can see Paul, Ollie's dad, in my mind's eye, telling him these words, the words Ollie is repeating to me right now.

'Are you okay with this?' I say.

Ollie exhales deeply. 'No, but I don't really have a choice. My final year here, saying goodbye, watching everyone go to university . . . It's like my last year of being a kid has been taken away from me.'

I feel the tears rise. I've always been an easy crier. Anger, sadness, happiness, you name it, I cry at it. And even though I'm furious he didn't tell me, I give him a hug. Because that's what friends do.

He grips me, and I remember what I was going to tell him. How I was going to tell him he was the one. And maybe I still will—

'Selena,' Ollie says into my hair.

'Yes?' I say, looking up at him, into those green eyes of his. We're so close now, I can feel his breath on my skin, it is pulling me closer and closer to him. This is it, even though he's moving away, he's realised how he really feels. I tilt my head up, lean in even closer and then—

'That garlic dip is pretty strong on your breath.'

Four

The change is comin'
This change is really summin'
No more wasting time, pretending it's fine
And now we're here, intertwined

'This Change' from *Roses*

THE NEXT DAY the sign appears in Ollie's front garden: *SOLD*. As if it had just popped out of the ground from the seventh circle of hell.

Mum pats me on the shoulder.

'Did you know this was happening?' I ask her.

'Meredith told me, but we wanted Ollie to tell you. The house has been sold for the past month, but they had been refusing to let the estate agents put up the sign until Ollie told you.' Mum shakes her head. 'It looks like the estate agents want the advertising now.'

Mum and Meredith are old friends. It's how Ollie and I became so close. Two next-door neighbours with children the same age. We did absolutely everything together growing up. From sleeping next to each other in a cot, to holding hands taking our first steps.

And now he's stepping right out of my life.

Tears start burning in my eyes again. 'I want him to stay.'

'Maybe you should tell him that,' she says. 'It might not change anything, but it could help give you some closure.'

Damn, she's perceptive. I have a strong feeling Mum might know I'm in love with Ollie, but I'm not about to confess it to her. Not when I've not even confessed it to him.

A week later, it's the last flavour of the summer at Annie Banannie, and the day before Ollie moves away. Ollie and I pay for our pink-grapefruit sherbet ice creams and receive the final stamps.

'Time to hand them in,' says Kristy. 'A full stack.'

Ollie and I look at each other. This is what we've been working towards all summer. Every week, coming here, collecting stamps, spending time with each other. These cards feel like more than just an entry into a competition.

'I want to keep mine,' blurts out Ollie.

'Are you sure?' says Kristy, looking at him confused. 'You do know you need to give it to me to enter the competition?'

'I like having all the stamps,' he says.

'Yes,' she says slowly, as if she's talking to a seven-year-old, not a seventeen-year-old. 'But the point of collecting all the stamps is so you can enter the competition to win the ice cream.' She points at the faded flyer behind her.

'I'm sure,' he says.

'I want to keep mine too,' I say.

'No, you should enter, Selena,' he says.

'Nah, I can't eat all that ice cream myself. And you won't be here to help me with it,' I say lightly. Plus, winning would only remind me of Ollie and make me sad. And potentially give me diabetes. At least now I can keep the stamp card as a memory.

'This is wild. You both were in here every week!' says Kristy.

'Ha, you do remember us,' I say. 'Why did you act like you've never seen us before?'

Kristy shakes her head and wanders off, muttering something about teenagers.

'Let's get out of here before the ice cream melts,' says Ollie, nodding towards the door.

We walk outside.

'You didn't want to enter just in case?' I say. 'I'm sure they would have sent the ice cream to Manchester.'

He shakes his head. 'The card feels more important right now. Our final summer.'

Our final summer.

We walk in silence for a bit, making our way home. From tomorrow, it'll no longer be his home. I need to tell him.

We face each other when we get to the front of our houses.

'Well, this is it,' he says, stuffing his hands into his pockets, ice cream finally gone.

I meet his eyes. *What if he rejects me and moves away tomorrow?*

The thought burns into my mind, outweighing the need to tell him. I can't bear the thought of him leaving and breaking my heart. What if he doesn't want to talk to me when he moves, because I'm so embarrassing and he doesn't feel the same way? Maybe closure is overrated.

'We'll say goodbye tomorrow,' I say softly.

'Come on, let's go sit in the garden,' he says, nodding his head. 'Got to have as much time as I can with you.'

It turns out there's no preventing heartbreak in this situation, as I can feel mine start to fracture at his words.

I stand on the curb, rocking backwards and forwards on my feet, feeling like I might fall over at any point. It's the day the Pointer family moves out.

Ollie walks over to me, dressed in tracksuits and one of his dad's freebie work T-shirts. It's a long drive up. He places his hands on my shoulders.

'So this is it,' he says.

I swallow, nodding.

'Come here!' says Mum, pulling us into a hug. 'I remember

when you two were small babies. You would throw your food at each other and then hug, making the mess worse.'

What a weird thing to get sentimental about.

'Mum,' I say, pushing her off.

'It's the end of an era,' says Meredith, walking over. '*I don't know how I could have survived the last seventeen years without Kajal.*'

I look at Mum, who is clasping her hands together, looking tearful. She might have said she was fine with the move, but looking at her now, I think she was saying that for me. Classic Mum, always trying to make me feel better.

Ollie grabs my hand, pulls me aside. He looks at me tenderly. A small part of me shrieks, *This is it! Confess your love.* But it is overruled by the more rational side of my brain which is shouting, *You can't confess your love in front of your mum!*

He touches the side of my face. 'I guess this is goodbye, Selena Pia,' he says.

'But not forever,' I say.

'No, not forever,' he says, kissing the top of my head. 'Just for now.'

He squeezes my hand, lets go, and heads back to his family.

For my whole life our two families have been intertwined by friendship and shared history, and now we're about to be ripped apart.

The Pointers get into the moving van.

I take a deep breath and say goodbye, and watch the van take them away. And a little piece of my heart with it.

Five

Carry me home
Like you did at the start
Carry me home
The first woman I loved

'Mama' from *Roses*

I**T'S THE FIRST** weekend since Ollie left, and it's nearly a week until school starts. Faye and Kira are over, trying to cheer me up. I've not told them about my crush on Ollie, but I'm starting to feel it might not be as much of a secret as I'd thought.

'Come on, Selena,' says Faye.

I am lying horizontally on my bedroom floor while they flick through YouTube videos on my laptop.

'Look there is a new *Date in the Attic* with Anu Kapoor. You love him.'

'I don't have time for love,' I say, a tad too dramatically. 'I'm in mourning.'

'And it's the actual morning,' says Kira, 'and one of the last few days of summer! I think we need to go outside and you need to see the sun.'

I grab my phone and turn up the volume, so Rose Conrad's 'I Loved You Like That' plays out louder.

'Okay,' says Kira, getting off the bed and grabbing my phone. 'That's enough Rose Conrad for now.'

'Guys . . .' says Faye, from the bed.

'But she sees into my soul,' I say, waving my arms around but still not getting up.

'Guys!' says Faye, shouting, which is unlike her. 'Someone is moving into Ollie's house.'

I'm up so fast I could break the world record for standing up, if there is one. All three of us kneel on the bed, our noses pressed against the window.

There is a black people-carrier in the drive of Ollie's house, and a large white van parked behind that. Suitcases are being wheeled along the driveway by men in overalls.

An older white man in chinos and a shirt is pacing the front of the house, speaking on the phone, with his other hand in his pocket.

A Black woman dressed in an expensive-looking summer dress comes out of the house and taps on the car back door.

The window rolls down, she bends over it.

'God, I wish this had audio,' says Kira.

'Do you think we should open the window?' I say.

'Shhh, look,' says Faye.

The door of the car slides open and a mixed-race boy gets out, heavily side-eying his mother. He barely looks at her as he saunters into the house.

'How do you get all the fit neighbours?' says Faye. 'I have two grandmas on either side of my house!'

'We don't know he's fit,' I say. 'We can barely see him.'

'He has fit energy,' says Kira. 'You can tell by the way he walks,' she adds seriously.

'We're really showing that we go to an all-girls' school,' I say. 'You're acting as if you've never seen a boy before!'

A younger boy gets out of the car and says something to the mother, looking apologetic, before following the older boy into the house.

The mother throws up her hands into the air in exasperation, then follows him inside. The older boy may be fit, but it looks like he may be a bit of a dick.

One thing is clear, though. These are definitely my new neighbours.

It's been a week since the new neighbours moved in, and I'm dying to know more.

'Have you met the new people next door?' I ask Mum, as nonchalantly as I can. Which is hard because we're trying to put up a metre-long painting on our living room wall and I'm breaking out in a sweat.

'I've seen them walk in and out. Think there's another boy your age there,' she says, looking at me knowingly.

'Whatever,' I say, as we finally catch the back of it onto the nail. 'They're no Pointers.'

We stand back, and Mum adjusts the painting.

'Where did you even get this from?' I say. It's an abstract painting of people in various positions.

'It's a modern interpretation of the twelve Olympians. I like it,' says Mum, standing back and surveying.

'That's because you like anything to do with Ancient Greece,' I say, pushing her on the shoulder.

'Exactly,' she says, pointing to the fireplace below, where a terracotta vase sits. 'I think it's a nice contrast with my amphora.'

The amphora is Mum's prized possession, and from what I understand, worth a lot of money. She got it when she left home, taking a solo trip to Greece against her parents' wishes. She never turned back. We now see Nani and Papa twice a year, for their birthdays. They live in East London and every time we go over it feels formal and stilted.

Mum sits down on the sofa. She struggles getting down, because of the stiffness in her knees.

'Do you want help?' I say, rushing over to her, just as she manages to sit.

'I've got it,' she says, holding a hand up.

'How are you feeling?' I say. 'It looks worse than normal.

Do you want me to get you some painkillers?' Following Mum's diagnosis I've become an expert on the different types of painkillers you can get. I also know where to find them on each floor of the house.

'I'm just having a flare-up. Good old rheumatoid arthritis. I'll be fine, Selena. You need to stop worrying about me. I'm your mother, not the other way around.'

Easier said than done: I know I'm all Mum has. What would she do without me?

Six

He was a young boy
Chasing dreams through the starlight
Until one fateful night
He saw the girl with the blue eyes

'A Night In Hollywood' from *Dreamers*

AFTER NODDING POLITELY along to one of Mum's speeches about art, I head to the garden to sit in the sun and read. I'm meant to finish *The Great Gatsby* before term starts in a couple of days, and I have a few more chapters left.

As I get to the part where Gatsby is clearly never going to be called back by Daisy, a voice calls to me from over the fence. An American voice.

'Hey.'

My new neighbours are American?

I get up and walk over, and see the younger brother on the other side.

'Hi,' I say, waving at him.

He's small and young, with a temple fade and big eyes. He's wearing a long-sleeved top and cargo shorts.

'I saw you over the fence,' he says. He looks at me curiously. 'Do you live here?'

'Well, I didn't break into a random garden,' I say, smiling. 'Yeah, we're neighbours. My name is Selena.'

'I'm Daze,' he says. 'I wanted to say hello, since we've moved here and all.'

'Paul!' shouts out a voice from the house. 'Dinner is up in ten minutes!'

'Thanks!' he yells back. He looks back at me, abashed. 'Okay, my real name is Paul.'

'That was poor timing for you.' I laugh.

'I'm really trying to get Daze to stick,' he says, waving his arm around. 'It feels, y'know, cooler. Like a stage name. And as we've moved here, it feels like a good time to, what's it called . . .' he pauses, scrunching his face up in concentration, 'reinvent myself.'

I hold back a laugh. 'Okay, I'll call you Daze,' I promise, although I can't help thinking this kid is going to get caught out on his first day of school at registration.

But there's a confidence to him. I'm sure if he told everyone that's what he wanted to be called, they would do it.

'Have you always lived here?' he says.

'Yes,' I say. 'I've lived in this yellow house my whole life. And before you moved here, my best friend lived in your house his whole life.'

'Where did he move?'

'Manchester.' I sigh.

'Like the soccer team?'

'Kid, you're going to need to start calling it football here. You use your feet to kick the ball, it's football.'

'I'm not a kid.' He winces. 'I'm eleven now. How old are you, anyway?'

'Seventeen,' I say. 'Literally nearly an adult.'

'My brother, Ty, is seventeen,' he muses. 'But the point, is I'm not a kid. I'm going to high school this year. Do you know how cool that is? Back home we don't go to high school until fourteen.'

'Talking about me?' says the older brother, appearing from behind Daze. Like Daze, he has a lazy grin and sparkling eyes. And he's handsome. Really handsome. Broad shoulders, tall, and he is, as Kira sussed out from my window, hot.

'You must be Ty,' I say.

'I am. And who are you?' he says, his grin getting tighter. He puts a hand on Daze's shoulder.

'This is Selena,' says Daze. 'She lives next door.'

'Do you normally talk to eleven-year-olds over the fence?' says Ty. His voice is still light, but I get the vibe he does not like this.

'Your brother called me over!' I say. 'We're neighbours, after all.' No point taking offence, I'm going to live next to him. Although I miss Ollie, it's not a betrayal to be friends with his replacement. His very hot replacement.

'Daze, I told you,' says Ty, putting his hands on Daze's shoulders and turning him around. 'You can't talk to strangers here. This isn't suburban San Francisco. This part of suburban London is full of drug dealers and people who have knives.'

'Woah!' I say. 'I am neither of those things. And also, Croydon isn't that bad.'

'Really?' says Ty. 'Yesterday on the way downtown, we saw a woman throw a trash can at another woman.'

'I'm sure she had a good reason,' I say, feeling strangely defensive about it.

'For minor assault?' says Ty.

Who is this guy? It's not like I agree with what he's describing, but this is my hometown. 'Well, I don't think San Francisco has the best reputation,' I say. 'I saw a TikTok on it.'

'There's one shitty area,' says Ty, rolling his eyes as if I should have known that. 'The rest is pretty great. Much better than this place, which seems to be entirely shitty.'

'You know what,' says Daze, edging away, 'I'm going to head inside and leave you guys to it.'

'Then why did your family move here?' I say.

'Because my dad got transferred to a company head-quartered here and thought this was a good idea. Good for his career. Thought we should live in the suburbs so we can still have a normal life. But what's the point of moving to London when we're too far out to even experience it? I actually like the main part of the city: the sights, the restaurants. But . . . this whole thing has been a bunch of arbitrary decisions, with him deciding what to do with our lives.'

I blink at him. Wow, that was certainly a speech.

Ty raises an eyebrow. 'Nothing to say?' he says.

I feel taken aback, unable to say anything to a person who just used 'arbitrary' in casual conversation.

'My best friend used to live here,' I say finally, gesturing to his house.

'What's that got to do with anything?' says Ty, looking confused.

'You're not the only person who's going through this,' I tell him.

'Well, it still sucks,' he says.

'Yeah, but you might make some new friends, see a new city.' I don't know why I'm hyping this guy up, all he's done is shit on my hometown.

'I wasn't good at making friends in San Francisco,' he says. 'It's not going to be any different here.'

'I'm getting that vibe,' I say, dryly.

He shakes his head. 'You don't get it. My dad made us move to the other side of the world, away from the life I had. Then to top it off, he wants me to apply for colleges on the side we left. Which means there's no point making friends, as I'll have to go back anyway."

If there's one topic I don't want to get sucked into with a

stranger, it is university applications. Especially with someone who is as unreasonably angry as this guy.

'I think I'll go now,' I say. I pause. 'I would say it's been nice meeting you, but you know what, it hasn't.'

And with that, I turn around and head back into the house, thinking about what a downgrade my new next-door neighbour is.

Seven

Let's get going
It's time to bust out of this town
Let's get going
I'm going to take the crown

'Let's Get Going' from *The In-Between*

'MY NEW NEIGHBOUR is the worst,' I say the next day to Ollie on FaceTime.

'And here I was worried he's going to replace me,' says Ollie, grinning at me through the screen. My heart feels like it's physically hurting in my chest.

'No chance.' I snort. 'He's completely pretentious and angry.'

'Wow,' says Ollie. 'I don't think I've ever seen you get so worked up about someone before. About other stuff, sure, but not other people. You're normally Ms I-Want-Everyone-To-Get-Along.'

'That's because I don't like arguments. But all this guy seems to do is cause arguments!'

'He really hit a nerve, didn't he?'

'It's annoying, this American guy landing here and making all these judgements, without even knowing anything.'

Ollie laughs. 'Don't you see the irony? You send your friends Selena Says all the time with your judgements!'

'That's different,' I say. And it is. My Selena Says aren't said to anyone's face. Which, okay, makes it sound worse, but I'm not going around picking fights. 'Oh, I need to remind you, Rose Conrad tickets are going on sale at the end of the month.' Maybe he won't notice I've changed the subject. 'You need to register for the access link.'

'Okay, send it over.'

'Amazing, thank you,' I say. Ollie doesn't have as much skin in the game as I do, but it's important to have as many chances as possible to get the tickets. 'How are you finding Manchester?'

'Oh, you know,' he says. 'It's fine. Not as cold as everyone said it would be.'

'It is August.' I laugh. 'Well, the last day, but still.'

'I'm just a bit . . . lonely, I guess?' he says. 'I don't know anybody here.'

'School's starting tomorrow,' I say. 'You'll meet people there.'

'Yeah, and I'm sure that'll go well. The new southerner boy. The people here really make fun of you, you know?'

It strikes me then – for the first time in his life, Ollie is in a minority. Me, on the other hand, I've always been conscious of being a bit different. The Indian one. The tall girl. So at school

I've always tried to blend in and be like everyone else.

But I don't know how to articulate any of this. Ollie always shakes his head when I bring up being a minority, saying there are tons of Asian people in London, the world is different now. But he doesn't see the subtlety – how I'm the only Indian girl at some of my cross-country sessions. How people sometimes assume I'm vegetarian, for no given reason. How I don't always feel connected to being Indian, because we don't speak another language at home or practice any religious or cultural events, but that's still what everyone sees when they look at me.

How I don't even know my dad or who he is or where he came from – except he must be ethnically Indian like me.

How, a lot of the time, I feel split in two.

But now's not the time to get into that.

'Sounds really hard,' I manage. 'But you should keep an open mind about school.'

The first day of term. The first day of the last year at school. The beginning of the end.

This is the year I'm going to turn eighteen. This is the year I apply to university. This is the year I try to work out *what's coming next*.

And it makes me feel sick.

I quickly message Ollie, wishing him good luck. He responds, saying the same thing back. I sigh. I can't believe this year we won't be able to hang out, telling each other about our day. We're relegated to text message and FaceTime.

My phone buzzes again; it's the Neapolitan group chat. I grab my bag and head down. Faye is parked at the bottom of the drive, Kira already in the front seat. Faye getting a car might be the best thing that's ever happened to us. Especially since we go to school in the neighbouring borough. And, sure, Faye's car is a billion years old and feels like on the edge of a breakdown all the time, but it's still a car.

I have yet to pass my driving test. My instructor calls me 'too timid on the road'. Kira has the opposite problem, she's failed two tests and on the last one even gave the examiner a heart attack. She claims it wasn't her, and he had an underlying health problem, but an ambulance had to come at the end of her test to take him away, which she's not managed to live down. (Apparently the examiner is fine and lives on to be terrorised by more seventeen-year-olds.)

'Can we play *Dreamers*?' I say, sliding into the back seat. It's Rose Conrad's third album, taking place at a time when her life turned upside down. Kira dutifully changes the song playing.

'Feeling sentimental?' says Kira. 'You always want to play *Dreamers* when you're feeling sentimental.'

'Don't make the first Selena Says of the year too depressing,' says Faye. 'They're best when they're funny.'

'Yeah, unlike the time when you mourned them taking out curly fries from the lunch menu,' says Kira.

'To be honest it was such a depressing read about curly fries, it did become funny,' says Faye.

'It's the first day of our last year at school!' I say. 'What's not to feel sentimental about?'

Kira gestures around her. 'Look, I love school, you know it. But this is the beginning of the rest of our lives!' She punches the air with her hands. 'And I am ready to get started on it. I cannot wait to go to uni. I'm going to send off my UCAS as soon as I can.'

'Don't you have to send it early anyway?' I say. Kira is, without any question of a doubt, incredibly smart, good at school and ruthlessly ambitious. So naturally, she wants to apply to Oxford university and get started on her way to political greatness.

'Yes, but I think the sooner I send it in, the better. You both should do that too, so you can get your places early.'

'I still haven't decided where I want to go . . .' I say. 'Or even what I want to do . . .'

'Girl, are you okay? You're running out of time here,' says Kira, turning around to face me.

I shrink into the seat. 'It's the first day of term,' I say. 'I've got loads of time.'

Kira shakes her head. 'What about you, Faye? You decided what you want to do yet?'

I'm curious about this too. Faye has always been more on my wavelength than Kira. She's the most laid back of us. The most go-with-the-flow.

'Yeah, I think I've made my choices, but I want to think about it a bit more.'

'What does that mean?' asks Kira.

'Well . . . I really enjoyed helping my parents out in *Thrifted First* this summer. I started embroidering some items to upcycle them, and they're selling really well. I've even started making my own dresses . . . I guess it's been cool to learn about the business side of things, how to do it practically.'

'You should study Business,' says Kira, excitedly. 'I don't think you need to have done the A level for it. Let me look it up.'

As Kira starts googling entry requirements for university courses on her phone, Faye and I make eye contact in the rear-view mirror and share a smile. We both know Kira's pushes come from a place of love, even though they're not always helpful.

Eight

And they ride their bikes
In the middle of the night
Down country lanes
Under starry lights
And she knows – that's how the story goes

'How The Story Goes' from
The Brink of Teenage Freedom

MY FIRST CLASS of the year is English Literature. My safe zone. I'm also taking History and French, but I'm most happy when I'm reading and writing about stories. I know this probably means I should be looking at English Literature for uni, but there are so many options: English Literature, English Literature and English Language, English Language, English Literature and French. Then the English tangential courses: Journalism, Creative Writing, Linguistics, Publishing.

The choice is overwhelming. And I guess I don't feel strongly enough about any of them right now to commit for the next three years. But I'm hoping as I get closer to the deadline, I'll have a revelation.

I head to class and sit in my preferred spot: second row. Close enough to see what's going on, but not look too keen.

Tori Corner sits in front of me. Tori is a lot like Kira, if Kira was annoying. She is the top student of every class I'm in (we share English and History); she answers every question first, leaving no one else a chance to give an opinion; and she has a general sense of superiority, which makes it impossible to argue with her.

Granted, I'm not a fan, but at least she and Kira are in separate classes for everything now, because during our GCSE years they were almost ripping each other's throats out with how competitive they were.

Today, she smacks down a ringbinder with about a hundred different coloured tabs poking out. Who even uses ringbinders any more?

'What's that?' says Farah from the desk over, which I know is exactly what Tori wants to be asked, considering she's made such a display of it.

'Oh, it's all my plans for *The Common Room*,' says Tori, flicking back her hair. 'I'm the editor this year.'

I shake my head. As soon as Tori found out she was the editor of our school newspaper, at the end of last year, she wouldn't stop going on about it. Clearly this hasn't changed over the summer. If the ringbinder's anything to go by, she's got more obsessive.

'I'm still on the fence over whether to apply for Journalism or straight-up English,' says Tori. 'Although my mum's friend is an editor at *The Chronicle,* so he's going to give me some advice next week.'

Tori's mum is some kind of well-connected exec in London who, according to Tori, seems to know just about any person you name. I'm sure if I wanted to meet the King, Tori's mum could arrange it.

'I thought I was dead set on Journalism, but Mum is concerned it's not prestigious enough,' says Tori, very seriously. 'But all I want is to be an on-the-ground reporter breaking big stories. With a Pulitzer Prize someday. And whatever will get me there is what I will do.'

While I'm googling what the Pulitzer Prize is (it's a Journalism award apparently), Ms Harkness walks in.

Ms Harkness is also one of the reasons I love English. She's younger than the average teacher and always dresses boldly: today she's wearing a flowy black dress and a leather jacket.

'*The Great Gatsby,*' says Ms Harkness, walking around the room. 'Is the book we're studying this term. I hope you've all read it.'

I finished it a couple of days ago. It has a depressing ending, which is what I took away from it.

We start discussing the novel, going through themes and

other devices. I enjoy the discussion, but mostly it's Tori's strong views that come through, and I'm too afraid of being wrong to argue with her when I disagree.

At the end of class, Ms Harkness asks for our attention as we pack up.

'As you know, the student newspaper, *The Common Room*, is starting up again this year—'

'Miss, I can do the announcement,' says Tori, her hand flying up.

'Okay, Tori,' says Ms Harkness. She's the teacher sponsor of the newspaper.

'So we're looking for contributors,' says Tori, animatedly. 'I am the editor. I want this to be the best year ever of *The Common Room*, so please email us any ideas, articles, pitches you have. I'm so excited to read them. Also if you don't have any ideas but want to write or put it down on your UCAS form, I have a tonne of ideas.' She gestures at her ringbinder.

'Thanks, Tori,' says Ms Harkness. 'But I hope everyone who submits does have original ideas. Journalism is a great way to express yourself and your point of view, not just write about what is going on in the world. Feel free to speak to me if you have any questions.'

As we pack up, Ms Harkness calls me over.

'How was your summer, Selena?' she says warmly.

'Good thanks, Miss,' I say.

'I wanted to talk to you about your university application. You're thinking about applying for English, right?'

'Yeah, Miss, I think so. I just don't know what course. Or where . . .'

'You know the deadline is in January? And you should apply earlier if possible.'

'I know, Miss.'

She squints at me. 'Is there something else going on?'

Yes! I want to say. *I am deeply afraid of the future and losing my friends and family, and completing my UCAS form cements the deal. I don't particularly want to leave home because my mum has a chronic condition and I want to be there for her. Selecting a course is a huge commitment to the future that I'm not ready to make, and I don't know where to start!*

But I don't say any of this. Instead I say, 'No.'

'You can talk to me if you want,' she says, and she looks like she means it.

And instead of denying any more, I say, 'I'll think about it, thanks.'

Selena Says: Ringbinders belong in a museum. Get in the 21st century and put everything on the Cloud. There's no need to carry a kilo of paper around any more. Think about the trees!

Nine

'It's Love' from *The In-Between*

'M STARING OUT of my bedroom window, thinking about what Ms Harkness said earlier today. My desk overlooks the garden. Mum put it there because it has the best lighting for when I study, but it also provides plenty of distractions.

Our garden is narrow but long, and there's an oak tree at the end. The main distraction is that I can see into next door's garden, which means I spend a lot of time people-watching. On one side is an older couple, whose children have moved out. If I have the window open in the summer I can sometimes hear Mrs Chang gossiping on the phone about her daughter, her daughter's friends and any celebrity online. On the other side, it's the Pointers. Or rather, it *was* the Pointers.

The thought makes my heart ache a bit. I look at their garden, or rather the side of it I can see. There's a fresh lawn, a pond and—

Ty taking *photos* of the pond?

Not even with his phone. He has one of those big fancy cameras. One that actual photographers use. He's lunging onto the floor, squatting down and peering through the lens. I'm not sure what he's looking at. There's not been any fish in that pond since the Pointers got a new cat and it killed all their expensive carp. But the way the sun comes from our side of the garden gives his garden an amazing golden-hour look at this time of day.

I watch him there, my laptop open, essay partway written. He stands up, starts looking at the screen at the back of the camera, before turning around and starting to photograph some plants. He moves so slowly, focused on one thing at a time.

Before I know it, I'm heading downstairs to the garden. As I step outside, I pause. A song is playing, 'It's Love'. One of the songs from Rose Conrad's latest album. Did I leave a speaker out here and it's still attached to my phone? But I haven't been out here all day. Mrs Chang is certainly not playing it – I once overheard her calling Rose Conrad 'salacious'.

Then I realise: Ty is playing it while he's taking photos.

I walk towards him slowly. Almost like I'm at a safari and

I don't want to disturb an animal in its natural habitat. Too late – the twig has snapped and the antelope rises.

Which is to say, I trip over a basketball and stumble forwards with a yelp.

I get to my feet and pick up the basketball. Ty is looking at me, bemused.

'I guess this is yours,' I say, throwing the ball over the fence.

'It's Daze's. He's trying to learn some new tricks,' says Ty. He picks up the ball and starts spinning it on his finger, a trick I've only seen in a movie. 'He's not very good at them yet.'

'Huh. I thought that trick was CGI every time I've seen it,' I say.

'Nah, like most things, it's just practise,' says Ty. 'I got very obsessed with learning how to do it, and now Daze is the same.'

'How about the photography,' I say, gesturing to his camera. 'Is this your new obsession?'

He looks down at the camera and laughs. 'I do get a bit obsessed with things. But I've liked photography for a while. And the light here is so good, I had to take a photo of something, you know?'

'And what about Rose Conrad?' I say. 'I didn't realise you were a fan.'

A stony look passes his face. His guard is now back up.

'I can be a Rose Conrad fan,' he says.

'Sure you can,' I say, and I know I'm pushing him a little. But he pushed me first, last time. 'But why *are* you a Rose Conrad fan?'

He bounces the ball on the ground. 'I don't think that's any of your business. Especially if you want to make fun of me.'

'Woah, what's this deep dark origin story of how you became a Rose Conrad fan?' I say. 'I thought you were going to tell me she is a lyrical genius and the best singer-songwriter of a generation.'

'And that would be enough for you?' he says, starting to dribble the ball, not breaking eye contact with me. It feels strangely intense. 'Because for some reason, as a guy, if someone finds out I like Rose Conrad, I get a grilling about it.'

'Well, maybe it's hard to believe she would speak to guys as much as girls.'

'But wouldn't you argue her music is universal?' he says, throwing the ball behind him with one hand and walking closer to the fence. 'That her songwriting is so good anyone can like it?'

I stutter. I agree with him, but I can't believe he thinks the same.

'So there's no origin story?' I say. We're almost face-to-face now by the fence. 'You just like her for her artistry?'

He laughs, looks away. 'Oh boy, there is an origin story, I was messing with you. But I don't think I need to share it with you.'

Bastard. He's toying with me, messing with what I think.

'Are you getting ticket codes tomorrow?' I say. 'Registration starts at ten.'

'Oh, I know,' he says, holding up his phone. 'I have a calendar reminder and an alarm.'

'I have three other people helping me,' I say. 'Potentially more, if I can round up some people at school who don't want to go.'

'Well it must be fun to be so popular,' he says. 'Good luck to you.'

And with that he turns around and leaves.

Talk about a sudden exit.

Ten

Wild horses won't hold me back
I'll keep going on this track
Gotta fight, gotta give, gotta make it
Right from the start . . .
Because I ain't giving up

'Right From The Start' from
The Brink of Teenage Freedom

'D ID YOU REGISTER?' I ask.

'Yes, Selena, I registered before I even got out of bed this morning,' says Mum, spreading butter on her toast. 'It's not like you to be anxious about things.'

I sit down next to her at the table with my breakfast. 'It's the first tour where I've been able to make it. She only toured *Dreamers* at Glastonbury in the UK, which is impossible to get tickets for, and the tours before you said I was too young. Plus this tour is a few weeks after my birthday – it feels like a sign.'

'I know you're bitter about the earlier tours, but I didn't fancy my chances taking an eleven-year-old to London by myself to see a concert,' says Mum, shaking her head.

'The point is, it's important,' I say. 'I can't imagine a future where I will not go to this concert. It's as if my life has been leading up to this moment, and I need to maximise the chance I will get to go, you know?'

'I know, that's why I registered,' says Mum. 'I don't really understand why you love Rose Conrad so much, but I know it matters to you. Now don't you have to get to school?'

I look at my phone: Faye's outside. Before I go, I put Mum's plate in the dishwasher, to stop her from bending over, even though she protests against it. I then hug her, hold my toast in my mouth, grab my bag and jacket and run out of the house.

'Today's the day,' I say, sliding into the back of the car.

'Today's one of the days,' corrects Kira. 'The ticket sale day will be *the* day.'

'But there will be no ticket sale day if we all don't have registration codes—'

'Before you ask, we have both registered,' says Faye, pulling out of my driveway. A grinding sound starts as she reverses, which in classic Faye fashion, she ignores.

'Okay, good,' I say. 'So I think we need a strategy to get as many other people to sign up for us. For example, I know Katie Becker and her group aren't fans. Pretty sure she said she thought Rose Conrad is "overrated" once. And she owes me because I covered for her in French when she skipped to go meet her boyfriend.'

Kira shakes her head. 'You know, Selena, if you put this much effort into thinking about your uni application, you would probably have already got three offers by now.'

Faye parks the car and we get out in silence.

I look at Kira, a range of emotions running through me, making it difficult to form actual sentences. I settle for, 'I'll do my university applications in my own time, you know.'

'I don't get it,' says Kira, shaking her head. 'You clearly have the drive. Look at you and the Rose Conrad thing.'

We head to the common room.

Kira looks at me seriously. 'I want to ask you something. No jokes.'

'No jokes' is what we say when we want to get a real answer from someone. It means serious business. Faye and I glance at each other.

'No jokes,' I say back.

'Do you actually want to go to university?' says Kira. 'Like, you don't have to, there's apprenticeships and all this other stuff you could do.'

My chest feels heavy, but again I'm struggling to say how I feel. In truth, I don't want to tell Kira all my concerns. Leaving Mum, committing to the future, feeling afraid that this marks the beginning of the end of everything I know: in my head it sounds too silly to say out loud. I can see a future where Kira meets a bunch of new, smart, exciting people at whatever prestigious university she gets into, and leaves me behind.

Filling in the UCAS form itself feels like stepping off the edge and into the unknown, and I'm too scared to begin.

Instead I say, 'No, I do want to go to university. I like English and want to study it further. And I want the experience of university. I just need some time.' And it's true. I want to try it out and see what it's like. I am excited by the prospect of meeting new people. I just want to hold on to the present for a bit longer. Is that so bad?

'I'm still thinking about it too,' says Faye, touching my arm. 'If it makes you feel better.'

'See, that's two out of three of us,' I say to Kira. 'You're one extreme, you got to remember.'

'Fine, fine,' grumbles Kira. She looks at her phone. 'Hey, have you seen this?'

'What?' we say.

'They're looking for contributors to *The Common Room* for this year,' she says, reading the email on her phone.

'Oh, I thought it was going to be Rose Conrad-related news,' I say. 'Yeah, Tori and Ms Harkness mentioned it in English.'

'You should do it,' says Kira.

'Do what?'

'Write for *The Common Room*,' she says.

'I can't write for *The Common Room*,' I scoff. 'What would I even write about?'

'Oh my God, yes,' says Faye, grabbing my arm. 'Your Selena Says are basically breaking news.'

'You think I should send my Selena Says to *The Common*

Room?' I say, incredulously. 'They're three lines long. It's not exactly journalism.'

'Journalism looks different in this day and age,' says Kira, excitedly. 'You manage to convey a strong opinion in a few lines – I would say that's a talent. Also, I bet it would spark talk.'

'Nobody would publish it. Tori definitely wouldn't. She'd probably see my name, three lines of text and ignore it.'

'But if you want to do something English-related at uni, this will look so good on your application,' says Kira. 'And you could take the idea of Selena Says and make it into a different format. How will you know if you don't try?'

'Trust me,' I say, crossing my arms. 'I know there's no point here. I have a better chance of getting a hundred Rose Conrad tickets right now than getting published in *The Common Room*.'

Eleven

Wildfire eyes
Pulling me deeper inside
Ashes and embers
Keep me alight

'Wildfire Eyes' from *Roses*

ARRIVE HOME AFTER a long day of persuading everyone I possibly can to register for an access code. I called in every favour I could, which is saying quite a lot after being at the same school for the last seven years.

Selena Says: FACT: There is no better place to gather IOUs than in an all-girls' school. From forgotten homework to forgotten tampons, you can rely on someone owing you something at some point. Better yet, if you have a secret you're holding on to, is it blackmail or friendly fire?

Kira who messages back, 'Send this as a long-form article for *TCR*!'

I ignore her.

Ollie messages me confirming he's signed up for the access code, and I breathe a sigh of relief. I'm desperate to FaceTime him, to see his face, to talk to him, but he says he needs some time to get used to his new schedule first. I don't take it personally: Ollie is a big fan of routine, and not having one is probably stressing him out.

It's unseasonably warm for September, I definitely didn't need to wear a jacket today. And after all that hard work corralling people, I need a break. So I head out to the garden with my phone and a book.

Within ten minutes, a basketball lands at my feet. I look up and see Daze waving from across the fence.

'You really have a habit of getting the ball not in your garden,' I say, throwing the ball back at him.

'I'm practising trick shots,' says Daze. 'It's hard work.'

'Ty mentioned,' I say.

'You've been talking to Ty?' he says.

'Not if I can help it,' I say. 'He's just *here* a lot.' I wave my arms at the garden.

'Well he does live here,' says Daze.

'Okay, no need to state the obvious,' I say with a laugh. 'Have you started school? How's reinventing yourself going?'

'Actually pretty hard. It turns out everyone already knows each other,' says Daze, looking down at the ground.

I feel sorry for the kid. It's true, most people go from the same primary schools to secondary.

'But you're really easy to talk to,' I say, throwing the ball to him. 'You've got to put yourself out there.'

'Yeah, but how?' says Daze, throwing the ball back.

I think about it, bouncing the ball a couple of times. I have never bounced a basketball before, but the rhythm is soothing.

'I think the best way of making friends is by finding some common ground. My two closest friends, we bonded because we all like Rose Conrad. And then with my friends from school, we bonded because we were in the same classes. And girls in cross-country, we spend our time together running long distances in the cold. Which, I admit, is a bit masochistic.' I throw the ball back to him.

'Basketball doesn't even seem to be a thing here. There's no school basketball team or anything.'

'Football is. I bet if you go up to some guys at school and say you're American and want to learn the rules of football, they'll explain it to you. And then, bam, new friends.'

'But what if I'm not interested in football?'

I walk up to the fence, so we're closer together. I'm still a head taller than Daze, but I sense that in a few years he'll be as tall as Ty.

'Daze, sometimes you have to try new things to make friends. Also you don't know, you might be interested in football. Keep an open mind.'

'Do you have a lot of friends?' asks Daze.

I think about it. 'I have two very close friends, but I'm friendly with a lot of people at school. I've learnt that if you are a good person and don't cause any fights, people will like you. And I'm sure people will like you, Daze.'

'Fine. Seeing as you sound like a pro on this, I'll listen to you,' says Daze.

'I don't think you can be a pro at making friends.' I laugh.

'It must be nice, being popular,' says Ty, walking up to us. I remember he said he hadn't had many friends in San Francisco.

'I wouldn't call myself popular,' I mumble. For some reason it sounds like an attack, coming from him. Like I'm a mean girl or something. I snap myself out of it; there's no need for this guy to get under my skin. 'How are you doing in the making-friends department?'

'Luckily I am friends with everyone in my class,' he says.

I look at him, surprised.

'Ty is homeschooled,' says Daze. 'The only person in his class is Mom.'

'Oh,' is all I say. I don't know anyone who is homeschooled. Maybe because nearly everyone I know is from school . . .

Daze rolls his eyes. 'Ty is being so dramatic. He makes out that because he wasn't homecoming king he is bad at making friends.'

Ty rolls his eyes in exactly the same way. 'I'm bad at making friends because I tell people my thoughts too much.'

'That is not true,' says Daze.

'No? How so?' asks Ty.

'You don't tell Dad how you really feel about anything.'

Ouch. I can tell a killer blow when I see one. Ty's mouth tightens, his gaze gets more intense.

Daze shakes his head. 'Sometimes the truth hurts.' He bounces the ball and starts heading for the house. 'Thanks for the advice, Selena. I'll tell you how it goes.'

I look at Ty. 'Is he right, about your dad?'

I thought he was going to get defensive, but Ty shrugs. 'Yeah, he's right.' He must see my shocked face, because he gives a small smile and says, 'What? I'm many things, but I'm not a liar. Maybe that's why people don't always gravitate to me.'

'You don't have to be a liar to make friends,' I say. 'You have to care about what people think.'

'Ah, but that's the other problem. I don't want to care about what other people think of me.'

'Except your dad.' It's a statement, not a question.

He looks away. 'I don't want to talk about him.'

I leave it. If anyone knows wanting to be left alone about certain topics, it's me right now.

'Did you register for Rose Conrad?' I say instead.

'Yeah, did you?'

'Nope, I let the day slide after spending so much time talking to you about it yesterday.'

'Ah there's the famous British sarcasm.'

'Are you going to tell me why you like Rose Conrad yet?'

He shakes his head. 'It's not a big deal. My ex was really

into her. She discovered her when *Roses* came out. I was having a tough time and she played me the album, and since then . . . Well, Rose Conrad has spoken to me, y'know.'

'What happened to your ex?'

Ty gives a small smile. 'We discovered we were better off as friends. That and she was clearly in love with her lab partner.'

I make a face.

'I didn't take it personally, she was good to me. But I don't know. She wasn't the one, you know? When Rose Conrad sings about love, I feel it's got to feel bigger than anything I've ever felt before.'

'So you lost a girlfriend and gained Rose Conrad?'

'Something like that.'

Looking at Ty's pretty face and listening to his clever words, right now it's hard to imagine anyone leaving him. But then again he does have a very prickly personality.

'Why are you homeschooled?'

'Because I'm in the last year studying for my High School Diploma, so I can't take whatever levels you have here.'

'What do you study in the diploma?'

'A bit of everything: Math, English, Politics. All AP.'

'What's AP?'

'Like advanced classes, they get you more credits for college.'

'And your mum teaches you?'

'Oh no, I have an online school which I'm finishing up with. Not as good as a real school, but sometimes Mom comes and keeps me company if she thinks I've not seen a real person in a while. She's working weird hours because she's kept her job back home, so is free most mornings.'

'Do you like it?'

'Do I like not being in a real classroom, with my real friends, in a time zone eight hours ahead?'

I feel myself getting hot. 'You're really taking to that famous British sarcasm.'

'It helps when people ask me stupid questions,' he says serenely.

Harsh. One minute, we are having a nice chat, the next he goes and lashes out again.

'Must be such a tough life getting to see the world,' I say in a mocking voice that comes out of nowhere.

Ty's face is suddenly enraged. 'Yes, it must be so hard getting to stay where you live, not getting ripped away from your friends and family.'

'In case you didn't remember, I have been ripped away from my best friend. He used to live in the house you are now living in.'

'Good for him. Sounds like he got out and away from a very annoying neighbour,' he says, a smile playing on his face.

I've had enough of this guy now. 'Isn't it exhausting, being such a knob?'

'Knob?' he says. 'How British of you.'

What.

A.

Dick.

I step forwards, getting closer to the fence.

'How is Daze so nice?' I say. 'Are you sure you're brothers?'

'Coming from an only child,' he says. He's also come closer to the fence. It's the first time I've seen him so up close in a while. His skin is this amazing tan colour, and way too clear for a teenage boy. Honestly, it infuriates me how attractive he is.

'How do you know that?' I say. 'Been watching us?' And by *us*, I mean *me*.

'I'm not the only person trying to get to *know thy enemy*.'

'I didn't realise we were enemies,' I say softly. I look at his lips, and force myself away. *We are enemies. He said so.*

'Well our run-ins haven't been exactly . . . friendly. And you've also been watching my moves.'

He saw me watching him the other day? 'I didn't realise it was a military tactic to look out of a window.'

Somehow we're now so close that I'm tilting my head to look up at him. The only thing between us is the garden wire fence.

'Why, you're so damn angry,' he muses. For a second, I think Ty is about to touch me. Grab my face in his hands. And for a second, I want him to.

No, I think, shaking myself out of it. *Absolutely not.*

'I'm angry? You're the one being so . . . vitriolic,' I spit out, clutching for words.

'Big word,' he says, raising an eyebrow. 'Someone's read a dictionary.'

Everything about this boy annoys me. His condescension.

His jibes. The fact he's the person living next door to me, not Ollie.

'I'm doing English A level. I like to write,' I say, stepping backwards, wincing at the sticky feeling.

'A writer.' He laughs. 'So what do you write?'

I don't want to tell him about Selena Says. He would use it against me. I'm pissed he laughed at the thought of me writing.

'This and that. I'm not just some stupid, popular girl.'

'No,' he murmurs. His eyes are dark in this light. I've noticed sometimes they look green, sometimes brown. 'I suppose you're not.' He laughs again. 'Okay, Writer, I'd like to see what you've got.'

And he turns and heads back into his house.

I've really got to stop him having the last word.

Twelve

It's sweet, it's salty
It's kind of bitter
It leaves a taste in your mouth
That you'll always remember
Oh baby, that's revenge for ya

'Taste' from *The Brink of*
Teenage Freedom

'K NOW THY ENEMY,' I say, pointing at the whiteboard in my room. I'm hosting this important meeting after school, and everyone is tired after a long day.

'Are you quoting the Bible?' says Faye.

'I don't think that's the Bible,' says Kira.

'Oh you're right,' says Faye, looking at her phone. 'It's some Chinese military guy. Sun Tzu. *The Art of War.*' She looks at me. 'Don't you think you're being a bit dramatic?'

'Focus,' I say, pointing at the whiteboard. 'We need to think of the things we know about Ty.'

'He's hot?' says Kira.

'Apart from that,' I snap. 'And he's not *hot* hot. He just has a nice face. Not a nice soul.'

Faye shakes her head at Kira. 'Definitely a bit dramatic.'

'Once again, people, focus.' I walk up to the whiteboard and write 'Ty' in the middle. I start drawing out arrows from it. 'We know he's American.' I say, writing it down and underlining it. 'He is cocky. He doesn't like Croydon. He photographs his garden.'

'Seems like a good place to start,' says Kira.

'The cockiness?'

'No, the photographer bit. Can't you . . . wreck his camera or something?'

'I want to piss him off, not wreck his property,' I say, thinking how expensive the camera looked. 'Isn't that a crime?'

'Okay, maybe not the best idea,' says Kira.

'How about wrecking the photos?' says Faye.

And with that, I have an idea.

My Amazon delivery arrives the next day. Ty always takes photos at the same time every day, when the light is the best. So as soon as I see him in the garden on Saturday afternoon, I head outside. He's focused on what he's doing, which is taking pictures of the pond again. The light is glittering on the surface, creating an ethereal glow around the water.

I start putting up the privacy screen. The screen is a pop up, meant to block sunlight or nosy neighbours.

It's opaque, so I can't see him after I put it up. But I can hear him.

'Writer!' says Ty, his voice raised. Looks like the nickname is sticking, but I don't feel mad about it. 'What are you doing?'

I pop my head from around the side of the shield. He looks mad.

Excellent.

'How did you know it was me?' I say. 'It could be my mum putting this up.'

'I can see your hands. I don't need to be Sherlock Holmes to work this one out,' he says. 'What are you doing?'

'Just putting up this privacy screen,' I say. 'You know, on my side of the fence, so I can.'

'But why?' he says.

'For privacy, duh,' I say. Bet he doesn't like being made to feel stupid.

'You need privacy?' he says, eyebrows up. 'From us?'

'Well, I wanted to stop having conversations with annoying neighbours,' I say sweetly. 'This feels like a good solution.'

As soon as I say this, I catch the screen on the fence at an awkward angle, causing me to stumble and drop it. This is a mistake because now the golden hour light has hit Ty's face, lighting him up like an angel.

An angel with a devil's heart, I have to remember. He made me feel so bad yesterday.

'Really?' he says. 'You want to stop talking to me?' He leans forwards. 'I must have made quite an impression.' His eyes flicker over me. 'Are you sure this isn't to do with me taking photographs?' He gestures at his camera.

'You take photos?' I say, feigning ignorance. 'I hadn't noticed at all.'

Within seconds he is over the short fence, and straight up in my space. I feel my throat get dry with his proximity. But I can tell my aim has been accomplished, he looks irate.

'Stop this stupid act,' he says.

'You were the one calling *me* stupid,' I say.

He frowns, those green-brown eyes narrowing.

'No,' he says slowly, 'you're the one who accused me of calling you stupid. I never said that.'

I think back to our conversation. It's true he never said it, but he made me feel it.

He shakes his head. Lifts up his camera.

'Do you know why I like photography?' he says.

Now it's my turn to shake my head.

'May I?' he says.

I nod, mostly out of curiosity of where this is going. He takes a couple of steps backwards, lifts up the camera, twists and taps on the settings. Then he looks through the viewfinder and takes a photo of me.

He looks at the screen on the back, nods, and then comes over to show me the photo.

It's me, but not as I know. It's my dark wavy hair, loose around my shoulders, lit up by the sun. My brown eyes, glinting in the light, and even though I'm frowning, there's no doubt, I look good.

I look up at him. 'So what?' I say.

'I like photography because it captures things as they are. Not just beauty, but what's inside. It's a way of cementing what's real. And you don't look stupid, Selena, not at all. Those are the eyes of a smart person.'

He closes down the camera sharply. 'Which is why I know you're fucking with me. You may not be stupid, but you sure are annoying.' He walks back over to the fence and hops across it. 'The sun has now gone, so thanks for wasting my time. Mission accomplished.' He crosses his arms and stares at me belligerently.

I meet his eyes. Smile. 'I would say "take a picture, it'll last longer". But oh wait, you've already done that.'

And feeling pleased with the burning fury in his eyes, I turn around and head back into the house, exhilaration shooting through me.

Thirteen

'Midnight Musings' from *Dreamers*

'Y OU'RE GOING TO try for tickets, right?' I ask Ollie. It's the first time I've managed to get hold of him on FaceTime since school started over a week ago. I miss talking to him every day, but once a week will do. He's still my Ollie. I've grabbed him on a Wednesday evening, after school. It seems to be the only day he doesn't have any after-school activities.

'Of course,' he says, with a million-watt smile that tugs at my every nerve. 'It's your favourite artist. I've registered. How could I not help my oldest friend in her quest?'

'Okay, because this is a really big deal, and it's in exactly two days, and I'm slightly panicking.'

'You'll be fine. You've got, like, ten people trying for you.'

'It still might not work out,' I say.

'It'll be fine,' he says. 'You love Rose Conrad, surely that alone should go far.'

'It doesn't work like that,' I say impatiently. 'Loads of people love Rose Conrad. She's the biggest pop star in the world! But you'll still try, right?'

'Yes,' he says, laughing. 'Selena, how many times do I have to tell you?'

'Have you met anyone in Manchester who loves Rose Conrad?' I say.

'Er,' says Ollie thinking, and I immediately know the answer is no, otherwise they would have been talking about the ticket sale. 'No, I don't think so. The friends I've made are really into electronic music.'

'What, EDM?' I say, confused. Electro music to me sounds like noise. How am I meant to scream my heart out when there aren't any lyrics?

'Yeah, or DJs. I actually don't mind it – it's kinda soothing. I've started working to it.'

'What? Since when have you been into electro?' I say, dumbfounded.

For as long as I can remember, Ollie has loved indie and rock bands. Men singing about smoking cigarettes and swooning over their girlfriends who eventually break their hearts. When he was twelve he tried to dye his brown hair black in ode to his favourite band singer, Damien Dylan. I never let him live it down. I've tried to get him to listen to my music for years, but he always said he was set in his ways.

And now he's listening to *EDM*?

'I realised I needed to loosen up a bit. And my new friends, they've been helping me to realise that . . . well, I don't need to be so uptight, I guess.'

'Ollie, you've been at the new school for less than two weeks. How have you had some life-changing revelation?'

It's not that I'm not happy for Ollie . . . it's more that I'm jealous. He's had a breakthrough and I've not been a part of it.

'It's not a life-changing revelation as such. I'm trying to fit in here. The rules are different at this school. The people are different. And I want to get along with everyone, which means following their rules, not the ones I had before.'

This sounds more like Ollie. He wants to be a lawyer; he likes rules. And if in his new school the rule is to like electro music, then Ollie will learn to like electro music. He sees order in following the majority.

'Makes sense. Just don't change too much, okay?'

It sounds like I'm joking, but deep down, I don't think I am.

The next day, I walk into the common room after French. There's a stack of printed papers on the front table. The first edition of *The Common Room* of the school year, released every Thursday. I grab one as I wait for Kira and Faye to meet me for lunch, and turn to the opening page.

★ THE COMMON ROOM ★

NEW SCHOOL YEAR - NEW LOOK - NEW FEATURES

CONTENTS

- Inside the staff room: Mr Edwards tells all
- Our favourite 10 apps to help with focusing
- Today's Take: All-girls' schools are the best for IOUs
- Into the archives: Weird school rules of the past

I immediately turn to 'Today's Take'. There it is, word for word – my Selena Says from last week. Underneath is a note from the editor:

> *I absolutely loved this take from an anonymous*
> *writer. Short, sweet, to-the-point. And it raises a few*
> *different topics for discussion. Our secret sender*
> *has some interesting points on women . . .*

Tori proceeds to go off on an editorial rant about women's rights and feminism and solidarity, using my words as a springboard for an opinion piece that has nothing to do with my initial point.

My first thought is *How did my Selena Says get into The Common Room?* Followed immediately by the answer.

Faye and Kira walk in together, and I beeline for Kira.

'Did you do this?' I say, pulling them to the side and pointing at the article.

She glances down at it, looks back at me and shrugs.

'Yeah,' she says.

'Why?' I demand.

'You're the one who said they'll never publish it. I wanted to test out the theory. So I submitted it from an anonymous email account. And look, now it's published.'

'You can't take our texts and publish them,' I say. 'That's like . . . an invasion of privacy.'

Kira rolls her eyes. 'I don't know why people think *I'm* the dramatic one out of the two of us. Look, I know it's a bit morally sketchy to do this without telling you in advance, but I did it for your own good. You were never going to submit anything by yourself. And look, it's in print – and also, nobody knows it's you.'

'But what if they find out?'

Kira shrugs. 'It's a harmless opinion,' she says.

'But it's still *my* opinion. Also one I amped up for comic effect – I don't really believe in blackmail. And I wasn't planning on sharing it with the school!'

'Okay,' says Kira, holding up her hands. 'I am sorry I did this without telling you. But look around, people are discussing it.'

She nods towards Alia and Tasmin, who are having a very animated discussion.

'Look, if someone used something I told them in secret against me, it would be blackmail.'

'But what if they witnessed you doing something bad, is that not fair game?'

'Two wrongs don't make a right!'

'It's not that straightforward.'

'Who are you blackmailing?'

I watch them animatedly discuss my Selena Snap. They're discussing my thoughts, my words.

'I mean, the blackmail point wasn't really the take,' I say. 'The point was I thought all-girls' schools were a good ground to get favours.'

'Well, if *you'd* actually written the opinion piece afterwards, and not Tori, maybe you could have said that,' says Kira.

'Tori's piece is garbage,' I say. 'It's not what I was writing about at all.'

'You do realise there's a way of correcting that,' says Faye.

'How?' I say.

'By submitting a follow-up,' says Faye, with a coy smile.

Fourteen

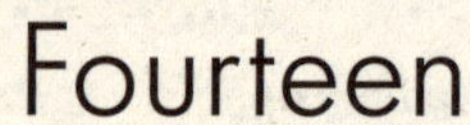

All I have is my pen
It can create or break open
Worlds of my choice
With wicker words that
Set alight when spoken

'Creation' from *Dreamers*

THAT AFTERNOON AFTER school, I'm sitting at my laptop, overlooking the garden. No sign of Ty out there.

I'm trying to avoid Ty. I haven't talked to him since our interaction last week. Partly to keep a sense of mystery going. But mostly because I'm worried he'll retaliate. Giving him some time to cool down may be a good thing for us both. But I can't stop myself from watching him when he's out there. And what's most annoying is that I can tell he knows I'm doing it.

I didn't bother putting up the privacy pane. My point

was made. And it's good because it means I still have an unobstructed view into his garden. We're hitting the last of the September warmth, and I know our garden meetings will soon be over.

I turn back to my laptop. Kira gave me access to the anonymous email account she used to submit my Selena Says. There's one email in it, Tori acknowledging receipt and asking a string of questions: what year of school I'm in, what classes I'm taking, if I want to write a further expansion of my piece . . . She's attempting to respect my anonymity, but I can tell she really wants to know who I am.

There are some things that bug me about the Secret Sender piece. One is Kira sending it in the first place, although I know she had my best interests in mind. The second is everyone misconstruing what I said.

I tap my desk with my fingers. Can I really send in a follow-up? Won't it make it all worse? But part of me enjoyed that people were talking about what I wrote, dissecting the meaning. It was like I was the subject in an English class. Being a writer feels powerful.

I open an email up and start writing:

Dear Tori

No that doesn't sound right—

Hey Tori, It's time to get down to business . . .

I delete it. Too aggressive.

Honourable Tori, I have a bunch of stuff I would like to clarify . . .

I close my laptop and look out of the window, hoping for inspiration.

Instead, I see Ty.

But today, he's not with his camera. Instead he is dragging a sun lounger across the garden, towards the pond.

Weird.

I sit up, leaning closer to the glass. What is he doing? Firstly, it's September and four p.m., it's not exactly sunbathing time. Secondly, the sun on that side is pretty bad, which is why the sun lounger was on the other side of the garden.

Ty's dressed in a long-sleeved top and gilet. He doesn't look like he's come out to catch some rays.

He lies down on the sun lounger, directly facing me. Then he picks up the other thing he was carrying.

It's a newspaper.

What seventeen-year-old boy reads a *newspaper*? I don't even know where you can buy a newspaper around here.

I look closer. At this point, my nose is pressed up against the glass pane.

SAN FRANCISCO RANKED BEST CITY.

CROYDON RANKED WORST.

Ha. He clearly made this newspaper himself, the writing

large enough for me to read. It's a way of winding me up.

I can't help it: I smile to myself.

And the next thing I know, I'm downstairs and marching towards the fence.

'You made a prop?' I yell over the fence.

'Do you like it?' he says, looking up at me.

'Bit immature,' I say. 'And factually incorrect. Croydon isn't even a city.'

'What, unlike buying a privacy shield to stop me taking photos?'

'I didn't make that. I ordered it off Amazon. Plus, I could have been wanting privacy.'

He shakes his head, still lying on the sun lounger. In all his layers, he looks so ridiculous.

'Well if you don't mind, I have a paper to read,' he says.

'No teenager has read a paper since 2003 – well, maybe except a school newspaper,' I say, climbing over the fence. 'I bet there's nothing even in there.'

'What a wild statement,' he says, looking up, surprise on his face as he registers me coming closer to him. 'What are you doing?' he says.

'You came into my garden,' I say, making some strides. I grab the newspaper from him. 'Aha! This is completely empty.' I shake it at him.

'Well done, Sherlock Holmes.'

'You're not exactly some criminal mastermind.'

'I knew it would wind you up, based on our first conversation.'

He shrugs. 'Why are you so protective of this place anyway?' He looks genuinely interested, and against my better judgement, I find myself perching on the end of the sun lounger.

I look at my house.

'We don't really get a choice where we're from, do we? And the places we're from, we're the only people who really know what it's like. The media can paint whatever statistics, bring up whatever images, but only we really know it.'

'I didn't realise you felt strongly about it,' says Ty, looking at me abashed.

'This is my home,' I say as genuinely as I can. 'It's the only one I've ever known. So I'll defend it. And it's definitely not the worst city in the world.' I brandish the newspaper.

He takes it from me. 'That was very poetic, you know. I can tell you're a Rose Conrad fan.'

I feel myself turning red. 'My words are nowhere near as good as hers.'

'Give yourself some credit, Writer,' he says with a smile. 'They're much better than most people's.'

'My friend submitted something I wrote anonymously to the school newspaper,' I say.

He raises his eyebrows. 'And is that good or bad?'

'I don't know. Initially I thought it was bad, but there was something cool about everyone talking about it. Like I left a mark, you know?'

'I get it. It's how I feel about photography. When I look at the images, I know I did something.'

'It just feels . . . a bit public, you know? Like I'm exposing myself.'

He grabs the newspaper back from me, taps it on my head. 'But isn't that how anything great is done? Look at Rose Conrad, how her lyrics expose her. It's why people love her, they see themselves in her songs. When I hear 'Right From The Start' it really pumps me up – I can see myself taking on anything . . . or anyone. Or when I heard 'Mama' the first time, I just saw my mum. I'm sure Rose Conrad wrote those with her life projected onto it, but when I hear the songs, I can only see mine. That's the power of words.'

'I never thought about it like that before,' I admit. 'That different people can hear the same thing and take wildly different things from it. The way I view it isn't the only way of viewing it.' I pause. 'I guess you're trying for tickets tomorrow then.'

'Oh absolutely,' he says.

'Are you going to go by yourself?' I say, curiously.

'I'm not swimming in friends right now,' he says. He sighs. 'I'll try for multiple tickets, and if I get more than one I'll hold it above your head for the next few months so you become a nicer neighbour to me.'

I may not know Ty well, but I know he means that he'll give it to me if he has a spare.

'Thank you. I'll do the same. If I have a spare ticket lying around.'

He laughs. 'I'll take the if. What are you going to do then, about the writing thing?'

'Submit a follow-up. You've just given me an idea,' I say. I look at the newspaper. 'Got to correct all the poor and lazy journalism out there.'

He laughs at that.

'I'll be taking this with me,' I say. 'Might burn it before anyone else can see it.'

'Until next time, Writer,' he says lazily from the sun lounger.

'You don't need to pretend to lie down here any more,' I call back without looking around. 'It's bloody cold out here.'

I hear his laughter as I head back inside. It makes me feel lighter.

— ★ —

A week later, the next issue of *The Common Room* comes out:

TODAY'S TAKE: *Hometown Glory*

But first, a response to the response. I never thought I'd need to print this, but I don't support blackmail. If anything, my last article is a lesson in being careful with your words. And how once they're written down, they're out of your hands. Another thing my last post was not about is the feminist nature of IOUs. You can take some things at surface level, you know? And now that's out of the way, today's take is:

Hometown glory is more than watching the local football team win. It's quirks and foils and everything between. Take this place, Croydon. For me, it's knowing what it's like to see a sunset from the viewpoint of Lloyds Park, or the church ladies volunteering to raise money for their friends' care. How on the bus you can see every race and ethnicity sat next to each other in perfect harmony. The history of the Brutalist architecture and the weddings by the library. The beauty of haggling at Surrey Street market. Maybe it's a romantic way to view it, but it's my home.

Fifteen

Energy bites
It fizzles, delights
Oh . . . I think this is the start
Of something electric, magnetic
I hope I don't regret it

'Electric' from *The In-Between*

ON SATURDAY MORNING I'm as prepared for these Rose Conrad tickets as I'll ever be. I've watched several TikToks about the North American sale, read every internet forum, and have a set-up including my laptop, my phone and my mum's laptop and phone.

An interesting piece of post arrived for me this morning. In a brown envelope with only my name written on it, a collection of photos had been posted through our letterbox. It was pictures of Croydon, taken all over the city. Ty had captured every part of the town, from good to bad: graffiti, shops, people who live

84

here. And he managed to make it all look beautiful. There was one small note with it: *I spent a week looking around. I can see why you like it here so much.*

I read it and smile. Maybe Ty is having a change of heart. Maybe this is a good omen for the ticket sale. I grab the school paper, slide my article about hometown glory into the empty envelope and quickly run out to post it back to him.

Kira and Faye are logging into the sale from their own homes, because having different IP addresses is paramount to success. Armed with our parents' credit cards and hyper speed Wi-Fi, there will be no stopping us.

The countdown is on until 10 a.m., when tickets go on sale. I'm jittery, I've barely slept and have accepted a rare coffee offer from Mum.

The group chat is pinging off between me, Kira and Faye.

9.57 a.m..

I enter the online waiting room. Five times, with every electronic device in the house. I breathe out a sigh as my access code works. As does Mum's. Faye and Kira confirm they're in too. No word from Ollie, but no doubt he's as nervous as me.

And now the ticketing gods will sort us into a random place in the queue as soon as it it hits—

10 a.m..

I squeal as the page refreshes. I don't even think I'm blinking.

My heart drops when I see the page.

You are 72,345 in the queue.

I let out a sound I can't describe. Like a strangled shout.

I look at the other screens in the room.

90,372

63,587

22,485

104,572

My best shot here is the 22,485, which is on Mum's ancient and unreliable laptop.

I feel like I'm going to throw up.

I immediately go to the group chat.

Kira has 45,293 and 35,587.

Faye has 33,485 and 102,874. Across everyone else I had asked, there is no good news. So much for those IOUs. My only hope is Ollie.

I message Ollie, asking him what his queue number is. Surely now he should reply.

Nothing.

It would be great if you could tell me now, as I'm stressing, I message, gritting my teeth. 'Stressing' is a loose word for what I'm feeling. But 'on the edge of a breakdown' doesn't have the same ring to it.

Still no reply.

I look back at my queue positions. They've all started to tick down, but none are anywhere close to zero. I go on the forums online. People are starting to post about getting tickets, some people are also raging about the long queue.

I think I *might* throw up.

Kira and Faye both tell me that theirs are still nowhere near the end.

Mum comes over. Puts her hand on my shoulder. 'It'll be okay, Selena.'

Part of me wants to wail and scream, but I close my eyes, take a deep breath, and nod. What use is screaming when the outcome is so obvious? It won't change anything.

Ten minutes pass. Ten minutes of agonising waiting, watching everyone get tickets. I see other people at school post their victories and I want to delete all my social media and throw my phone into the void.

Instead I send them party congratulation emoji responses.

And then it's over.

And I don't have tickets.

And Ollie never responded to my message.

Sixteen

It's a bad dream
That you're not with me
The nightshade envy
Leaves its marks

'Nightmare' from *Dreamers*

LATER THAT DAY, Ollie's response left me confused.

Sorry, I completely forgot! I was going to Scott's birthday bash – he wanted to get a McDonald's breakfast to start his 18th lol. Shame about the tickets, better luck next time!

There's a few things my overthinking brain reads into.

One: Ollie's friends now have names. Scott. Ollie's mentioned friends before in passing, but it's now moved from 'a friend' to an actual name, as if Scott is part of my life too.

Two: It's an 18th birthday. I can't have a go at him for not trying for tickets instead of going to an 18th birthday. He'll tell me how hard it is to make friends in upper sixth, at a new school. Although it would have been good if he had remembered yesterday.

Three: *Shame about the tickets.* It doesn't even come close to the magnitude of devastation I am feeling about not going to see Rose Conrad. Which he knows I must be feeling.

But I don't want to upset him by bringing this up. I don't want to push him away. So instead I decide not to reply and get through my emotions by going for a run.

I don't run frequently, but when I do, it feels like the most freeing thing in the world.

I'm turning all my anger and sadness into a pure physical feat, while Rose Conrad blasts out of my headphones.

By the end I'm pelting home at full force.

I'm so caught up in my head I run straight into Ty as he heads out of his house.

Literally. I faceplant his chest and we both go stepping backwards onto his front lawn, and then down . . . down . . . down.

And now I'm lying on top of him on the cool autumn grass.

I freeze, staring right into his eyes. My mind goes completely blank.

'Mind getting up?' he says, with a small smile.

I snap back to reality, and jump off him.

'You know, I thought we were starting to get along better. But I didn't realise you literally wanted to knock me off my feet,' he drawls, standing up after me.

'This is an accident,' I hiss.

'Well, an apology would be nice then,' he says, smirking at me.

'I don't have time for this,' I say, my voice increasing in volume. 'I am having a terrible day as it is.'

'You didn't get Rose Conrad tickets,' he states. 'Even with your army of people trying?'

I nod.

'That sucks,' he says, and he looks like he means it.

I sigh, shaking loose the tension I feel inside of me.

'How about you?' I say.

He shakes his head. No.

I'm glad it's not only me who didn't get the tickets.

'Is that all you're sad about?' he says.

I inhale sharply. 'How do you know? That I'm not just sad at the tickets?'

'Because you look hella mad, rather than devastated. Really pulling out your Olympic sprinter for those last few hundred metres, I saw you fly down here.'

I smile and shake my head. 'I am devastated, and kind of mad too. My best friend let me down today. He was meant to try for tickets for me . . . and didn't.'

'He,' he says, crinkling his forehead. 'So not the Black girl in the dungarees or the blonde, hippy one.'

'What a way to describe them,' I say, letting myself smile at him. 'You got all of that from looking out of the window?'

'They always look like they have your back, for sure,' he says. He looks down at the ground. 'I still haven't made many friends here. Being homeschooled, moving to a new city, a new country, there's not much opportunity.' He gives a small laugh. 'You feel like my closest friend, Writer, and half the time we're hating each other's guts.'

I feel a wave of sympathy towards him. 'That's only half the time.' We both laugh. I hesitate, then say, 'It's the opposite with Ollie, he's made all these new friends and is forgetting about me. I feel . . . I feel like I'm being left behind.' Now I'm not looking at him, this choking feeling rising in my chest. 'But it's fine.' I say, forcing myself to believe it, like I always do.

Ty catches my eye. 'Is it?' he says. He steps forwards. 'You know it's okay not to be okay? I was devastated when my parents told me we were going to move here. And I made it known.'

'I'm not like that,' I say, wringing my hands. 'I don't want to be a pain to anyone. I don't like the confrontation.'

'So you won't tell your friend he let you down? Because you don't want to be a pain?'

'I . . . I feel there's a lot of pressure on me to be good, you know? A good daughter, a good friend, a good person. And being good sometimes means putting others in front of yourself.'

'Sounds tiring,' he says.

'Don't you care? About what others think?'

Ty shrugs. 'To an extent, but not at a cost to myself.' He hesitates. 'And maybe I care too much about what Paul thinks.'

'Who's Paul?'

'My dad,' he says with a small smile. 'Not that I call him Paul to his face.'

'Why do you care what your dad thinks?'

He scrapes the toe of his shoe on the ground. 'I don't know. Because it's so hard to impress him? Because he says he's given us so much, we should make the most of it. I don't know, but whatever his standard is, I don't feel like I'm meeting it.' His voice breaks at the end.

'Has something happened?' I say.

'We're arguing about college, whether I stay here or go back to the US.'

'What do you want to do?' I say.

'I don't want to leave Mom or Daze,' he says. 'So I want to stay here. And it's not like I had a load of friends back home. I want to try from scratch here. And for all the complaining I did about Croydon' I laugh at that 'after my trip around this last week, I realised it's not so bad. There's more to it than I thought.'

'I liked your photos,' I say. 'Thanks for sending them to me.'

'Well, you're the person who inspired me to go explore. I loved your "Hometown Glory" article, by the way. Why was your name not on it? I knew it was you because you used the same envelope I sent my photos in.'

'I'm anonymous . . . It lets me be more myself.'

'Anonymity is cool, you can start out like this and have a grand reveal later. And your article was really good.'

'It's nothing on your photos. They were really something! I actually have no idea how you managed to make some crappy graffiti look interesting.'

'Hey, they don't call it street art for nothing!'

I smile at him. 'Or maybe you're the artist.'

He looks away, with a small smile. 'And London itself – well, I still haven't explored there yet. I want to try taking photos in central London. I bet it's beautiful. When I was walking around Croydon, I was thinking there's so much of the world I haven't seen yet. Why would I want to go all the way back to California, to be miles away from my family? But Paul thinks it's better if I go back home for college. It's why I think I lashed out so much about the place. Because, y'know . . . what Paul says, normally goes.'

'Sounds tough,' I say. Ty's angry persona, his walls, it's starting to make sense a bit more now. If you feel like you're constantly on guard at home, anyone would be like that.

'Anyway, we were talking about your friend problem, not mine.'

'It's all right, there's not much to talk about anyway.' I shrug.

'You know, Writer, you aren't that bad when you're being real.'

'And you're not so bad when you're not being an arse.'

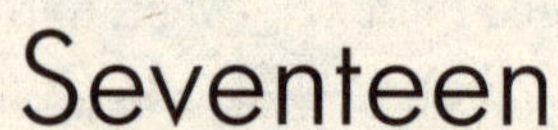

Seventeen

I want to know
What's going on in your head
I want to comb through your mind
See what I can find
A catacomb of memories
To make mine instead

'Catacomb' from *The In-Between*

TODAY'S TAKE: *Forgive and Forget?*

Call me Ms Chances, because I'm forever giving them out. A friend recently betrayed me, but is it bad to not want to deal with the drama? The easy route would be to cause a scene, blow up in their face. The high road is the uphill one, and I'm willing to climb it to save a friendship. Yes, it was something important to me, but our friendship is bigger than that, and I can be the bigger person.

PS. Thank you for responses to Hometown Glory! We've set up SecretSender@chschool.com if you want to write in directly. For those who agreed with me, I loved reading your favourite parts of Croydon. I forgot about the ice rinks and small parks and charity shops! And for anyone who wrote in saying it was a ****hole . . . well, you're wrong.

'You're really getting into being the Secret Sender,' says Kira under her breath as she sits down next to me with her lunch and her copy of the latest *The Common Room*.

I shrug. 'It was your idea. And turns out I like expressing myself.'

'Do you think you might be expressing yourself a bit too much?' says Faye, looking at my article. '"If you disagree with me, you're wrong" doesn't sound a lot like you.'

I shake my head. 'You should have seen some of the emails Tori forwarded to me. Kathleen Turner bloody hates this place, which is a bit rude, because she's so rich and lives in the nicest neighbourhood!'

'It's interesting gossip, for sure,' says Kira. 'But do you think doing this anonymously is making you write things you wouldn't normally?'

'But isn't that the point?' I say. 'It's freeing to be able to write what I think, and to have everyone read it. People are talking about my words.'

'But no one knows it's your words,' says Kira.

'I don't need the fame,' I say. Kira doesn't get it, she loves credit. She loves being in the spotlight. I'm perfectly happy to be in the shadows. I don't need the attention.

Kira shakes her head.

'What else is going on?' says Faye.

'I'm stressed about sending in my UCAS,' says Kira.

My fight or flight is suddenly on. I can't help it, every time someone mentions those four letters I want to run for the hills.

'You've still got nearly three weeks,' says Faye. 'I know you want to send it earlier than the deadline. But it's not the end of the world if you don't.'

'I think I'm nervous about actually sending it off. And then that's it. There's nothing more I can do.'

'But you've done everything you can do,' says Faye, patting Kira's hand.

'Yeah, you'll be fine,' I say. 'You're the most prepared person I know.'

'How are your applications going?' says Kira.

Faye hesitates. 'I actually have something to tell you guys. I don't think I'm going to university.'

'What?' says Kira. I'm shocked, I know Faye's been on the fence like me, but I thought she was also being indecisive about what to study, not she didn't want to go.

'I thought about it, and I want to continue to learn to dressmake and help run my parents' shop. I've found an apprenticeship I can do with this seamstress in Chelsea, and maybe I'll go and study, but first I'm going to build up my portfolio.' She tugs at the jumper she's wearing. A distressed-hem forest-green sweatshirt. It looks pretty cool. 'Look, I made this.'

'That's amazing, Faye,' says Kira, hugging her.

'I'm really happy you've worked out what you want,' I say, and I mean it. Out of all of us, Faye has never really cared too much about academia. And I never got the impression she really wanted to study any more.

'How about you, Selena?' says Kira.

'Oh I don't know yet,' I say.

'Are you still sure you want to go to university?' asks Faye.

It's a good question, after Faye's revelation. But I know the answer.

'Yes, I do,' I say. 'I like learning stuff, I want the experience.' That much is true. When I think of what's ahead, it feels right that it's uni. I just can't put together any more of the details of what I want.

'Then why aren't you getting your shit together, girl?' says Kira.

'I have until January,' I say, crossing my arms.

'Have you decided what course you want to do?' asks Kira.

'No, but—' I say.

'Time is running out!' says Kira.

'Why are you so invested? It's my life,' I say.

'Because you're my friend and I want to help you,' says Kira.

'But it's not helpful that you're always nagging me,' I say. 'As you say, you're my friend, not my mum.'

'I wish that my mum would push me like this,' says Kira aggressively. 'Instead she keeps telling me to be realistic and get my degree and find a good job. She doesn't believe *I* can do it, because no one else can.' Sometimes I think Kira's mum has a point. 'But how am I meant to achieve anything if I set my expectations low? I'll end up being like everyone else.'

'Is that so bad?' I say. 'To be ordinary?'

Kira looks me dead in the eye. 'It's the worst thing I can imagine.'

'But that's you,' I say, standing up. 'Maybe some of us are okay wanting the ordinary.'

'But Selena, how can you know you want the ordinary, when you don't know what you want at all?' Kira touches my arm sympathetically.

I pull my arm away. 'Then give me the time to work it out.' I understand Kira is trying to help, but why can't she see not everyone is like her? That we're different and that's okay?

Eighteen

This pen is a weapon
Ink for bullets
Bleeds deception
Don't mess with me
Or you'll end up stained
With my treachery

'Stained' from *Roses*

ARRIVE AT ENGLISH and Tori is already there with Farah and Mia. I take a spot at the desk behind her. Not because I'm a creature of habit, but because I can hear they're talking about the Secret Sender and I want to eavesdrop.

'She's so good,' says Farah. 'I found *Hometown Glory* so inspirational, and the friendship one so funny but true.'

'"Call me Ms Chances" is such a line,' says Mia, clicking her fingers. 'She can write for sure.'

I feel a swell of pride at the girls' comments.

They think I'm funny.

'That line is like a Rose Conrad lyric,' says Farah. 'It's so witty.'

I could kiss Farah. My writing, compared to Rose Conrad's? My ego is inflating so much it might pop out of the classroom.

'Do you know who the Secret Sender is?' Mia asks Tori. 'You're the editor. She must contact you.'

Tori nods, and then to my complete shock says, 'I know who it is.'

I feel my body tense. How? How can she know? She keeps asking questions every time I submit something, but I never reply. Can she track my IP address or something? Is Tori part-time student newspaper editor, part-time hacker?

'Who is it?' says Farah, leaning forwards. I'm also leaning so far forwards I'm basically hanging off the front of the desk.

'Oh I can't tell you,' says Tori, looking at her fingernails. 'Source confidentiality and all that.'

'Is she in our English class?' says Mia.

'No,' says Tori. 'And that's the only question I'll answer on it.' She looks smug. 'But the Secret Sender and I have a good relationship. You know, editor-journalist brainstorming and so on.'

That's when I know: Tori does not know I am the Secret Sender, and she is bullshitting her friends, probably to look more important than she is. Classic.

Ms Harkness arrives in the classroom. Still in a leather jacket. I'm starting to think it's welded to her.

'How's it going, girls?' she says.

'We were talking about the Secret Sender,' says Farah. 'Tori says—'

'Her latest article is very thought-provoking and she's a great contributor to *The Common Room*,' says Tori, smoothly interrupting Farah.

Farah glances at Tori but says nothing.

Ms Harkness shakes her head. 'Well you know my opinion on anonymous contributors, Tori. But as you're the editor, I think it's good for you to take responsibility.'

'What's your opinion, Ms?' says Mia.

'I think,' says Ms Harkness, taking out some papers and laying them out on her desk, 'that if you're going to write personal and sometimes controversial opinions, you should be held accountable to them by putting your name on it.' She looks up, and for a second catches my eye. I look away in a hurry. 'I don't think anonymity is a good thing in this day and age. It can create cowards who hide behind it.' She starts handing out the papers. 'But then again, the Secret Sender hasn't written anything against school policy or horrible or defaming, so I can let it slide for now.'

'True,' says Farah. 'I think that it was a bit much to call out the people who sent her disagreements. It sounded like she was making fun of them.'

I feel myself sweat as Ms Harkness passes me. What would she think if she found out the Secret Sender was me? What would everyone else think?

One thing is certain: no one can find out it's me writing the articles.

'Oh Selena, I want to talk to you later,' says Ms Harkness.

My mouth goes dry, my heart is hammering.

'No need to look so afraid.' She laughs. 'I want to talk to you about your UCAS.'

Any relief I had about not being unmasked as the Secret Sender is replaced by annoyance. Can I not catch a break?

I'm in a foul mood when I get home. Between Kira and Ms Harkness, my UCAS form seems to be everyone else's business. I want to talk to Ollie, but he says he's busy and he'll call me soon.

'I don't get it,' I say to Mum. 'You don't even care as much as Kira does.'

I'm helping her make dinner. She's sat down at the counter, chopping vegetables, I'm starting to fry them. Our kitchen is open plan, joining onto our dining room, which faces out to the garden. Throughout all of our time here, our routine has remained the same: Mum making dinner, me watching her and asking her advice. Recently, I've started helping out more and more.

What has remained constant over the years is the art hung up on the walls – paintings from Thailand, India and more that she collected in the years before she had me.

'You don't think I care,' says Mum, raising an eyebrow.

'Well, you never really say anything about it,' I say.

'I ask you all the time about what you want to do!' says Mum, aggressively chopping a carrot.

'But conceptually, not concretely.' I start to temper the spices in the pan, like Mum taught me.

'What does that mean?'

'Like "What do you want to do in the future" is a bit vague compared to "What do you want to study at uni? Shouldn't you be prepping your UCAS by now? You needed to have chosen three days ago".' My voice turns more and more into Kira's as I say it.

'Just because I don't ask you specifics doesn't mean I don't care,' says Mum, her voice level.

I turn off the heat and turn around to look at her.

'I know you care, Mum. You're constantly showing me you care. But it's low pressure, you know. You get that it doesn't matter *that* much.'

'No, Selena,' says Mum, looking up from chopping onions. She puts down the knife. 'It does matter, but I wanted to give you the space to figure it out yourself, rather than have you looking to me for advice. But don't you think Kira has a point? Time is starting to run out. You don't want to rush making these decisions.'

I take a step back. 'You agree . . . with Kira?'

'Selena, my whole life I've had direction,' says Mum urgently. 'I didn't go to university, and I decided to study later. I chose a career I wanted. I hope you'd follow the example. Not making any choice and running out of time . . . that's not courageous. It feels like you want someone to tell you what to do, so you don't have to make a choice. I don't know why you're avoiding choosing options for your future, but whatever the reason it's not right to avoid it like this.'

I'm shocked. Mum has always gone along with what I thought. And I was hoping she would have my back with this against Kira. And now she says she thinks I'm being a coward by not making a rash decision? If it's my choice to make, I deserve the time to make it.

'I thought you were on my side,' I say as I walk out to the garden.

Nineteen

'Specimen' from *The In-Between*

I IMMEDIATELY REGRET WALKING outside. It's sunset and it's starting to get cold. The air has a chill, but I don't care as I angrily stomp up to the oak tree at the base of the garden. As I pass the fence, I see Ty.

He's lying down on his front, camera pressed to his face. As far as I can tell, he's zooming in on some blades of grass.

'Don't you ever stop taking pictures?' I say.

He rolls over, so he's facing upwards, camera still hovering over his face. The top of his head is facing towards me, I'm looking across at him, almost like he's in a movie still. He's wearing a white T-shirt, now marred by grass stains, that is pushed up past his waist, and I feel the tug of attraction again, the one I'm desperately trying to resist.

'Do you ever stop asking questions?' he says.

'He asks with a question?' I say, knowing I sound petulant.

He sits up and spins around, camera hanging around his neck. 'What's got you today?' says Ty.

'Nothing,' I say, turning around and walking off. 'I'm in a bad mood and I came out here for some space.'

A few moments later I can hear him jump over the fence and run over to me. 'Hey, tell me what's going on.'

I sit under the oak tree, ignoring his question. I really don't feel like talking right now.

Ty sits down next to me, touching my shoulder. I shrug off his hand.

'Come on, Writer. Use those words of yours,' he says.

I look at him. 'You really want to hear me moan about my problems?'

He smiles at me, taps my knee. 'Considering how bad a mood you're in, yes I do.' He looks like he means it.

I sigh. 'Everyone is on my case about the future,' I say.

'In what way?'

I look at the ground. 'I haven't figured it out . . . you know, post this year. What I want to do at university. If I even want to go to university.'

'Do you want to go to university?' he says. I can still feel him grabbing on to my wrist, shooting pulses of electricity up my arm.

'I think so,' I say. 'But . . . it's always been abstract, you know? Like it will inevitably happen, and I've not thought too much about it. What it actually means, to grow up, to move on. I don't feel . . . I don't feel ready for it.'

'So you're avoiding thinking about it?' he says.

'Yes, but everyone else is thinking about it for me. Kira, now Mum, Ms Harkness.'

'Who's Ms Harkness?'

'My English teacher.'

'That makes sense, surely you're going to major in English.'

'But even that isn't straightforward.' I can feel myself getting worked up about it. 'There's a lot of options there too. You know how I've started writing for the student newspaper? For the first time, I feel I'm really good at something. People are talking about what I've written. I want to do this more. It's made me even more confused. Do I want to be a journalist? I'm not like Tori, who has her whole life planned out—'

'Who is Tori?' says Ty, cutting through my monologue.

'This girl in my English class who's the editor of the newspaper. She's wanted to be a journalist forever. She was basically prepping to be editor for the past three years. I think she scared off anyone from also applying to do it, as she ran uncontested.'

'She sounds like a lot.'

'She is. But how can I also do journalism or something, when I haven't spent my life preparing like Kira and Tori? They've had everything figured out for so long, I can't compete. I feel I'm so behind, and I'm only seventeen.'

Ty grabs my wrist and squeezes it. For once, I don't pull away. 'You know what I think?'

I shake my head.

'I think you're trying to compete when there's no competition here. Do it because you like doing it. Apply for it because you want to. Don't worry about other people, worry about yourself.'

'But what does that look like?'

Ty shrugs. 'Only you can answer that. But whatever it is will be better than being paralysed by indecision.'

'That's what my mum was saying.'

'She sounds like a wise lady.'

'She is.' I sigh. 'But I got really mad at her for telling me.'

He nods. 'You didn't want to hear the truth. She probably understands.'

'You're not bad at giving advice, you know?'

'Turns out you're not the only person good with words. I'll be giving you a run for your money soon.'

'What do you want to do anyway? Photography?'

'No, this . . .' he says, holding up the camera, 'this is a hobby to me, I don't want to study it in case it becomes less fun. I want to study Chemistry.'

'Chemistry?' I say. 'You've never mentioned anything about Chemistry before.'

'Well organic compound reactions don't really come into daily conversation, which is a great shame.'

'British sarcasm really is growing on you.'

'I would say I'm fluent now.' He laughs. 'I like understanding how the world works. And Chemistry does that. When you boil everything down, it's tiny atoms making everything up. I think it's fascinating.'

'And do you want to be a chemist?'

'I don't think so,' he says. 'But like you, I don't know exactly what I want to do. But I know I've got to start, and that'll help me figure it out.'

I look ahead. Makes sense to me. I just need to start.

Probably with apologising to Mum about yelling first.

Twenty

'What Happened Next' from *Roses*

REALLY NEED TO talk about this to Ollie, who has become more and more distant since the ticket incident. Shockingly, I manage to get hold of him on FaceTime on a Friday night.

'I can't believe it's now October. Time has gone by so quick,' says Ollie.

And it has, we've barely spoken in the last week. It's hard to believe, since we used to talk to each other every day.

'I know,' I say. 'It's so dark now.' I'm trying to not watch myself in the tiny corner screen and focus on Ollie's face.

'How have you been?' he says, the camera suddenly moving as he rolls to his side on the bed.

I inhale deeply. If anyone knows me the best, it's Ollie.

'Right now, focusing on uni,' I say. 'I should apply after Christmas.'

'I've sent mine off,' he says. 'Getting a headstart and all that.'

'Lawyer Ollie incoming,' I say.

'Oh yeah,' he says. 'Have you picked yet?'

This is what I like about Ollie. No assumptions, he knows me.

'I'm thinking about doing English,' I say.

'Great,' he says. 'You've always liked reading.'

I think of Ty, how he calls me Writer, how he says I know my words. Ty knows I like to create, build with language.

'Actually,' I say, taking a deep breath, 'I've started doing some journalism for the school newspaper.'

'Really, that's great,' says Ollie. 'What are you writing about?'

I explain how I've turned my Selena Says into an anonymous column. At the end he is silent.

'What do you think?'

'Is this not like a gossip column?' he says.

'No!' I protest. 'It's my opinions.'

'Then why not do it with your own name?'

I fall silent. This is not the response I want. Because I'm afraid of expressing my opinion out loud? But how could someone like Ollie, who is so confident in what he thinks, and never is afraid to say it, understand that?

'Never mind,' I say. 'It's a side thing. My classes are the main reason I want to do English.'

'What are you reading now?'

'We're doing *The Great Gatsby* at school. It's pretty good.'

'Ah, we've started with Shakespeare. Good old *Romeo and Juliet*.'

'Enjoying reading about star-crossed lovers?' I say, my breath hitching a bit. Maybe this will trigger something in Ollie. Maybe he'll see us in the text. Without the tragic ending.

'Not particularly,' he says. 'I wanted *Macbeth* or *Hamlet*.'

'Fair enough.' How could I have imagined he would say something else? 'How's school, then?'

'It's getting better. I've actually made a few friends. None of them on par with Selena Pia, of course.'

But I don't want to talk about Ollie's new friends. Especially as it was because of them I didn't get the Rose Conrad tickets. I move on. 'And how's Manchester?'

'It's so cold here,' he says. 'Much more than down south. But all the lights are coming out now, and it looks really nice.'

'The way Ty complains about the weather, you may as well think it's Siberia down here,' I say.

'Ty?' says Ollie, looking confused. 'Who's Ty?'

'The new neighbour,' I say. I feel a slight sense of panic about bringing him up. It doesn't feel right and I don't know why.

'I thought you disliked him?' says Ollie, raising his eyebrows.

'I do!' I say, and I watch as my eyes become wider in the corner screen. I need to make myself look more chill. 'He is egotistical and annoying and has this really specific way of saying the wrong thing, but . . .'

'But what?' says Ollie.

'But I see him all the time, so he's impossible to ignore,' I say.

'That's good,' says Ollie. 'I would hate to think someone's replaced me.'

'Oh, absolutely not,' I say. Is Ollie . . . jealous? I smile at the thought. 'You know you can't be replaced. Even with a few weeks apart.'

'Oh, which is why you should come to Manchester for my birthday! The first of November is on the last weekend of half term too, so hopefully you'll be able to travel. It's my eighteenth, after all. What do you think?'

'Really? Are you sure you want me there, not your new friends?'

'Well, yes, but you should come too, so you can meet everyone. What are you thinking about doing for your birthday?'

I feel a surge of delight. Ollie hasn't forgotten about me after all. 'Oh, you know I've got until the beginning of December to think about what I want to do about mine. But I will be there for yours.'

Twenty-One

Notes on a postcard
Etched in forever
I'll keep these words
For worse or for better

'Postcard' from Dreamers

To Secret Sender,
Please do not forgive your friend. If it's important
to you, they should have remembered.

Dear Secret Sender,
Your latest post worried me. It's not about
being the bigger person. Did your friend
acknowledge what they did wrong?

Secret Sender,
GIRL cut out this toxic boy. And I can tell he's

a boy. Not revealing the gender was a sign of
boy problems. And the best way to get out
of boy problems, is to get rid of the boy.

ID YOU WRITE this last one?' I say to Kira, who's
peering over my shoulder to look at my inbox. It's
Monday and it's filled up over the weekend.

'No, but I kind of wish I had,' she says. 'They have a point.'

'I didn't realise I was going to receive so much unsolicited
advice,' I say. The messages don't make me feel good. They
don't know the full story, and I can't reply back with it, so it
feels unfinished.

'Not only that, you've managed to divide the school,' says
Faye. She holds out two badges in her palm. One says *Team
Sender* and the other says *Team Friend*. 'People are literally
picking sides.'

'People have too much time,' I say, picking up the badges
and throwing them into the bin.

'It's because Secret Sender doesn't feel like a real person,'
says Kira. 'This is the problem with anonymity. The person
behind the mask feels less human.'

'Hey, you're the person who gave me the mask,' I say. 'And
it's fine. I can handle some unsolicited advice and some stupid
merch.'

Just then Mia comes running up to us. Kira and Mia were
in a lot of classes together during our GCSE years, and they

bonded over the teachers mixing them up because their names sound similar, despite the fact they look nothing alike.

'What's going on?' says Kira.

'I need some advice, quick,' says Mia, 'and Farah and Tori are in Spanish class.' Mia looks around. 'It's just that my friend – she's my friend from when I was a Brownie, she doesn't go here . . .' She pauses, collecting herself. 'I found out there's this story going around her school and it's about a girl who mistook an "Around the World" dress-up theme and instead of coming as a specific place, they bought an inflatable Earth costume and couldn't fit through any door of the church hall.'

We all start laughing. 'That is pretty funny,' says Kira.

'The person was me,' hisses Mia. 'I got confused about the "Around" part of "Around the World". Anyway I told her not to tell anyone, and it turns out she has.'

'Is it that big a deal?' says Faye. 'It was a while ago, no?'

'Yes, but it's hurtful because I told her not to tell anyone, and she did.'

'Ah, so she betrayed your trust,' says Kira. I narrow my eyes at the turn of phrase.

'Exactly,' says Mia. 'And normally I would tell her how I feel or, you know, ignore her for a bit so she can tell I'm pissed, but the Secret Sender is saying we should all be bigger women!'

'It sounds like you were pretty big in that globe costume,' says Kira with a smile. 'But seriously, that is rough. You know you can do what you want and not listen to the Secret Sender, right?'

Mia shakes her head. 'I know,' she says. 'But I feel this girl knows something, you know? That we don't. It's why she's so mysterious.'

'*Or,*' says Kira, 'she could be a normal person.'

'Yeah,' I say. 'You should do what's right for you.'

'Okay,' says Mia, smoothing down her top. 'Thanks, guys, I'll think about it. I just needed to get it off my chest.'

After Mia walks off, Kira turns to me. 'With great power comes great responsibility,' she says.

'That wasn't a big deal,' I say, rolling my eyes.

'It starts with no big deals, then it ends up with your words doing some real damage,' says Kira. 'You've got to be careful.'

She's right, I am a bit shaken at how Mia took the Secret Sender like gospel, not as some random thoughts I had. I look back at the emails in my inbox, and shut down the laptop.

'I need to talk to you about something else.'

'You've decided what course you want to do?' says Kira excitedly.

'No,' I start, then I pause. 'But I feel a bit better about it after talking to Ty.'

'So you're friends now?' says Faye, raising an eyebrow.

'No!' I say instinctively, then immediately reconsider. 'We're friends, but friends who are constantly annoying one another.'

'Sounds hot,' says Kira, laughing and kicking her legs out.

'It's not like that,' I insist. 'I don't like him like that.'

'Girl, he's hot,' says Kira.

'Yeah, are you blind?' says Faye.

'I don't feel like that about him because—' I cut myself off, and look at my two friends, waiting expectantly.

'Because?' says Faye, motioning her hand.

'Because . . . because I like Ollie,' I finally splutter out.

'Still?' says Kira.

'What do you mean "still"?' I say. Deep down I thought they knew, they've just never said it out loud before.

'Selena, you're so bad at expressing yourself sometimes – we've become experts at reading you,' says Kira.

'Yeah, we could tell you liked Ollie,' says Faye. 'But do you still like him after he's been gone for so long?'

'You have to tell us everything,' says Kira, leaning forwards.

'Of course I still like Ollie,' I say, feeling a bit stung they hadn't told me that they knew I liked him. 'I've liked him for the past two years.'

'Why didn't you tell him then!' says Faye. It's one of the most animated I've seen her.

'Because I'm afraid . . .' Isn't that obvious?

'Of what?' says Kira.

'Rejection? What if he doesn't feel the same?' I say.

'But you won't know if you don't try,' says Kira, raising her hands in the air.

'You don't even like Ollie,' I say, shaking my head.

'No, I don't. Mostly because I think he's a presumptuous arse,' says Kira. 'But I like you. And I wish you had put yourself out there. You've been pining after him all these years and never told him how you feel!'

'Okay, well I'm going to Manchester at the end of the

month,' I say, crossing my arms. Why does Kira have to always make me feel like I've done something wrong? It's not like she's so perfect.

'So what,' says Kira. 'You're going to go all the way to Manchester to win him back?' She pauses. 'Selena, I have to tell you this, but that is batshit. You can't do that.'

'Just a second ago you were telling me I need to put myself out there!'

'Yeah, when he was living next door! Not when you have to trek across the country to do it.'

'I think it sounds romantic,' chips in Faye.

'Ollie invited me,' I say. 'I'm going to Manchester because he invited me! It feels like we're growing apart, but he's still one of my best friends. My oldest friend. I'm not going to confess my undying love to him.' I pause a beat. 'Potentially.'

Kira and Faye exchange a look. 'Okay,' says Kira. 'You have our full support.'

'Yeah, it makes total sense you want to see your friend,' says Faye.

'But think about what you're going to do before you go,' says Kira. 'Hey, I'm in full support of you telling that waste-of-space you have feelings so you can get it off your chest, but I don't want you to do it in a way where you get hurt.'

'I'll be fine,' I say. 'Even if he rejects me, he won't hurt me. It's Ollie!' I look at the National Rail site on my phone. 'What's more at risk of hurting me is the cost of these train tickets! How does anyone ever afford to go to Manchester?'

Twenty-Two

My nerves are on fire
This is desire
Oh . . . I think this is the start
Of something electric, magnetic
I hope I don't regret it

'Electric' from *The In-Between*

'M IN THE kitchen, with my laptop open, ready to book the world's longest coach to get to Manchester. It's now mid-October and Ollie's birthday is three weeks away, and the train tickets are eye-wateringly expensive. And for every day I've not booked, the prices have climbed higher and higher. The coach may be a lot cheaper, but what it doesn't cost me in money, it costs me in time. Seven hours, to be precise, because of a 'route diversion' which means they've added five more stops than usual. Wonderful.

Luckily Ollie's birthday has timed with half term, which

means I can afford to spend a full Friday travelling to Manchester.

That's when I notice the basketball in the garden. I see it as a signal that Daze wants to speak to me. He simply can't be this bad at basketball, no matter how hard the tricks are.

I walk outside in a puffer jacket, pick up the ball and throw it over the fence.

'Aren't you cold?' I say. Daze is dressed in a basketball jersey, but with leggings under long shorts.

'Hell yeah,' says Daze. 'But it keeps me moving.' He starts dribbling aggressively, then stops suddenly, walks away and picks up a jumper. 'But I guess to talk to you I should put this on.'

'How's it going? How's school?'

'I like it,' he says. 'I took your advice to make some friends, and now I think I like soccer. Well, football.'

'That's good!'

'You should write an advice book or something. Ty told me you like to write.'

'I'm not that good.' I laugh. 'I barely know what I'm doing tomorrow.'

'But you're so . . . cool,' says Daze. 'Like, nothing gets you. You didn't get Rose Conrad tickets and you seem fine, even though I know you must have been sad.' I decide not to tell him how I wept to *Dreamers* for several hours in my room.

'I'm definitely not as cool as you think,' I say. 'But it's nice of you to say anyway.' I pause. 'In fact, I spend a lot of time in my head and I keep putting off the big decision about the future. I don't think any of that is cool. Plus, I cried for hours after not getting Rose Conrad tickets, you didn't see it.' So much for not telling him.

'Well, that sounds like . . . a lot,' says Daze, scrunching up his face.

'I shouldn't be telling my life problems to an eleven-year-old.' I sigh.

'It's all right, people end up telling me things.' He shrugs. 'I have that type of face.'

Suddenly I see my shot. 'Does Ty tell you things too?' I ask, as innocently as possible.

'Naw, Ty actually tells me nothing. He's easy to read though,' says Daze, starting to bounce his ball around again.

'Oh, in what way?' I say, leaning on the fence, trying to fake nonchalance. Good thing my target is an eleven-year-old boy, I don't think anyone else would be convinced by my acting skills. But hey, I want to write, not be on stage.

'He gets kinda obsessed about things. Right now, he's trying to beat Level 17 of this video game and that's, like, all he does apart from school and the gym.'

I make a mental note: *Into video games.*

'And what does that mean?' I say. 'Since you said, you know, he's easy to read.'

'It means he's trying to avoid something,' says Daze. He looks at his phone. 'I've got to go, it's my turn now to play on the PS5. Ty said I could have a go after an hour.'

And before I can even say bye, Daze legs it back to the house.

I'm about to turn around, when Ty calls out my name.

'Hey,' I say. 'I was giving Daze his basketball back. I think he uses it as a way to talk to me.'

'Interesting communication form,' says Ty. 'He mentioned you were out here, so I came out.'

'Without a jacket?' I say. Ty looks cold, in tracksuit trousers and a T-shirt.

'I was in a rush,' he says, sheepishly. 'I didn't want to miss you.'

I feel a rush of emotion. He ran out for me.

I walk towards him. 'What did you want to talk about?'

He looks surprised, as if he didn't expect the question. 'Well – er . . .' he stumbles.

'It's rare for you to lose your cool.' I laugh.

'Maybe because I'm freezing,' he says.

'It is impressive you are standing out here in the cold like this.' I want to reach out and put my hand on his bare arm, but I hold myself back.

He staggers back, as if he's been wounded.

'Writer called me . . . impressive? I think that's the most complimentary adjective you've used yet.'

'And you know what an adjective is.' I smile. 'Even more impressive.'

We're flirting. I know we are now.

He smiles at me, and picks up the basketball, bounces it a couple of times, then throws it to me. I catch it.

I'm frozen, not sure what to do next. I should do something impressive, like dribble it myself, but I've never played basketball and I don't want to embarrass myself. Or maybe I should throw it back at him.

Instead, I stare at him.

'Are you not going to throw it back?' he says, walking up to me.

The fence reaches our waists, my hands holding the basketball over it.

He's close to me now, so close I can see the stubble on his chin. So close I can smell the spice of his aftershave. I look into his eyes, and I feel my words catching on my tongue.

'I wouldn't know where to start,' I say.

Ty's mouth curves into a smile, his eyes on my mouth. I tilt my head up, never breaking eye contact. The electricity is tugging me closer to him.

He reaches out his hands, grabbing the ball by putting his hands over my own. I feel electric pulses run up my arm. I drop the ball.

This is a boy who knows he's attractive. A boy who probably has never been told no before. A boy with eyes that can melt you and a smile that draws you in.

So I get drawn in. Ty's head is dipping lower and lower, my eyes flutter close, and in the last moment, I—

He moves away.

'Sorry,' he says, throwing the ball on the floor, not looking at me.

I feel a wave of frustration and rejection crush through me. What was he doing? What was I thinking? Then a roil of guilt; I'm meant to like Ollie.

'My mind is all over the place,' he says, looking up at me. He looks lost.

I take a deep breath. 'I don't know what you're talking about,' I say. Better to move on. It was a moment of thoughtlessness for both of us.

He blinks, looking a bit stunned, then regains himself.

I need to break this weird silence. 'What's going on? You're acting . . . strange. Stranger than usual.'

He looks around. 'Do you want to go for a walk?'

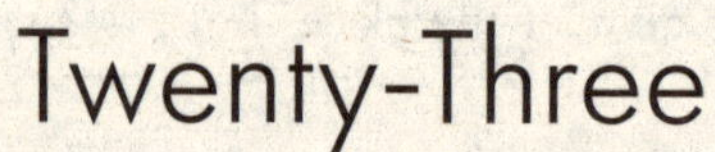

Twenty-Three

Tell me a secret
I promise I'll keep it
Throw the wish into the well
I'll believe it

'Secrets' from *The Brink*
of Teenage Freedom

AS WE START walking away from our houses, the sun is beginning to set.

'You know, Writer, you may be the best friend I have in this city. Hell, in this country,' says Ty, staring straight ahead. The last of the sun bathes over him, and for a moment, he looks serene.

'Isn't that something?' I say, lightly. 'You know with this streak of befriending my neighbours, maybe I don't have anything to worry about at university.'

He shakes his head. 'You really don't. People like you.'

'You've rarely seen me outside my back garden, how would you know?'

'Because you're magnetic,' he says, looking very seriously at me.

My heart feels like it's jumping out of my chest. I don't know how to respond.

'Anyway,' says Ty, looking ahead. 'As I said, I've got a lot on my mind.'

'Like what?' I ask.

'My parents . . . have a lot of expectations.'

'Is this about your dad again? About how he wants you to go to America?'

'It's more he . . . he just wants me to be successful.' Ty is still not looking at me, only at the horizon.

'Isn't that what all parents want for their kids?'

'Yes, but my dad has a very rigid definition of success.'

'And what's that?'

'He thinks being successful is having a lot of money, being in charge, being powerful.' He pauses. 'You can see some of that thinking in Daze. His disregard for authority is him trying to look powerful.'

'You don't think it's a good idea?'

'I don't know, it's such a part of who he is. Because he was raised like this, because we were raised like this . . . How can we separate ourselves from the people our parents shaped us into?'

'And what did your dad shape you into?'

'My dad made me become this person who needs validation. Everything I do, I need to feel like I've done a good job. Even with my photography, I want to get so good at it I can enter competitions, rather than do it for the sake of doing it.'

'I don't think there's anything wrong with wanting to be good at things,' I say. 'I'm pretty easy-going, but I want to feel like I'm doing well. It's why I feel so self-conscious sometimes. That I'm not good enough.' My voice cracks at the last line. I stare firmly ahead.

'I guess that makes both of us. No matter what I do I can't please him. I told him I was going to apply to US universities, but he wasn't happy I'm not applying to The Ivies. Wasn't happy I want to take photographs instead of study the stock market with him. Not happy I don't care about golf or cars or any of the things he cared about at seventeen.'

'Your dad was into golf at seventeen?'

'Yeah, his dad took him. And he tried taking me as a kid but all I did was complain about how heavy the clubs were and how I couldn't hit it far enough. Daze at least likes basketball.'

'You think Daze is living up more to what your dad wants?'

Ty laughs. 'Which is weird, because his attitude drives Dad mad. Eternally optimistic, defies authority, cares so little about school. He's doing it his own way.'

'And what would doing it your way look like?'

'Taking my time to work out what I really want, not what he expects.'

'To go to university in the UK?'

'Yeah, and more than that. I told you I want to study Chemistry. And if my dad had it his way, I'd be doing Business or Economics. He says he doesn't see a future in being a chemist, but that's not the point. I don't need to have figured out what I want to do with my life at eighteen.'

It feels like he's mind-read me. 'I get that. I feel so anxious having to even pick what I want to do in the future. Do you know which universities you want to apply to yet?'

'I'm actually going to drive up and take a look around Liverpool on the first of November,' he says. 'Get out of London for a bit. Have you looked anywhere?'

'No, I think I want to stay in London but haven't decided yet. Like most things.' I pause. 'Wait, did you say you're going to Liverpool for the first of November? That's near Manchester, right?'

Ty shrugs. 'I think your UK geography is better than mine.'

I'm aware things are currently a bit strange with Ty, but the opportunity is too good to miss . . .

'Can you drive me up too? I need to be in Manchester that weekend. And right now I'm looking at a seven-hour coach ride . . . A car ride from you sounds much more enjoyable. And with less stops.'

Ty side eyes me. 'Sure,' he says slowly. 'Why are you going?'

'To see a friend,' is all I say.

We walk in silence for a bit, heading into the park.

'It's funny how you feel you have too much direction and

I don't feel I have any at all,' I say.

'But isn't it nice? To feel like you could do anything?'

I pause, thinking carefully. 'I always thought I could do anything. But I think I would also want someone to tell me I'm on the right track. That everything will be okay, no matter what I choose. Because even though there are a lot of choices, it doesn't always feel like I'm making the right ones.' Now it's my turn to pause. 'I never knew my dad, you know.'

Ty nods. 'I've only seen you and your mom around.'

'The rough story is, Mum met him on one of her trips when she was young, got pregnant, he didn't want anything to do with me or her, and . . . now I'm here.'

'That's . . . I can't believe someone would do that.'

I wave my hand at him. 'Don't worry about it. I don't really mind. Mum has been enough for me. Enough for two parents. And we barely see my grandparents at all. But Mum's a strong person, you know? And I want to make the right choices, so she knows . . . well, she made the right choices with me.'

Ty grabs my wrist, squeezing it. 'You and your mum are great. I'm sorry for complaining so much about Paul.'

I let him hold on to it. 'No, don't worry about it. I wanted you to know I get it, about how our parents shape us. Who would I be if my mum wasn't so decisive, so independent? I think she expects me to be the same as her, but I'm not, and I feel I'm letting her down sometimes. And now her arthritis is getting worse, I feel like I'm not doing enough for her. Just like you feel you're letting your dad down.'

'I think the difference is my dad is a hardass, while your mum is badass.'

I laugh and pull myself away, spinning myself around in the autumn sunshine. I feel lighter than ever before.

Twenty-Four

They say I'm all about the
Drama!
So good at acting this part
I might just get an
Oscar!

'Drama!' from *The In-Between*

TODAY'S TAKE: *Haters gonna hate*

My last article caused quite a stir, so let me address that here. Unlike your social media posts, I don't need everyone to like me. I'm not your god, your therapist, your mother. I am here, telling my story and sharing my thoughts. You're your own person, you can think for yourself. And if you're going to be a group of snivelling lambs following a wolf – well, that's your own prerogative.

'What is this?' says Kira, putting down *The Common Room* in front of me.

'Looks like a copy of *The Common Room*,' I say.

'"I don't need everyone to like me",' reads out Kira. She looks at me. 'Selena, you care deeply about being liked. It's why you won't put your name against this.'

'But it's not my words, it's the Secret Sender.'

'You are the Secret Sender,' hisses Kira.

'Shhh,' I say. 'I know, but nobody else does.'

'So what, you're going Jekyll and Hyde and this is a new identity for you?'

'No, it's not that.' I stop. 'I want people to not take me too seriously, so I was sending a message. And yeah it may be a bit extreme, but at least that way people will listen.'

Kira shakes her head. 'You've got to be careful, girl. People are dying to work out who you are. In Economics I overheard some wild theories flying around about the Secret Sender.'

'I'm an anonymous writer, not Batman,' I say. 'I've got to get to English, I'll see you later.'

Class actually starts in ten minutes, but I want to shake off Kira's words first. She doesn't get it. Kira's so confident, she doesn't need anything to boost her.

When I get to the classroom, Tori and the newspaper staff are all in there. Ms Harkness is there too. They must be wrapping up a newspaper staff meeting. I stand outside, listening to Tori's booming voice.

She's boasting about something new. 'The *Croydon Post*

only takes three work experience students every year from across the boroughs, and I'm definitely going to get it. This is my stepping stone to the real news. Then TV, maybe.'

I roll my eyes and start scrolling on my phone. I don't want to go in early.

'I wonder what her next article is going to be,' I hear Farah say a few moments later. My ears prick – are they talking about me?

'Yeah, this one is pretty biting,' says Mia. They are, so I decide to slink into the back of the classroom.

'She really has a way with words,' agrees Connie, the sports editor. '"I am not your god." Wow.'

Once again, I feel a bump of delight at that. People enjoy my work!

'I think we need to get her out there,' says Farah. 'School exclusive. It'll be big news.'

'What will be big news?' says Ms Harkness, looking up from her desk.

'If we unmask the Secret Sender, Ms,' says Farah. 'What do you think?'

'Do we know who the Secret Sender is?'

'Tori does!' says Mia. She looks at Tori excitedly. 'Do you think you can get her to reveal her name?'

'Er—' stutters Tori, who has been silent for this whole conversation, very unlike her. Probably because she's backed herself into a corner. 'I can't reveal it publicly,' she says.

I raise my eyebrows. Tori admitting to not being able to do something?

And then she says, 'Because I am the Secret Sender.'

I smack my hand on the desk.

Luckily the noise is drowned out because all of the newspaper staff are in uproar. Everyone is yelling at each other, at Tori, or are making noise.

'Stop!' yells Tori, drawing focus to herself again.

I am raging in silence. I can't believe Tori has taken the credit for being the Secret Sender. For my words. How dare she?

But what am I going to do? I can't reveal myself. So I watch and wait.

'Why didn't you post under your own name?' says Mia.

I cross my arms. I'm interested to hear Tori's take. Part of me wonders if she planned to do this, or she panicked. Either way, she hasn't planned for the questioning, she looks like she's making up the answers on the fly.

'I was doing an editorial experiment,' says Tori. 'I wanted to see how readership is affected by writing anonymously. It's for my university interview discussion.'

I'll hand it to her, Tori can bullshit.

'So that's why we can't reveal it's me,' continues Tori. 'Because I haven't concluded the experiment yet. I want to see how far I can take it with my articles. But as you're my writers, I thought now is a good time to let you know.'

'So what you wrote about betrayal—'

'I'm not ready to talk about my Secret Sender posts just yet,' says Tori, overtly theatrically. 'All shall be revealed in due course.'

The bell goes, and as the rest of the class filters in, some of the newspaper staff filter out, muttering secretly to each other. No doubt they think they have something juicy.

Never mind the secret they've uncovered is actually a lie.

Ms Harkness starts handing out essays she's marked. She puts mine down on the desk. A shiny red A* marked on it.

'Well done, Selena. Top marks in the class,' she says, looking at me. I see Tori turn her head around at that, looking at me with surprise. I feel smug. 'I saw you listening in on our newspaper meeting,' Ms Harkness continues.

I shrug. 'I got here early.'

'Did you ever contribute anything?'

'No,' I lie.

'Interesting,' she says. 'I could have sworn I've read something in there that sounds like your writing voice.'

And with that, she walks away to hand out more papers. I touch my forehead. I'm sweating.

Twenty-Five

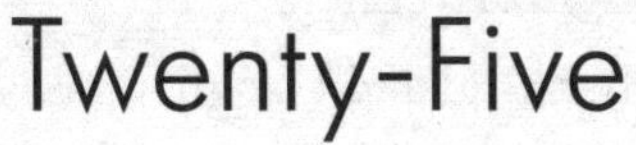

A new day is coming
The golden glow of sunrise
Finally appears
I've been waiting
To make it here

'New Day' from *The In-Between*

ON THE FRIDAY of the October half term, Rose Conrad releases a bonus track for *The In-Between*. I listen to it first thing in the morning, as I finish packing for Manchester. The last week of school and the whole of half term have been uneventful, bar Tori continuing to keep up her Secret Sender charade.

So if anything, this is a sign. Rose Conrad only releases new music when something pivotal is about to happen in my life.

And today is the day when I confess how I feel to Ollie.

I look out of the living-room window; Ty's not out yet.

'You're both going to be okay driving up?' says Mum.

'Ty is driving, and in America they apparently drive all the time. From when they're fifteen. If you think about it, he's more like a twenty-year-old driver here.'

Mum shakes her head and I laugh.

'It'll be fine. Ty's driving us to Liverpool, I'll get a train to see Ollie. Ty's going to spend Saturday exploring Liverpool, then on Sunday we'll meet up and he'll drive us both back down. Easy.'

'This does sound thought through,' laughs Mum. 'Just text me you're okay, right? You've not really gone this far before.'

'You went all the way to Greece around my age,' I say.

'Well yes, which is why I'm not stopping you. Go out and see the world, that's what I want you to do. But text me when you get there?'

'First Manchester, then the world,' I say, hugging her. I pause. 'Are you sure you're going to be okay without me? If you have any flare ups or anything, call and I'll come back. I've left some meals in the fridge in case you don't want to cook.'

'I'll be fine. I keep saying you don't need to do all of this,' she says, shooing me out of the door. 'Go have fun.'

I walk outside as Ty leaves his front door. He's dangling car keys from his hand.

'You're driving that?' I say, pointing at the black 4x4 in the driveway.

'Paul's away this weekend, what else would I drive?' he says.

'Something smaller?' I say, as he unlocks the car and I get

into the passenger seat.

'I'm from the land of the big car,' he says, starting to reverse out. 'I'm not concerned about the size of the car, more about driving on the right side of the road.'

'Wait, what?'

He turns and gives me a brief smile. 'Selena, I'm joking, it'll be fine.'

He makes a right out of the drive and we're off.

'Why don't you put on some music?' he says.

'You know what I'm going to put on, right?'

'Rose Conrad?'

'You got it.'

I connect my phone and start building a playlist up. I don't want anything too romantic, which is a bit difficult with Rose Conrad.

'Are you sure you're okay listening to only this for 250 miles?' I say.

'I told you, I'm a big fan,' says Ty, lazily. Then he starts singing along to 'This Change'.

'I can't believe you know all the words,' I say, as he croons out the final wobbly note. Ty may be many things, but a good singer isn't one of them.

'You know how I get real obsessive about things?' he says.

'Like trying to complete Level 17 of a video game?'

'Did Daze tell you? He's ruining my image! But yes, I fixate on things I like. So that summer when I got dumped—'

'I thought you broke up amicably with this girlfriend?'

'I might have edited the story a bit to reduce how heartbroken I was. Anyway, after she ran off with her lab partner, I listened to Rose Conrad obsessively to remind me of her. And then I got really into the lyrics, and learning the lyrics, and the next thing you know, Rose Conrad became my thing, not hers.'

I am quiet for a bit. I know other people like Rose Conrad, she's on a sell-out tour. But for some reason it's making me feel annoyed that Ty's ex also liked her. As if she's taken that from me.

'What was her name?' I say.

'May.' He glances over. 'You got any exes?'

'No,' I say honestly. 'All girls' school and all that.'

'What about this guy you're visiting?' he says, looking at me out of the corner of his eye. 'Ollie? The old next-door neighbour?'

I squirm in my seat. I don't want to get into all the details of this with Ty. I want to go and talk to Ollie, and figure out how I feel and how he feels. Simple.

'He's just a friend,' I say honestly. 'My oldest friend.'

'But he didn't help you out with those tickets.'

'You forgive friends,' I say quietly.

'Okay,' he says, nodding. 'I'll leave it alone.' He shakes his head. 'What do I know about friendship anyway?'

'You said before you didn't really have many friends in your old school,' I say. 'Is that true?'

He shrugs. 'I had acquaintances. Guys I hung out with. But they never got why I wanted to teach myself photography, or learn every element in the periodic table, or when I tried to perfect baking San Francisco sourdough bread. They wanted to play video games or go to the movies, which I liked, but there's other things I like too. So I kept drifting to the sidelines. Finding it hard to connect, you know? Until I met May.'

'And she saw you?' I can't help but want to know more. And it feels nice Ty is opening up to me like this. It feels like he really cares about what I think.

'She was interested in everything, like I was. But ironically, considering she left me for her lab partner, I don't think we had real chemistry.' I laugh. 'It's true, I think we found things interesting. When I saw her with Jordan, the lab partner, I could tell there was something different there.' He looks at me. 'That's why I appreciate you.' I think he can see my startled look, because he quickly says, 'Because you also find things interesting. You ask me a lot of questions. There's more to you.'

I get a faint, buzzing feeling whenever he says something nice to me. Like he really sees me. I catch his eye, he gives me a faint smile . . .

We need to move on – I'm going to see Ollie, I can't feel like this. 'Is that why you want to stay here for uni? So you can meet more people?'

'And for Daze and Mom. They're more than my family, they're my friends too. I don't know what I would do without them. Mom's the one who spent all that time baking bread with me. She's never doubted me or asked questions. And Daze can be the most annoying person on the planet, but he's so smart, so funny. I don't want to be on the other side of the world from them.'

'How does your dad feel about you going on this open day?' I say.

'Oh, Paul doesn't know,' says Ty.

'Then what does he think you need the car for?'

'He thinks I'm taking you to the open day because I'm such a good friend,' he says. 'So he knows we're going to Liverpool. The car has a GPS tracker anyway.'

'Ah, so you lied,' I say.

'More bent the truth.'

I raise my eyebrows. 'You are going to the open day though,' I say.

Ty shrugs his shoulders. 'It's not worth rocking the boat with Paul. He doesn't need to know.'

'So when you miraculously decide to go to university here, what, he won't know?'

'Paul believes he knows what's best for me. I like to keep him believing he does.'

'Even though you disagree.'

'Selena, we've been through this. My dad is . . . how do you say it here . . . an arsehole. But I need to keep him happy. It's not worth the stress otherwise.'

'Okay,' I say, and smile at him. 'I'll leave it alone.'

Ty turns up the music. He laughs. 'Maybe this is what friendship is. Knowing when to not talk about things.'

Friends, that's what we are. If that's the case, why is my heart beating so much? I turn back to the window. Things felt a lot less complicated when we were fighting.

Twenty-Six

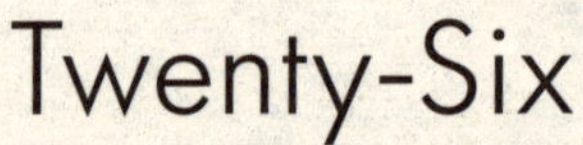

Because I'm torn
Split in two
With a jagged line
When I think of you

'Torn' from *The Brink of*
Teenage Freedom

SETTING OUT EARLY pays off and we make it to Liverpool in the afternoon.

'Do you want to take a look around before you go to Manchester?' he says.

I look at my watch. 'Yeah, I have some time.'

We start walking around the university.

'This architecture is amazing,' says Ty. 'I wish I had my camera.'

We pass a girl with an open day T-shirt on and a witch's hat for Halloween. She hands us a prospectus each. My immediate instinct is to refuse, but it seems to cause more confusion and I leave with the prospectus in my hand.

'Sure you're not interested in coming here?' says Ty, nodding towards the prospectus.

'It's so far from home,' I say, shaking my head. 'That's my whole problem. I don't want to leave Mum to go to university. Not because I need her and I'm scared of going. But because she needs me. What is she going to do when I'm not around?'

'She'll live her life like she's always done?'

'I have images of her being alone in the house without me.'

'Your mom is super independent. Don't you think you're finding more excuses to put this off?'

'No,' I say, grasping his arm. 'Mum's been injured for years. She's been unable to do her dream job in London since her knees got so bad. She needs me. But both choices seem awful: go away, have fun, leave her behind. Or stay at home, become a nobody, don't make anything of myself and watch everyone I know grow up and leave.'

'Or,' says Ty, taking the prospectus away from me and tucking it under his arm, 'you could go to university in London. You could even stay at home if you wanted to.'

'Would it be the same?'

'It would be something. But if she's such a big factor in your decision, I really think you should talk to your mom about it.' He hands me back the prospectus.

— ★ —

Ty drops me off at the train station, a bit later than planned, but we got carried away looking at Beatles memorabilia.

'So what are you doing tonight?' says Ty, as we wait for my platform to appear at the station.

'Tomorrow is Ollie's birthday. I think he's going to show me around Manchester. Not really sure exactly what he's planned.'

'And he's meeting you at the station tonight?'

'Yup,' I say. Ollie texted me earlier to confirm.

My platform appears. 'See you on Sunday for our next roadtrip,' he says, giving me a hug. 'Let me know if you need anything before then.'

'It'll be fine,' I say, running for the train.

I am excited to see Ollie, even though I am feeling confused about Ty. It feels like we're just friends, and that near-kiss . . . I banish the thought from my mind. The truth is, liking Ollie is easier. I know him better. We've been friends longer. Ty is kind of cranky, obsessive and has baggage about his dad.

He's also sweet, thoughtful and funny. I push aside the voice in my head.

I need something to distract myself with, so I pull out the prospectus and start flicking through it. It's the first time I've read about a university in any detail. I read about campus life, places you can stay, what sports and clubs there are.

Then I start reading through the English course options. Modules and options on everything from Shakespeare to banned books. What makes good writing. How analysis can make you a better writer. A note from the lead lecturer on how words have power and it's an honour to teach us all how to use them. They show alumni who have gone on to become novelists, journalists, CEOs.

As I read I imagine myself in the future, making my writing a reality. It's the first time I've really imagined what it could look like. And maybe studying English Literature and Language together would give me the best of both worlds.

— ★ —

When I get off the train, I can't see Ollie by the barriers. Around me is a swarm of people in different Halloween outfits, heading into Manchester for a night out. My gut plummets. Has he forgotten about me the way he forgot to get the Rose Conrad tickets?

'Selena,' yells a familiar voice. I turn around and Ollie is there, in the same wool coat he's had for the past two winters.

My heart soars and I run into his hug.

'I can't believe you're here,' he says. 'It feels so strange to see you outside of Croydon!'

'I can't believe I am here!' I laugh. I look around. 'Your new home!'

'Well, not right here, this is Manchester Piccadilly.'

We both laugh, and I'm at ease. This is how I remembered it. How we fit perfectly together.

We get the tram to Ollie's new home on the outskirts of Manchester. The whole journey we're catching up. He tells me about his new friends. I tell him how Kira and Faye are doing. He tells me about his university interviews. I tell him I think I want to study English Literature and Language at a London university. He tells me he's on a rugby team now. I tell him I'm still skipping cross-country practice. He tells me he's missed me, and I grip his arm so tightly I might burst.

Ollie's new home is in a fancy part of Manchester. The Pointers have definitely gone more upscale than where we used to live. On this road, everything is basically a mansion.

'You can get more for your money in the north,' says Ollie sheepishly as he leads me up the driveway to a house that is double the size of his one back home.

Any unease I feel about its grandeur is put aside when Meredith greets me, hugging me close.

'Selena, we have missed you being next door!' she says. 'Our neighbours aren't the same as you and Kajal.'

'That's because our new neighbours are geriatric,' says Ollie.

'And who's replaced us?' says Meredith, whisking us to the grand kitchen-diner, where the table is all laid out for us to have dinner.

'Oh some Americans,' I say, taking some potatoes and avoiding eye contact with Ollie.

'But you know them, right?' says Ollie, looking over at me.

'Not well,' I say, becoming really interested in the vegetables now. I look up at Ollie. 'Not as well as I know you.'

He smiles at me, and I push all thoughts of Ty away. How

this morning he made out that I was his only friend. How I knew him like nobody else.

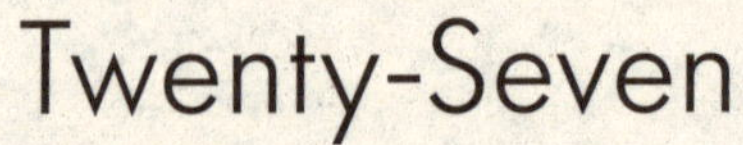

Twenty-Seven

'New Friends' from *The Brink
of Teenage Freedom*

T HE NEXT DAY, Ollie gives me a whirlwind tour of Manchester. We go to record stores, museums, eat street food on the side of the road.

In these moments, I forget about Ty, I forget about the Secret Sender, I forget about everything that's happened since August, without Ollie. It's like I've gone back to a time when everything was simpler, and I was much happier.

I start getting the familiar tingling sensation again, whenever Ollie is around me. Find myself catching his eye and then quickly looking away. I feel like I can and can't bear to be around him, without really knowing how he feels.

Okay, I have to tell him.

Tonight. It's his birthday, it's the perfect time.

'So what are we doing tonight, birthday boy?' I say, linking my arm through his. I feel overly flirty, but I need him to start seeing me in a different way. Hopefully he already has.

'Well, I've invited all my friends to Bravos. I think we're meeting them at seven?'

Wait, what? I think back to our original conversation – he had mentioned going out with his friends.

How am I meant to confess my undying love in front of a bunch of strangers?

It's okay, I can wait until we get back to his house. You can see stars in the sky at night, which would be a romantic setting. I can do this.

When we get to Bravos, I realise it's a pool bar, with some arcade games in the corner. I didn't know Ollie is so into pool. He had barely touched a cue when we lived next door.

'This is *the* cool place to hang out,' he says, letting me in. 'So I booked a bunch of tables for us to play at.'

Soon everyone starts to filter in.

There are three guys and two girls. One redhead girl, one blonde girl, two dark-haired guys and one blonde guy. With their pristine clothes and discerning looks, I feel like I'm standing out.

'Team, this is my oldest and dearest friend, Selena,' says Ollie. 'We've literally known each other our whole lives. Selena, this is Thom, Scott, Mike, Keeley and Diane.' He points at each one in turn but I have a hard time remembering the names, let alone remembering who they belong to.

'Nice to meet you,' I choke out with a smile.

The red-haired girl, who was pointed out as Diane, rushes to me and gives me a hug. 'We've heard so much about you,' she says with a northern accent.

I exhale. Okay, this will be fine. I hug her back.

'Really looking forward to hanging out with you this weekend,' I say. And I mean it.

'Let's get this party started!' says Ollie, holding up the cue.

Ollie and another guy start to play pool. I hover by the corner of the table. I had imagined more catching up time, but I guess we can do that later. A couple of people who have turned eighteen already grab alcoholic drinks, but I am not keen on breaking the law this far from home, so I stick with Coke.

'Hey,' says Diane. 'Do you know how to play pool?'

'No, not really,' I confess. 'But maybe tonight I'll learn.'

'I like the attitude,' she says, laughing. 'Is this your first time in Manchester?'

'Yes. I went to look around Liverpool uni yesterday – kind of by accident – then came straight here.'

'That's so funny, I'm mostly looking at London,' she says. 'Why?'

'Because I want to get out of here, you know?' She casts her arms around. 'There's got to be something more than the life I know. Not just London, but Scotland too. I want to get away.

If going abroad wasn't so complicated and expensive I would do it.'

I stare at her. 'I can't imagine wanting to leave anywhere that bad. My friend does too, but she's crazy ambitious.'

'Fair. It's not ambition for me, really. I think the future is wide and interesting, and if I don't grasp it now, when will I ever?'

When will I ever? The words ring through me, and I stare at her.

'Anyway, how's your time been exploring Manchester? We're so glad you're here.'

'It's been great to look around,' I say. I don't tell her I thought it was going to be just me and Ollie. I'm trying to get over how crushed I feel about it, by focusing on how nice Diane is.

'That's good,' she continues, oblivious to my feelings. 'I know tonight he really wants to celebrate his eighteenth.' She looks at me and smiles. 'I'm so glad you made it for him. It must be rubbish to turn eighteen and not have all your old friends there.'

'Well, it looks like you are all pretty close already,' I say, watching Ollie grab his opponent around the neck in a bear hug.

'Yeah, he's fit in well,' she says, as we watch Keeley walk up to Ollie, tugging him towards her by the arm. 'You can thank Keeley for befriending him. I think she has a thing for him. But you know, it's all will-they-won't-they right now."

It feels like the ground is spinning out underneath me. I grip the ledge behind me, as if it can anchor me upright.

'But,' says Diane, who now must have seen my feelings on my face, 'he's told us loads about what good friends you are.'

But why hasn't he told me about Keeley? I realise, with deep dread, what I had imagined would happen if I came up here. Ollie would realise he loved me all along. He would want us to be together. And despite all my mixed emotions and feelings with Ty, I realise it's what I've been hoping for all along.

But he has invited me as a friend.

'Are you okay?' says Diane, looking at me with worry.

'Perfect,' I say. 'I'm going to go play.'

I stride over to Ollie. 'My go,' I say, placing my hands on his shoulders. 'Shall we play?'

'Do you even know how to play?' He laughs, swinging me around by the waist, until we're both facing the pool board. I take the cue from his hand, rest my head on his shoulder.

'I hear you've been telling everyone how I'm a sporting legend,' I say. 'So I trust that I have an innate ability.'

'Let's go then,' says Ollie.

Out of the corner of my eye, I see Keeley. Her face is blank, but I can tell there's a quiet fury underneath it. I don't know what I'm doing any more. I want proof Ollie wants *me*. That I haven't come all the way here for nothing. And would telling him how I feel be the most rational thing to do? Maybe. But that would require confrontation and this feels more subtle. Who needs rational, when you could look cool?

I'm fed up of trying to please everyone, of always having to do the right thing.

Ollie and I start playing, and I contemplate faking being bad so he teaches me how to play. But it turns out I'm just bad.

'Come on, Pia,' says Ollie. 'What was that? Here, let me show you.'

He gets behind me and manoeuvres the cue. I feel hot under his touch. I feel his breath on my neck as he instructs me to pull back the cue and shoot.

The ball goes in.

I whoop, punch the air, and everyone cheers. Except Keeley, who now has her arms crossed.

I don't feel good about this. I know she's jealous of me. But I'm grateful for Ollie's attention. Maybe I am important to him after all. This is the way things have always been. She's the newcomer, not me.

Keeley taps Ollie on the arm. 'I think she's got it,' she says, with a strained smile. She glances at me. 'You said you were going to play that driving game with me. They've got it here.'

'Oh yeah,' says Ollie, laughing. 'Keeley claims she's a better driver than me, so we thought we could race and find out.'

Keeley looks at me pointedly. 'It's two players only.'

Message received. My heart drops a bit when Ollie leaves me to go play the game with her.

I start talking to two of the guys, Thom and Mike. Thom is quiet and doe-eyed, very sweet. Miles is brash, loud, and for some reason his accent sounds like Ollie's, even though he tells me he's from Chester.

'So what are you doing for uni?' asks Mike. He has one of

those voices which always sounds like he's yelling.

'I want to do English, but I've not sent my application yet.' It's the first time I've said it confidently to a stranger, and it feels good. I'm in control of my own future.

'Mine's already sent off. I had to put down some snap choices. Although fingers crossed for Oxford. To read PPE, of course.'

There's not much else to say, except I have no idea what PPE is. I thought it's what builders wore on construction sites.

'I'm so excited to get out of here,' says Thom. 'See the world, meet new people.' He's moving his hands around excitedly. I had taken him for an introvert with his quietness, but after two drinks he has become very talkative.

'I don't know, I quite like home,' I say, looking into my Coke. 'I like my family and friends.'

'Oh me too,' says Mike. 'I don't want to leave these buggers anytime soon. But don't you feel excited by it all?'

Just then Ollie appears, with Keeley and Scott at his side.

'Hope you're only telling them how I was the best neighbour ever, Selena,' says Ollie.

'Absolutely,' I say.

'Even more than Mr All-American?'

I flush. I feel a twinge of . . . I don't know. Guilt? Confusion? 'He's fine,' I say. I don't want to talk about Ty to Ollie.

'Well now both you and Ollie are here,' says Mike. 'You've got to tell us some stories about him as a kid. Was he always this cocky?'

'Ollie . . . cocky,' I say, tapping my finger on my chin, pretending to look contemplative. 'It is a word that has been used to describe Ollie before, I guess.' I get a lot of laughs. 'As for embarrassing childhood stories? Let me see . . .'

'Now this is what I'm here for,' says Diane, appearing back from the bathroom.

Ollie groans.

'Well, he had this little rabbit blanket he took absolutely everywhere, for one,' I say. 'It got so tattered its ears fell off so I had to convert it into a guinea-pig.'

'I had a rabbit blanket too,' says Keeley, touching Ollie's arm. 'When you come over, I'll show you some photos. I wonder if it's the same one!'

'I don't know if that'll make the story better or worse,' jokes Scott.

'Okay, I think that's enough.' Ollie laughs awkwardly. 'Why can't you tell everyone about some of my greater achievements? Like when I scaled that tree in front of the entire park. No need to ruin my reputation so early on. Keep some things a surprise.'

'Well, the biggest surprise is that she was coming here at all,' says Keeley, a bit too sweetly.

'Oh, I think I mentioned it,' says Ollie, putting his hand behind his head.

'Not to me you didn't,' says Keeley. 'I would have remembered.'

Ollie looks stricken. 'Come on, Keels, why don't you come with me to the bar and we can talk.'

Keeley gives me a smile as Ollie takes her by the arm.

As I watch him go, I feel the final pin of deflation. That look in his eye. The concern. I've seen it before. With me.

There's nothing more to do here except to accept tonight is not going to be the night I tell Ollie about how I feel. I can't, after I've seen him with Keeley. I need him on home ground, in the place where our connection feels the strongest.

I need to tell him back home.

Twenty-Eight

Friends grow old
Friends find each other
Friends never forget
Friends become lovers

'Friends' from *Roses*

T Y MEETS ME at Liverpool train station the next day. I'm feeling deflated. The rest of the night Keeley and Ollie laughed together like old friends, while I watched on.

'What's the matter?' Ty asks, as we walk to the car park.

'Nothing.' I shrug.

'What, the great Ollie Pointer's birthday party wasn't a hit?'

'It was good, it was nice to see him.'

'Then why are you acting like you went to a funeral?'

We get into the car and I put on my seatbelt with a small huff. 'I'm not,' I say. 'I had a good time. We spent some time together, I met his new friends, that was it.'

Ty starts driving us out of the city centre. 'Well, when you want to talk about it, I am here,' he says.

I look out of the window. 'It's just . . . Ollie's friends are not what I thought they'd be like.'

'And how were they?'

'I don't know, a bit much. Pretentious, some of them.' I think of Diane. 'Not all of them. But some of them.' I pause. 'Plus, I thought it was going to be the two of us this weekend. Not me, him and a bunch of strangers I don't know. He sees them every day at school!'

'And he didn't tell you?' says Ty.

I look across at him; his face is giving nothing away.

I feel uncomfortable now. I don't want Ty to think badly of Ollie. Especially after the concert-ticket thing. And Ollie didn't do anything wrong – it's not his fault I'm not a big fan of his friends.

'Well, it was his birthday. Maybe I misunderstood,' I say. 'It would make sense he would want all his friends to be there.'

'Did you have a good time with him at least?' says Ty. My Rose Conrad playlist is on again, and he is nodding along to the song and drumming his fingers on the wheel.

'Yes,' I say, and I mean it. 'On the first day, he took me around Manchester, and it was magical. We went to all these cool places, he showed me his favourite restaurants. It was so nice to hang out with him again, you know?'

Ty is silent. Then, 'Yeah I can see that.' He pauses. 'So, he treated you well.'

'Honestly, nothing bad happened this weekend.' I chew my lip, thinking of Keeley. 'He has this new female friend though . . . And I think I'm a bit . . .'

'Jealous?' says Ty, when I don't finish the sentence.

'Is that so bad?'

'It's only human.' He clears his throat. 'I didn't know you liked Ollie like that.'

Part of me wants to throw myself out of the moving car.

Do I deny it? Do I agree? Do I sit here in silence for the next two-hour car ride?

After moments that feel like hours, I come clean. 'It's been a long time building up. I don't really know when it went from us being friends to me feeling like this.'

'And he doesn't know?' says Ty.

'I don't think so. If he does, he's not letting on. But I should probably tell him.'

'Do you think he likes this other girl?'

'Not sure,' I reply, thinking back over the evening. 'He was behaving really weird – one moment he was all over me, then all over her. Maybe that's the way he is.'

'Or maybe he's trying to have it both ways,' says Ty. 'And leading you both on.'

'You want to see the worst in him.'

'And why would I want that, Selena?'

I flush, not wanting to voice my thoughts. Hidden looks and moments are one thing, but there's no coming back from saying this out loud.

'I know you're trying to look out for me,' I say quietly. 'But you don't know Ollie the way I do. He's not the villain you think he is.'

'Everyone is a hero in their own story,' says Ty. 'I'm sure Ollie doesn't think he's doing anything wrong.'

'But neither do I.'

Ty sighs. 'Okay, Selena. Well, I'm here for you.' My mouth feels dry, I can't believe he's this nice. He's really watching out for me. He cares about *me*. I don't really know how to put it into words.

We go back to sitting in silence, listening to my playlist.

'When's your birthday, anyway?' I say.

'Oh, it was last month,' says Ty.

'Wait, what?' I say. 'You turned eighteen and you didn't tell me!'

'Well, our friendship was . . . fraught.'

'You mean we fought.'

'Well, that too.'

'You should have still told me,' I say. I feel upset that he didn't. I would want to celebrate with him, show him he does have a friend here.

'Well, now you know. September seventeenth.'

'I'll memorise it for next year.'

He smiles. 'I hope I can celebrate with you next year. When's yours?'

'In a few weeks – December first,' I say. 'Ollie and I were born really close together. It's how our mums became friends, how we became friends.'

'You two are really tight, huh?'

I shrug. It's true. We are, or were.

'What are you going to do for your birthday?'

'I haven't really thought—' An idea strikes me. 'Hey, I should host a party.' It's perfect!

'Really?'

'Yes! And I'll invite Ollie, and then I can tell him how I feel.'

I blurt it out, and Ty is silent. Oops. I was so excited, and now I feel bad bringing it up. I feel torn again; I want to be able to talk to Ty about everything, but there's this unsaid undercurrent in our relationship. One that makes it hard for me to talk to him about Ollie. And I want Ty to know he matters to me too.

'Sounds like a plan,' he says after a moment.

We drive on for a bit longer in silence.

'Ty,' I say quietly, glancing at him. His eyes are on the road and it is really hard trying to work out what he's thinking.

'Yeah?'

'I'm glad we're friends,' I say. And it's true. He drove me all the way here and all the way back. He's the one who's listened to me rant about Ollie and my confusing feelings, with no judgement. He really cares for me, and I realise, I really care about him too.

I look at him, and for a brief second he catches my eye, and a jolt of electricity shoots down me. We both quickly turn away.

Immediately, the new Rose Conrad song comes on. New Day. He smiles, the lyrics playing softly in the background.

'I'm glad we're friends too, Selena,' he says softly. He shakes his head, as if snapping himself out of something. 'But you do have suspect taste in friends.'

I laugh and reach over and turn up the music. As it pumps out, I think about how I always associate a Rose Conrad song with a particular person or moment, and how I had thought this song was all about Ollie.

But maybe it's about Ty.

Twenty-Nine

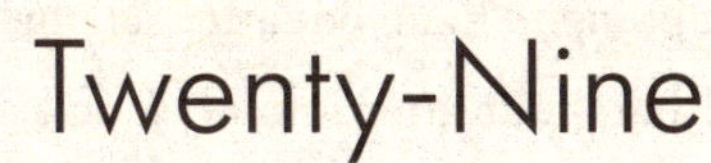

It's the time for
Champagne and party poppers
In the midnight rain
And we're never gonna stop, yeah

'Champagne and Party Poppers'
from *The In-Between*

'YOU'RE GOING TO host a party?' says Kira, doubtfully. We're sitting in the common room. It's been two days since I've got back from Manchester, and I've been thinking about it ever since.

'What's wrong with that?' I say.

'Well, for one, you've never hosted a party before, and two your mum loves her home. There's no way she'll be cool with people getting up-and-close with her artefacts,' says Kira.

'Okay, good point,' I say.

'Who are you going to invite?' says Faye. 'I think it sounds fun.'

'Oh I definitely think it sounds fun,' says Kira. 'And also a bad idea. But I'm here for it.'

'Why did you decide to do this, anyway?' says Faye. 'I thought we were going to hang out after school.'

'We can still hang out after school.' I pull at the sleeve of my jumper. There's no point lying to them. Kira is drawn to lies like a seagull to chips. 'In Manchester, Ollie seems to be a party person, so I thought I could invite him, and you know—'

'Show him a side of your personality that hasn't existed until now?' finishes Kira.

'I like parties and hanging out with people!' I say defensively.

'Yeah, but you've never thrown a party before,' says Faye.

'Who's having a party?' says an all-too-familiar voice. Tori has appeared beside us with Mia and Farah.

'Erm, me,' I say, caving immediately. 'Do you want to come?'

'Sure!' says Tori. 'Can I bring my boyfriend?'

'He goes to Benson's,' says Mia, leaning forwards.

'The more the merrier,' I say, shrugging. I need numbers for this party. And Tori is fine, I guess. In small doses.

'Oh, can he bring some of his friends?'

'Are they hot?' says Kira, leaning forwards.

'Er—' says Tori.

'Doesn't matter,' says Kira. 'We need boys at this party. Bring them.'

'Great!' says Tori. 'Send us the details.'

'I thought you were anti-party?' I say to Kira.

'Well, if you're going to go ahead with it, may as well make it good,' says Kira. 'Also we need more boys than the ones in your weird love triangle.'

'It's not a love triangle!' I say, pushing Kira.

'How long have you been with your boyfriend?' Faye asks Tori, thankfully digging me out of this hole before anyone can ask any questions. Luckily, Tori loves to talk about herself.

'Oh, a few months,' says Tori. 'He's the son of one of my mum's friends.'

Kira rolls her eyes. I don't blame her, almost all conversations with Tori include mention of her influential mother.

'Speaking of which,' says Tori, excitedly, 'his dad managed to upgrade our Rose Conrad seats. We now have a box!' She claps her hands together, and I have a strong urge to clap mine around her mouth. 'I'm so excited to sit in a box.'

'What's a box?' says Mia.

'It's a special area you can sit by yourself with a bar and food,' says Tori.

I can't even get a ticket to sit at the back of the stadium and Tori is getting table service at the concert. Of course.

'Can I have a party for my birthday next month? As my birthday is on a Friday?' I say. I'm leaning against the doorframe of Mum's office, watching her type notes on her laptop.

'Sure,' she says, squinting at a piece of paper, then putting it down. 'What do you want to do?'

'I was thinking of having a few people over here. Get some food, some drinks.' I feel very nervous right now, but I tell myself nothing I'm saying is a lie.

'Kira and Faye? You don't need to ask me that.'

'Maybe a few more people.'

Mum puts the paper down and turns around.

'How many people are we talking?'

'You know – some girls in my classes, some in Kira's classes, Ollie, so on . . .'

'I need a number, Selena.'

'I've only invited around five people!' I say. And it's true. They've invited other people.

'Okay, fine,' says Mum, nodding. She pauses. 'You know what, I'll see if Gina wants to go away that night. We wanted to go to a spa soon anyway. I could do with floating in some water and taking the pressure off my joints. Plus you're officially an adult then – I'm sure you don't want your mother hanging around for your party.'

This is even better! Mum won't even see the number of people there. I'll enlist everyone to help me clean. Everything will be fine.

The stars are aligning – that's got to be a good sign, right?

'Thanks, Mum,' I say, beaming. 'I'm glad you trust me.'

And even if I haven't been fully honest with the truth, it's true, she can trust me.

Thirty

My tears are
Salt on an old wound
Saline stinging harder
It tears me apart
To be without you

'Salt On A Wound' from *Dreamers*

TODAY'S TAKE: *Stop throwing salt on old wounds*
You know what I hate? People rubbing it in. I get it, your house is nicer. I get it, you got perfect marks in the test. I get it, you've got Rose Conrad tickets.

You know what? Nobody cares. Nobody wants to hear about your victories at their expense. I certainly don't. So keep your smug stories to yourself.

'ARE YOU REALLY the Secret Sender?' asks Farah to Tori. I'm walking behind them on the way to English. Close enough to eavesdrop, of course.

Tori splutters, but nothing she says is really coherent. 'Yes . . . but no . . . sometimes . . .'

'It doesn't sound like you,' says Farah. 'When it came into the main inbox, I was surprised.'

It's true. Why would Tori, queen of smug stories, write about being smug?

'Well, if you must know, it's not me,' says Tori.

'What?' says Farah. 'Why did you say it was?'

Tori shrugs. 'Because I thought it was cool. And at the time, it was. But now . . . she's just getting mean, right?'

I snort, and then pretend to be sneezing. But I know the only reason Tori thinks my latest piece is mean is because it's directed at her. Also, it's not really *that* mean.

'Are you talking about the Secret Sender's latest article?' says Paula Thomas, passing by. She's in our English class. I rarely speak to her, but she's pretty nice.

'Yeah, what do you think?' says Tori.

'It feels harsh,' says Paula. 'Don't you think she's getting harsher? Wanting to celebrate yourself isn't the same as rubbing salt into other people's wounds. You should feel able to be happy about your life, to celebrate it.'

What? Paula thinks it's too much?

'Yeah, I agree,' says Tori. 'If she keeps being like this, we'll pull her from the newspaper.'

'Don't you think *that's* an overreaction? She posted an opinion,' I say, before I can help myself. 'Thought you were pro freedom of press, Tori.'

'Well, I am,' she splutters.

'And Secret Sender is the main reason people are reading *The Common Room*,' says Mia.

'They are reading it for quality investigative journalism too,' says Tori. 'Last week I did an exposé on the sausages in the cafeteria only containing fifty per cent meat.'

'I think most sausages contain fifty per cent meat,' I say, swinging my bag onto my desk as we get into class.

'Either way, it's an exposé,' says Tori, her mouth curling. 'What would you know about journalism anyway?'

More than you, I think. *I'm your most-read feature by far. And my articles are only five lines long, not five pages.*

And I know it's true. All around me, people are talking about my recent take.

I feel a familiar buzz again, the one I get whenever I realise people are reading what I've written, that they care about my words.

After class ends, Ms Harkness calls me up to her desk.

'Ms, I'm nearly done on my UCAS, I swear,' I say. 'I'm whittling down my final choices. I'm sure I'm going to stay in London—'

'Amazing, Selena, but I need to ask you,' she interrupts. 'Are you the Secret Sender?'

Blood rushes to my ears. My first instinct is to deny it.

But then she says, 'I should say, I know you're the Secret Sender.'

'How?' I croak.

She pushes forwards the latest copy of *The Common Room*, and a copy of my essay from the week before.

'Because in both of these there is a metaphor of salt in wounds. One when you're talking about Tom's interaction with Gatsby at the Plaza hotel, the other one obviously in the header. Then I did some digging and found it's also the name of a Rose Conrad song. And, well . . . ' She points at the Rose Conrad pin I have on my bag.

'Doesn't really prove anything though,' I say, but my voice does not have the confidence of the words.

'Selena, we both know Tori isn't the Secret Sender. She's confessed to it now, but I always knew. I know Tori's writing. There's no way she could ever be this concise. It's very clearly your tone, your voice, your directness.'

I feel myself deflate. 'Am I going to get into trouble?'

'No, of course not,' says Ms Harkness, looking surprised. 'Selena, there are no rules against anonymous writing. It's why I didn't put a stop to it straight away. But if I were you, I would think a bit about the downsides to anonymity. Sometimes having your name attached can keep you accountable.'

'You sound a bit like Kira.'

'You don't need me to tell you Kira is a smart person.'

'Sure, doesn't mean I want to go public,' I say.

'You never know, you might find you like having your name

attached to your work,' she says. 'Which is why I also wanted to talk to you about the journalist work experience at the *Croydon Post*.'

'What about it? I heard Tori talking about it.'

'It's taking place in the last week of term. The timing coincides nicely with the UCAS deadline. It would be great to put on your application.'

'Now you're really starting to sound like Kira.'

'Selena, you're a columnist,' she says, pointing at the Secret Sender. 'I might not agree on how you're writing this, but you're definitely capturing people's attention.' She pauses. 'There're a lot of people like Tori writing in the world, fewer people with your point of view. You should put that out there. But with your name.'

'I'd never get it,' I say. 'Tori said they take three people. There'll be people from loads of different schools applying.'

'You won't know if you don't try, Selena,' says Ms Harkness. 'There's nothing to lose from trying. Have you thought about what you want to do next year?'

I nod, thinking about reading the prospectuses on the train.

'I want to study English Literature and Language at university, in London,' I say.

'Great,' says Ms Harkness, looking delighted. 'How did you decide?'

'I went to look at Liverpool university with a friend. A bit by accident, but I saw it. And when I was looking at the courses, it clicked that I did want to go, I just don't want to go too far from home.'

'That's totally fair,' she says gently. 'And even though you're not applying for Liverpool, it sounds like that experience was really useful.'

She pushes the papers towards me.

'Think about applying, okay? Applications close on Sunday.'

'Sunday is three days away!'

She gives me a small smile. 'What would the Secret Sender do?'

Thirty-One

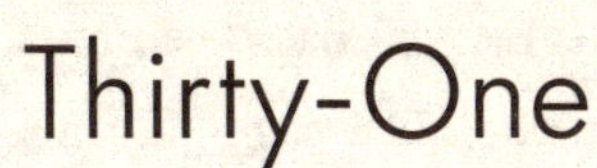

You're my . . . cheerleader
Standing on the side
Pep talks for miles
I couldn't do it without you

'Cheerleader' from
The Brink of Teenage Freedom

AM SHAKEN BY Ms Harkness knowing my secret. The next day, I keep looking around, as if the news will suddenly break and everyone will know.

'Why are you so concerned, anyway?' asks Kira, at lunch. 'I thought you stood by what you wrote.'

It's a pointed comment, and one I am going to ignore.

'It's part of the mystique of the Secret Sender,' I say. 'It's literally in the name, "Secret". Nobody is going to care if it's me.'

Kira rolls her eyes. 'They might care if it's you when they find out they're your opinions.'

'Let's not fight,' says Faye, holding out her arms. 'I have some news.'

'What?' we say.

'The Chelsea seamstress has taken me on for next year! I had to go there and beg, but I've got it.'

'Designer Faye, here we go,' says Kira, snapping her fingers. 'Hey, you can design all my power suits for when I'm running this place.'

'Why, Madam Prime Minister, I would love to be your fashion designer of choice,' says Faye, mock curtseying. I shake my head in bemusement.

'Now I've got into LSE, I feel much better about things,' says Kira.

'Wait – what—?' I say.

'I wanted to tell you guys in person,' Kira grins wickedly at us, 'and now seems like a good enough time.' She spreads her arms out. 'This girl is on her way out of here.'

I feel pure delight for Kira. Faye and I pull her into a group hug.

'This isn't gloating, is it?' says Kira.

I know she's mocking my article, but I'm too happy for her. 'No jokes. This is celebrating,' I say, holding her. 'I'm really happy for you.'

'See, Selena,' says Kira, grabbing my arms. 'Improbable things can happen. I can get into LSE, Faye can get her placement, and you can get this newspaper work experience.'

'You've been working hard for this your whole life! I don't think LSE was ever improbable.'

'Everything is improbable when it feels like the odds are stacked against you. Look at me – if I didn't try for any opportunity that didn't have people like me there, I wouldn't do anything. Just because you think the world is full of people like Tori, who have been prepping their whole lives, with contacts, doesn't mean you aren't good enough. You've got to try.'

'Yeah, now we've worked out what we're doing next year, it's only you left,' says Faye. 'And we've got your back.'

I nod, but inside I know, even though they've got my back, I'm the one who's got to do the work.

— ⋆ —

I don't know what to put on my application for the Croydon Post. Kira and Ms Harkness are right, I should apply and see what happens next. But now the question is: what do I say? I'm in a writing rut. And I need to submit this soon: it's now Saturday afternoon, the deadline is tomorrow and I've been working on it all day . . .

The application is a statement on why I want to do the experience, written as a column article.

But I'm blank.

Well, not blank, it's more that what I've written so far *doesn't sound good*. I've written about how much I like writing and English. I've alluded to the school newspaper, without calling out any specifics. All together the whole thing sounds vague and boring. I wouldn't give me a place with this! I've put

Rose Conrad on full blast for inspiration, and still nothing.

It's not just my work experience application that I'm lacking ideas for. I look at my latest draft for the Secret Sender next week. It's not good.

> **TODAY'S TAKE:** *It's time to take a break*
>
> Feeling burnt out? Like there's too much going on? You are not alone. Winter makes the days feel endless, and the constant pressure of school and deadlines doesn't help. So indulge yourself, take a break—

I stop reading. It's pretty garbage, and I know it. This isn't a unique point of view.

A point of view. That is what I need. Something that is mine, and mine alone.

I sigh and text Ty.

A few minutes later, Ty knocks on our front door.

I run downstairs to open it.

'Do you want to come in?' I say, stepping aside.

'Well, I have walked all the way here.'

'A long and treacherous way.' I laugh.

It's the first time he's been inside our house, rather than meeting in our gardens. November is truly here, the clocks have changed and it's perpetually dark and cold.

He takes off his shoes and looks around.

'Looks a bit different from your home,' I say, crossing my

arms. I've not been next door since Ollie left, but last time I was there it had a chandelier in the hallway, not an IKEA lampshade.

'Yeah,' he says, following me to the living room. 'It looks like a real home.'

We sit on the sofa, and I hug a cushion to myself.

'So why the mystery invitation?' he says.

I shrug. 'I wanted to talk to you, and it's getting too cold to randomly keep bumping into each other outdoors.'

'What do you want to talk about?' he says, leaning back into the sofa. 'I can't stay long, I have to help Daze with his homework before dinner. Dad wants to see it done by then and long division isn't Daze's strong point.'

'I'm applying for work experience at the local newspaper,' I say.

'That's great, Writer,' he says, a slow grin spreading over his face. 'I'm proud of you.'

I sigh. 'The trouble is, I need to do the application. Like, in a day.'

'So write it out, that's what you're good at.'

'I need to say *why* I want to do the experience. And everything I write about it sounds rubbish.'

Ty leans back into the sofa.

'Let's talk it through. Why *do* you want to do the experience?'

'Because I like writing for the school newspaper and it'll be cool to see what it's like to write for a real one.'

'So just say that.'

I shake my head. 'It's not that simple. No one knows I'm the Secret Sender. Apart from you, Faye and Kira. And Ms Harkness now, I guess.'

'Who's Ms Harkness?'

'My English teacher. She found out I'm the Secret Sender and said I should apply for the work experience.'

'Sounds like she's a good teacher,' he says.

'The point is, being the Secret Sender, is, well . . . a secret. I can't go and put it in an application form.'

Ty shakes his head. 'I don't think they're going to tell anyone. You need to put it in, because it's the truth and anything you write will sound fake without it.'

'I know,' I say and close my eyes. There's another weight on my chest, pressing down on me. 'What if I'm not good enough?' I say, quietly.

Ty leans forwards. 'Selena, I call you Writer because that's what you are. Didn't you say you liked writing for the newspaper?'

'Yeah, but . . .' I look away from him, towards the window.

'But what?'

'But no one knows it's me. And it's more freeing that way. This application, they'll know it's me, they'll judge *me*. And I'm no Tori.'

'Wait, who's Tori?'

'Tori is the editor for the newspaper. She's wanted to be a journalist her whole life. And it sounds like she has one of these three places in the bag already.'

'So what, there's still two other places.'

'Ty, I took this up a month ago. Because Kira submitted me without telling me! And I write five-line articles. It's not exactly investigative journalism!'

'But that's not what journalism has to look like. Most people are consuming a few lines of social media posts at a time. The fact you can capture people with a few lines, that's an impressive skill. Probably more than whatever Tori is doing.'

'People do talk about the Secret Sender the most,' I say thoughtfully.

'Writer, you've got to try.' He leans forwards, his eyes dark. 'Otherwise you'll never know. And the only way is to tell your story. The real reason why you write. The real reason you should be the person to get the opportunity to learn more about telling stories.'

'You've got all that from a couple of Secret Sender articles?'

'No, it's because . . . you're a natural storyteller,' he says, touching my hand. 'And I want to keep listening to you. You've got this.'

I nod, unable to rip my eyes from him. 'Okay,' I say. 'You're right. I can do this.'

He winks at me. 'I normally am right.'

I throw the cushion at him. 'You know, sometimes I forget how annoying you are.'

'But incredibly charming, right?' He grins.

'I wish I had another cushion to throw at you.' I go to pick up the cushion by him. 'Do you really think I can do it?'

He grabs me by the wrist, electricity sparking down my veins at his touch. 'I really do.'

'Why do you keep doing that?' I say, looking down to where his hand is clasped around my wrist.

'What?'

'Grabbing my wrist.'

He stands up, his eyes even darker, lets go of my wrist. 'It feels like the safest place to touch you.'

I feel there's layers of meaning to the statement, but I don't want to probe any deeper. If I'm honest, I'm afraid of what I might find.

'Thank you,' I say softly.

'Good. I now need to get to homework duty,' he says, smiling at me, before heading for the door.

'Oh, before you go, you're invited to my birthday party in a few weeks – it's on Friday first of December,' I say.

He cocks an eyebrow. 'I assumed I was invited, as you came up with the idea in front of me. And I live next door.'

'Take this as a formal invitation,' I say, unable to stop myself smiling.

'I'll be there.' He laughs. He turns around briefly, pauses. 'Is Ollie coming to your birthday?'

I look out the window. 'Yeah,' I say, 'he texted that he was really excited to come.'

'Good for you, Writer,' says Ty, waving a hand and leaving.

Good for me indeed.

SELENA PIA: Your future journalist

I've always been a storyteller. It's been a part of me as far as I can remember. From being sentimental over the change of seasons, and trying to understand people's motives and reasons, to giving overt meaning to ice cream flavour stamps (a story for another time). I've found stories, both real and fictional, a way to escape and a way to convey how I really feel.

I never realised that could be journalism . . . until this year.

For the past few years, I've been sending my friends these texts called 'Selena Says'. They were observations of what I thought and the daily news from around the school and our community. It became a discussion point for the three of us. A source of debate and laughter. Of keeping up with what was happening. It was a microcosm of news, but only the news that mattered to us.

When my friend suggested I should send them in to the school newspaper, I initially was resistant. Who would care about my mundane thoughts? Well, to cut a long story short, they ended up in the newspaper. And it turned out . . . a lot of people cared about my thoughts.

I write as the 'Secret Sender' in my student

newspaper, a columnist who has a lot to say on what's going on in the school. Every week, my short, five-line column is the most-talked about piece in the school. It might not be breaking news, but it's a pulse on what everyone is feeling at the time. A document of the current status of our corner of the world. And if that isn't news, what is?

I don't know if I want to be a hard-hitting investigative journalist – that's the truth. I don't have any connections, and I haven't been doing this for years. But I want to tell stories, and I want people to read them, and I want to get better at it.

So please take a chance on a writer like me.

I submit the application to the sound of Rose Conrad's 'Let's Get Going' echoing around my bedroom. Another big moment marked by another song. Let's hope it brings me luck.

Thirty-Two

I've been waiting and watching
My clock's been a-ticking
I'm feeling this itching
Right in my soul

'Let's Get Going' from *The In-Between*

TODAY'S TAKE: ***Let's get real on Rose Conrad fans***
Real Rose Conrad fans have been around since *The Brink of Teenage Freedom*, not since *Dreamers*. They know her lucky number is 8 and that even though she lives in LA, she calls Memphis home. Real Rose Conrad fans have sat down and gone through the song lyrics, looking for links between albums, notes she's laid down for us. We know her through the trail of breadcrumbs she's left for us, hints and stories unlocked through details. Real Rose Conrad fans are going to The In-Between

185

Tour not because it's a cool thing to do or because it's a world tour, but because it means the world to them. Let's hear it for the real fans.

OVER A WEEK after I send my application to the Croydon Post, I get a reply. I've been accepted.

I stare at my screen in disbelief, rereading the words over and over again. Then it hits me. I've got in.

I got in!

Pure, brilliant triumph surges through me.

'Holy shit,' I say to Faye and Kira. We're in the common room during the one free period we all have at the same time. 'Look at this,' I say, throwing my phone at them.

'Go, Selena!' says Kira, punching the air. 'I knew you could do it, girl.'

'I can't believe it,' I say.

'I can,' says Faye. 'You're so good at writing. Why wouldn't they take you?'

'Because I barely have any experience and wrote about how the Selena Says texts morphed into the Secret Sender! I thought they would have wanted something more.'

'You must have written about it well,' says Kira. 'And I'm also proud you put your name to the Secret Sender.'

A slight gnawing sensation appears in my stomach. Somewhere, someone, or even more than one person, knows I'm the Secret Sender. And I don't know who they are. What if they reveal it to everyone? Have I made the right choice?

I push it aside and focus on the good things. 'I can't believe they liked my work,' I say, excitedly. 'Someone read what I did and thought it was good.'

Faye grabs my shoulder. 'That's because you are good at this. You have to believe it.'

'You know, for the first time, I do.' I feel a bit uncertain. 'Although I'm not sure about telling them I write for *The Common Room*. What if it gets back to school somehow?'

'What's that about *The Common Room*?' says Tori, suddenly appearing. I swear, if anyone talks about something remotely related to her, she appears, like a vampire feeding off her own ego instead of blood.

'Nothing,' I say. 'Just saying how we're excited to read this week's issue.'

'Of course. There's a great article on the new uniform rules they're putting in. They're trying to standardise our skirts, you know. Next it'll be our socks!'

'You're doing the *Croydon Post* work experience, right?' says Kira, leaning forwards.

I shoot her a glare, mentally trying to communicate with her not to tell Tori.

'Yes! Finally got confirmation of my placement today, but I knew it was going to be a sure thing. I've been emailing the guy in charge of placements for the whole summer, sending him updates on my writing.' She actually tosses her hair over her shoulder. Unbelievable.

Kira nudges me, but I don't say anything, I don't want to tell Tori. Not yet.

'Good for you, Tori. Now if I could only bug someone into getting me Rose Conrad tickets,' I say, moving the conversation on.

Tori nods. 'Speaking of which, did you see the latest Secret Sender post, on Rose Conrad?'

'I think everyone's read every Secret Sender post,' says Faye.

Tori scowls. 'That's because people have short attention spans. She's certainly got a knack for grabbing people's attention. Between us, initially I thought the feature was a great idea, because loads of people were reading copies of *The Common Room* – but it turns out they're only reading the Secret Sender!'

'Maybe because people want to read about Rose Conrad and not about the latest cafeteria update or uniform rules,' says Kira, rolling her eyes.

'But her latest opinion on Rose Conrad was so aggressive,' says Tori. 'She's definitely got a holier-than-thou attitude.'

'What do you think, Selena?' says Kira.

I shrug. 'I agree with her.'

'Well, you're a huge Rose Conrad fan. Look at that pin,' says Tori, rolling her eyes. 'You're not going to be on the side of public opinion on this one. Trust me, how people feel about her is starting to change.'

'Any idea who it is yet?' I ask, feeling beads of sweat on my forehead again. Tori and I are doing the work experience together. With the newspaper staff who will know I'm the

Secret Sender.

'Not a clue,' says Tori. 'But everything comes out in the end.'

— ★ —

I tell Ms Harkness the *Croydon Post* news before I leave school. After all, I have her to thank for pushing me, but I have also asked her not to tell Tori. She'll find out eventually.

'Secrets always cost you, Selena,' she says. 'But I'm glad you got into the programme. You're talented.'

There is one person I am definitely not keeping this a secret from. I have to tell Ty as soon as I get home. I run to his door and knock on it.

A man opens it.

Paul. Ty's dad. Even though he lives here, I am surprised to see him, for some reason. He's dressed in jeans and an expensive-looking jumper. Normally whenever I've seen him, he's going to and from work in a suit.

'Hello,' he says. I can see a bit of Ty in him, the angle of his eyes, his high cheekbones. I would bet in his youth Paul Brown was a handsome guy.

'Hi,' I say. 'Is Ty home?'

'Ty!' he calls out behind him. He turns back to me. 'You're our neighbour. Nice to meet you,' he says.

'Yes, I'm Selena,' I say, realising I should introduce myself. 'Nice to meet you too.'

'Paul,' he says. 'I'm Ty's dad. My boys have been telling me all about you, the girl-next-door. They've become quite besotted with you.'

'That's enough, Dad,' says Ty, appearing. 'Hey,' he says to me.

'Come on in,' says Paul, opening up the door. 'It's freezing outside.'

He leaves us in the corridor and heads upstairs.

'I'll be quick,' I say. 'I didn't know your dad was home.'

'He's working from home today. But you know you can be here when he's here,' says Ty, rolling his eyes. 'Come in properly.'

I look along the hallway, and suddenly it hits me. All I can think about is Ollie. There are new photos on the wall, but the familiar corridor looks strange, and seeing Ty standing here . . . Well, it feels very disorientating.

'I need to get home for dinner,' I say quickly. 'I wanted to tell you I got into the newspaper internship.'

'Seriously?' says Ty. 'Selena, that's amazing!' He hugs me and I'm crushed into his chest. I wrap my arms around him, inhale. How does he smell this good?

'I wanted to thank you,' I say, still holding on to him. 'For believing in me and telling me I should do it.' My voice cracks a bit. 'It means a lot.'

'Selena, a lot of people believe in you.'

I think about it: Kira, Mum, Faye, Ms Harkness. And now Ty.

'You're right,' I say, 'they do. But you gave me a final push. When I needed it.'

I look up the stairs, the ones Ollie and I played on as kids.

We'd skid down them on our bums. Once I got carpet burn on the back of my thighs.

'I should go,' I say. 'But thanks again.'

I turn around and head home. As I do, I think about the list I made, and how Ollie wasn't on it. I haven't even told him about the work experience, because I haven't told him about the Secret Sender. The whole thing feels too long and confusing to explain to him. But it's more than that too, I think.

As I walk into my front door and take out my phone, I think about how Ollie would be pleased for me, but as I take a look at our text history, I can't deny it, we've been talking even less since my trip to Manchester.

What will happen when he comes to my party? Will we reconnect again? Will this be a love story for the ages? Will I finally experience the type of love Rose Conrad has been singing about?

Or is our childhood friendship a thing of the past? Will we keep growing further apart as we follow our own paths?

I look at the last message he sent me. It's about his weekend in Manchester. He filled me in on what he had eaten, where he had been . . . but things were left unsaid too. I wonder again if Keeley was with him, and feel that familiar twinge of jealousy.

I used to be so sure of how I felt about Ollie. How madly in love I was. And I thought we were this classic love story waiting to happen. Now I'm not so sure. Maybe it'll be clearer when we're together again. I'll have to see what happens at the party.

Thirty-Three

A force unseen, dragging me to you
It's just science baby, I can't fight it
Neither can you
This electro field it pulls
Magnets is all it is, with you

'Magnets' from *Roses*

SUDDENLY, I'M EIGHTEEN.

When I wake up in the morning, I kind of expect something special to have happened. That as adulthood is bestowed on me, my body and mind become something new. Instead I wake up to my school alarm as per normal, roll out of bed, and start my Friday, as I have done every other Friday before.

Mum greets me when I come downstairs.

'I can't believe you've not gone to work! Don't you have to be early on Fridays?' I say, spotting breakfast. It's smoked salmon and eggs, my favourite, and never seen on a weekday usually. 'You didn't need to do this,' I say, starting to eat.

'I wanted to. You don't need to try and do everything, Selena. Plus, I had some time as I've taken the day off for my spa date with Gina. We got a great deal because we're going on a Friday, and I can spend tomorrow with you,' says Mum, kissing the top of my head. 'I can't believe you're eighteen,' says Mum, hugging me. 'It feels like yesterday I was pregnant with you.'

She's got her bags packed for her night away, her walking cane leaning against them. I feel a pang of guilt about her going away because of me.

'I'd better head off, but I wanted to wish you a proper happy birthday. Especially since I won't see you until tomorrow. We're going to have our big day out then, but have a great day, and enjoy tonight with your friends.'

It's true, tomorrow Mum and I plan to go out for lunch at my favourite pizza spot and then go shopping. Mum picks up her bags and heads to the door, leaning on the cane.

'Are you going to be okay?' I say.

'The point of the cane is to help me be okay,' she says. 'It's fine, I'm taking it more as a precaution.' She swipes at the air with it. 'And it's a good emergency weapon in case I run into trouble!'

'All the trouble you're going to get into at the spa.' I laugh.

'You should be the one trying not to get into trouble,' she says. 'You're eighteen now. A grown-up!' She smiles at me. 'I'm so proud.'

'Mum,' I say, suddenly. 'Thanks for . . .' *The party, the food, raising me single-handed . . .* 'Everything.'

Mum smiles at me. 'Of course,' she says. 'Have fun!'

Before I leave for school, I open the A4 brown envelope Kira gave me yesterday. On it is scribbled in a Sharpie: *DO NOT OPEN UNTIL BIRTHDAY. OH, AND FOLLOW ALL INSTRUCTIONS.*

I roll my eyes and rip open the envelope.

A bark of laughter involuntarily escapes me.

It's a sash that says *BIRTHDAY GIRL* and a tiara that says *18*. There's a note attached.

Happy birthday, bitch! Instructions are to wear the sash and tiara. Do not protest, as you only turn 18 once! Live your best birthday life!

See you in approximately 15 minutes, as I bet you've only opened this before leaving the house. Well done for abiding by the first instruction . . . now you have to do the rest!

PS. Have a great day. We love you!

It is the most Kira thing I've ever read. And the last line is clearly Faye.

I sigh and then laugh. Kira's right, when else would I ever do this? So I put them both on, and wait for Faye to arrive.

Moments later, a text comes through in the Neopolitan group chat, after the flurry of birthday messages this morning. *Code red*, messages Faye, *my car finally has given up from the cold. It's refusing to start!*

Determined not to let anything ruin today, I let Faye know I'll get the bus. In all honesty, I'm not surprised it's not starting. The other day it was whining the whole trip.

As I exit my drive and turn right to walk towards school, Ty comes sprinting out of his door. He's in tracksuit bottoms, Crocs, and a faded Pokemon T-shirt. It's December, so it is, to say the least, not the most appropriate attire.

'Selena!' he calls.

'Ty?' I say. 'What is it?'

'It's your birthday,' he says, pointing at my tiara.

'Yes?' I say, bemused.

He pauses, looking abashed. And cold, he's starting to look very cold. 'I wanted to say happy birthday,' he says.

I smile at him. 'You ran out here in the cold to say that? You have my number now, you know?'

He starts rubbing his arms, hopping from one foot to the other, but still his cheeks turn a little pink. 'Well, it's a big deal. And it's not that cold.'

'I think you're changing colour.'

He looks down at his goosebump-covered arms. 'Come inside,' he says.

'What?' I turn around, look side to side. 'I need to go to school.'

'Come on,' he says, jogging backwards.

I follow him inside.

'Are your parents here?' I say as I walk through the front door.

'Nope, Dad's gone to work, Mum has a morning meeting with a London client.'

'Hey, Selena,' says Daze, appearing from the top of the stairs. He skips down them, holding on to the bannister.

'What's up, Daze?' I say, holding up my hand. He jumps up to high five it.

'How are you so tall?' he says.

'Born that way, I guess.'

'It's your birthday,' he says, pointing at my sash.

'Here comes Detective Daze,' I tease.

'Happy birthday, Selena,' he replies, so sincerely my heart melts a little bit.

'Go on, you've got to go to school,' says Ty, shooing Daze to the front door.

'So does Selena,' says Daze, as he backs out of the door.

'Yeah, and she'll be there soon,' says Ty. 'Go annoy your friends at school instead of us.'

'That's right,' says Daze, fist-bumping me on the way out. 'I've made friends now.'

'You love winding him up,' I say, laughing, once the door shuts.

'I was trying to get him to leave,' says Ty, tugging off his crocs.

'Didn't take you for a Crocs man,' I say.

'They're practical!' he says.

I sigh and pull off my shoes. 'Why am I here? I'm meant to be going to school.'

'It's your birthday,' he says.

'As we've established. Several times.'

'So,' he says, approaching me until we're inches apart. He looks down at me, at my lips. 'Let me give you your birthday present.'

My brain stops firing. I'm caught up in his eyes, this invisible string pulling us close together. All I can hear are the lyrics from 'Magnets' in my head.

And then he laughs and pushes me on the shoulder.

I flush. Why do we keep doing this game?

He moves around so he's catching my eye again, but this time it's friendlier rather than flirty, a sly sparkle in his eye. 'But I am being serious about the present.'

'What is the present?' I say, crossing my arms.

'The best present I could give to you,' he says, moving his arm theatrically with each word. 'The present of my presence.'

I roll my eyes. I thought we were done winding each other up by now. I wedge my shoes back on, pushing past him to the door.

He grabs me by the arm, and pulls me back. 'I'm being serious. Skip school with me,' he says.

'You don't even go to school,' I say, but I don't pull my arm back.

'Okay, well then skip school for me. Please.'

I catch his eye, and against all better judgement I say, 'Okay.'

Thirty-Four

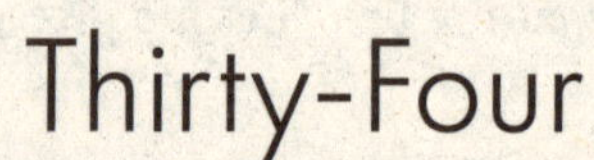

Home's not where the heart is
Home's not where they are
Home's not the place where you park your car
Home's a feeling
As deep as the midnight sky
Home is where I'm kissing you
*   hello and goodbye*

'Home' from *The Brink*
of Teenage Freedom

S O THAT'S HOW I end up on a train to London with
Ty. I'm still wearing my sash and tiara, getting some
interesting looks from strangers.

Kira and Faye are very excited that I'm going to spend the
day with Ty. I insist it's as friends, and Kira says something
about romantic gestures, which I ignore. Plus, I get a text from
Ollie that he's on his way down south. I don't tell him I'm

spending my day with Ty. I feel bad about it, but I don't want him reading too much into it.

'What exactly are we doing?' I say, as the train finally pulls into London Bridge.

'We are going to live my best British tourist life,' he says, getting up.

'Isn't it my birthday?' I laugh.

'Hey, you can live your best British tourist life too,' he says. He looks down at me. 'Unless you have anything you want to do. We can do whatever you want.'

I stand up. 'No, let's see what your plan involves.' I pause. 'Plus I've not really done most of the touristy stuff since I was a kid.'

'So, where's the bridge?' says Ty.

'Erm, not really sure,' I say.

'Don't you live here?'

'No, I live in Croydon. The same as you. A suburb of London. Do you know every part of San Francisco?'

'I would be able to tell you where the Golden Gate Bridge is.'

'Oh come on,' I say, marching on ahead.

We skirt past tourists and families, and I see an exit sign pointing towards London Bridge.

'What's the matter?' I say, looking behind to see Ty, dashing up to me.

He looks out of breath. 'There's so many people,' he says.

'This?' I say, looking around. 'This isn't even rush hour. People aren't even going to work now.'

'It's still busy!' he says.

'Is this your first time into London? You've been here three months!'

'I've been busy, you know, adjusting to the move.' He looks abashed. 'That's why I thought this was a good excuse. It's a good reason to go in, for your birthday.'

'Isn't San Francisco a city?'

'Yeah, but not like this, Selena. This is one of the biggest cities in the world. San Francisco is slightly bigger than Croydon.'

I shake my head. 'Well, I'm looking forward to giving you the full London experience. Come on, let's find your bridge.'

A few moments later we are at the bridge.

'Is this it?' says Ty, as we look at the slab of concrete in front of us. He takes a few photos with his camera, which is slung around his neck and held protectively every time it's not in use.

'What were you expecting?' I say, trying to hold back my laughter.

'I thought it was meant to be like, a thing?' he says, jabbing his hand towards the bridge. 'This is meant to be one of the best cities in the world, and that's London Bridge.'

'Maybe you were thinking of another bridge,' I say, trying again not to lose composure, while glancing behind him. 'How about that one there,' I say, pointing over his shoulder.

He spins around. 'Oh,' he says.

He's looking at Tower Bridge, with its ornate towers, blue-iron structure and famous pull-up bridge.

'Are you sure that's not London Bridge?' he says.

'Nope,' I say. 'Tower Bridge.'

'You knew that all along,' he says, accusingly. He takes his camera, focusing with more intent. He bends down on a knee, pointing his camera up. I wish I could see things the way he does.

'I'm not an expert, but I am from here,' I say, grabbing him by the hand. 'Now let's take a closer look.'

'Actually,' he says, as we start walking again. 'It's nice . . .'

'But . . .?' I say.

He swallows, I watch his Adam's apple bob. 'I know this sounds weird, but I think bridges make me homesick.'

I pause, raise my eyebrows.

'Because I live on a bay, and it's surrounded by bridges. And not any bridges, dramatic bridges, like this one is.'

'I knew about the Golden Gate Bridge, but I didn't realise there were more.'

'San Francisco is part of a big bay,' he says. 'Imagine if this river ran in a circle all around the city. And the river was the sea.'

'So nothing that alike, really.' I laugh.

'No, not quite, but my point is, it's a place surrounded by water.' He looks at Tower Bridge.

'Do you miss it?' I say.

'Home?' he says, still looking out on the water. 'It's part of my identity, it's part of who I am. But I don't think I miss it as much as I should.'

'Why do you think you should miss it more?'

'Because I love it. I love the sea breeze, the hills and the fact there's no seasons. And I miss my friends, I do. And cheetos, I really miss cheetos.'

'Pretty sure there's an American import shop somewhere we can go to.'

Ty laughs. 'For sure. But I think what I actually miss is the sense of belonging. I don't have that here.'

He looks so troubled, I feel compelled to say something. 'That's okay,' I say, grabbing his arm. 'Because this is London, full of people who don't quite belong. So maybe that in itself may make you feel more at home.'

'What do you think of the bridge?' he says.

'It's nice, but it's just a bridge.' I shrug. 'I think what is cool is not the design or engineering of it, but the amount of people that have crossed it, the history it has.'

'Do you like history?' he says, turning away from the bridge and looking at me. People bustle past us, as we crowd closer to the riverside.

'I like stories,' I say. 'That's why I want to study English. I like the idea that loads of people have walked this bridge before, that they will again, and they'll all have different stories, different places they've come from and are going to.' I pause and look at him. 'Don't you think that's brilliant?'

He catches my eye. 'I'm not sure, but I do think you're brilliant.'

He holds my gaze for so long, I start to feel myself blush.

I hope the fact it's freezing might stop my face from actually heating up and giving me away.

'So what now?' I ask him.

Ty stretches his arms wide to the sky. 'Let's go explore.'

Thirty-Five

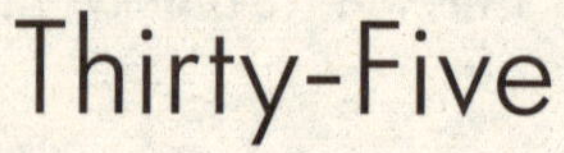

When the moment shatters
It leaves shards of what could have been
What would have been
If we had stayed there

'Shatter' from *Roses*

'WHY DO YOU love photography so much?' I say, as we're walking around an old museum. Ty is taking photos of all the architecture, I'm peering at artefacts in glass boxes.

We are crouched under a huge arch, where Ty is kneeling down, trying to fit the grand staircase into view.

'I like capturing the moment.' He pauses, flicks through the photos he's taken. Readjusts himself and tries again. 'There's so much . . . I don't want to say beauty, because it's not only that. You capture the essence of what's happening with a photograph. And there's so much to it, the skill, the technique.

I feel I'm constantly getting better at it. I'm nowhere near pro level, but I can see myself getting better.'

'You're really good at it,' I say softly, looking at the photo on his screen. The staircase looks dramatic from the natural light coming from the window in the arch above us.

'Go, get on it,' he says.

'What?'

'I want to take a portrait of you,' he says. 'It's your birthday after all.'

I go to remove the tiara and sash, but he touches my hand. 'Keep it on, I want to capture this day as it is.'

I walk to stand on the staircase.

'How should I model for you?' I say, striking a pose with my hand on my hip. He laughs and takes a photo, and I keep moving, throwing my arms and legs out in unnatural shapes, much to the amusement of tourists walking by us.

'Okay, enough,' he says, laughing. 'I think I've captured enough of the Selena Pia catwalk show.' He walks towards me, sits down on the step. 'Talk to me,' he says. 'I want to capture you.'

I feel very self-conscious, looking at him with his camera to his face. It's like I'm trying to see into his eyes, via the camera.

'What should I talk to you about?' I say.

'Are you excited for the newspaper experience?' he says. 'Selena the journalist.'

'I'm excited to learn more,' I say slowly. 'The last time I did work experience, I was mostly helping the council with admin and it was really boring. I'm excited to see what a job like this could be like. If I could write forever.'

I look above, into the dome above us. Seriously – dome, staircase, arches, this architecture really is wild.

'Kira always says there's got to be something bigger than this. Than the life we're currently living. But the life I live has always felt enough, you know? I can't imagine what bigger would look like. But I'm hoping this work experience gets me there.'

'I think I got it,' says Ty, who I hadn't realised has stood up. He shows me the pictures on his camera. There I am, bathed in a soft glow, looking up.

'I'll print this for you,' he says. 'So you can remember to think bigger.'

'I love it,' I say, touching the screen.

'I told you, photography is about capturing the moment. That's all I did here.' I catch his eye, and he smiles at me, and in that second, I don't want this moment to end.

We go to a bar. It's the first time I've ever legally bought alcohol. I hand over my ID, almost nervously to the bartender, after Ty orders two glasses of champagne. We managed to find it at the back of the menu. I don't think it's the average order of this bar with its sticky menus and drinks offers, but Ty insists.

'Happy birthday,' she says, after looking at it and giving it back to me. 'Although with all the stuff you're wearing, I had already guessed.'

'I really should take this off,' I say, touching the tiara, after she leaves.

'It's part of the day,' says Ty. 'You're going to have to keep it on. What would Kira say?'

'I've been hiding myself too much and I should let myself go a bit more?' I touch my chin and pretend to think about it. 'You're right, I should keep the tiara on.'

The bartender brings over the champagne.

'Hey,' Ty says, lifting up his glass. 'To turning eighteen.'

'To both of us turning eighteen,' I say, clinking my glass against his.

'How do you feel about it? Turning eighteen?'

'Well, this morning I was feeling a bit anticlimactic about it, as it was feeling like a normal day, but now it's a bit more than that.' He laughs as I signal around the bar. 'But I don't feel like an adult. I don't feel any different to yesterday. And somehow now I can legally do all these things like drink and vote and leave home, all from one day?'

'What is adulthood anyway?' says Ty, rubbing his face. 'I thought being eighteen would be some great relief from my parents, now I'm finally an adult, my opinions would matter more. But I still feel they have the same amount of say as I did when I was a kid.'

'Ty, your opinions *do* matter,' I say. 'Being a legal adult doesn't change that.'

'My parents have always given this vibe of "when you're older you'll understand" . . . and I've kept getting older and the goalposts keep moving.'

'Why are you so afraid of him?' I say softly. I say him, because I think there's one parent in Ty's mind that he's talking about.

Ty sips again at his champagne. 'Because I want his approval,' he says, shaking his head. 'How messed up is that? All Daze and I want is for him to see us. To feel we're enough.'

'I don't think it's messed up wanting your dad to care about what you care about,' I say. 'I don't know how I would feel if I didn't have Mum's support.'

'Your mom seems great.'

'She is,' I say, nodding. 'Which is why I find the idea of leaving her so hard. She's supported me my whole life. It's just always been me and her. And we only see my grandparents maybe once a year, if that.'

'Do you know what happened? Why doesn't she see them that much? My mum is still calling my grandma all the time and there's an eight-hour time difference!'

'She doesn't really talk about it . . . and I guess I've never really asked. It's the way it's always been.'

'Then how do you know how she really feels if you've never talked to her about it?'

I exhale. 'I have a hard time with . . . I don't want to upset people, you know. So it feels safer to keep things to myself, not to rock the boat. It's why the Secret Sender has been so good for me. For once I can really express myself, no catches.'

Ty touches my hand. 'I know what you mean about not wanting to rock the boat,' he says.

I look at his hand over mine, he looks down and then starts to withdraw it, but I grab it back, so we're now holding hands on the table. The electricity is unbearable, the air feels thick. We make eye contact and I can't turn away.

I move closer to him, so our faces are inches apart. 'But sometimes you have to take the leap,' I say.

I look at him, and in my head there's nothing else, there's no concerns, no worries, just this moment.

Then I lean up and kiss him.

Ty kisses me back, letting go of my hand, and wrapping his arms around my waist, his hands pressing on the small of my back. I feel electricity that's been building up between us explode, firecrackers through my whole body.

The moment between us is shattered by my phone vibrating loudly in front of us. Ollie's name pops up. I glance down at it. Ty also looks, removes his hand from my face.

'I'll quickly check what it says,' I say, opening up my messages.

'Ollie's train is a bit delayed, but he will be at the party,' I say, avoiding Ty's eyes.

'Cool,' is all Ty says, and I feel the guilt rise and fall in me. 'I'm glad he can make it for you.'

I want to go back to before Ollie's text, but the moment has passed.

'Look, Ty—'

Ty holds up his hand. 'It's your birthday – let's talk about it tomorrow. We're celebrating today.' He clinks his glass against mine again, and I exhale. For now we can pretend nothing has happened.

But do I want to?

Thirty-Six

Anticipation, can you feel it?
The moment before
Our hearts start racing

'Anticipation' from The Brink
of Teenage Freedom

'IT'S SO COOL your mum is allowing us to have drinks,' says Kira, twisting open the screwtop on a bottle of wine. I don't mention it's because Mum thinks there's only five people coming. Close friends. If she knew the truth, maybe she wouldn't have been so generous with the wine she's left us.

'Don't go too wild,' I say. Now we're here, I feel excited but also anxious about the lie. Nobody could turn up, I remind myself. But would that be worse?

'Oh, I'm going wild, baby,' says Kira, pouring some wine into a cup. 'What's the point of being at an illicit house party if not to get a bit loose.'

The anxiety returns.

'I'm looking forward to this,' laughs Faye, sipping her Diet Coke.

Right now, it's just the three of us, but I've invited more people from school to come over.

'Faye, are you sure I can't tempt you?' says Kira, waving the wine bottle.

'Although you are dressed like a devil, not now,' says Faye. She isn't wrong, Kira is wearing a scarlet sequined dress and is by far the brightest thing in the room. I've changed into my gold dress with a halterneck, and Faye has made her own outfit: a floaty blue dress, which I cannot imagine how she constructed.

Faye is not drinking. I've seen her take sips, but she likes 'the clarity of a mind untainted'. She said she would at the toast we're going to do later, and I told her no sweat. Kira, on the other hand, seems determined to get more than a toast glass into Faye.

I take a sip of the wine. It's less nice than the champagne I had earlier with Ty. We didn't talk about the kiss at all, like it never happened. But it did and I can feel it on my lips. He said he would still come by tonight.

'Selena, Selena!' says Kira.

'Yeah, what?' I say, coming back to reality.

'You've gulped half that glass down already!' she says. 'Are you okay?'

'Sorry, my mind is elsewhere,' I say, as the doorbell rings.

'I'll get it,' says Faye. 'Otherwise you're going to be getting the door all night and it's your birthday.'

Kira looks at me pityingly. 'Is it because Ollie isn't here yet?'

I want to say no, but instead I say, 'Yes. I miss him. We've basically done every birthday together since we were born.' I feel another surge of guilt. I haven't really thought about Ollie all day. Our traditions, how we've always spent my birthday together. I was too distracted by being with Ty.

It's not a lie, just not what I was thinking of.

'After you spent the whole day with *Ty*?' says Kira, elbowing me. Damn, how does she know me so well.

'It's not like that,' I say, looking away from her.

'Really?' she says.

'We're friends,' I say. 'It's all cool.'

Kira shakes her head. 'I can't believe how many boys you've got all over you. I don't know when a boy will even speak to me.'

'Tori's boyfriend is bringing a couple of friends, you'll talk to them tonight,' I say.

'I can't believe that Tori has a boyfriend and I do not,' says Kira, waving her glass around. 'We're both nerdy girls. I even have a good dress sense.' She gestures around her body.

'You've not met anyone yet,' I say.

'And nor will I ever, while my parents have me under constant house arrest. This is why I need to go to university.'

'University might not solve all your problems, you know.'

'Neither will staying here.'

'Guys, don't argue,' says Faye, coming up to us. From behind her I see a group of girls from school: Christina, who's in my

History class, and her friends Anushka and Jenny.

'We're not arguing,' says Kira, quickly. 'It's Selena's birthday. And on that note, I'm going to get more wine.' She waves her cup at me. 'Want anything?'

'I'm good,' I say as the three girls come up to greet me.

I've seen Kira drink before, and normally she becomes an extra version of herself: fun, outgoing, loud. But something is different tonight; it feels like a dark cloud is hanging over her.

'What's up with her?' I say to Faye.

'I think Kira is being Kira,' says Faye, shaking her head. 'Don't worry about it.'

Soon the rest of my guests start to filter in, and I don't feel so bad. This is manageable. There's maybe fifteen people here, max, but our house can hold them. And everyone is being very respectful. Mostly because it's twelve girls and three boyfriends hanging out. Including Mia who keeps barking at her boyfriend not to touch anything, which I very much appreciate, as I couldn't take any of the art down.

I've put the most valuable items upstairs, but there's a bunch of heavy stuff I couldn't carry, so I stuffed it into a cupboard in the living room. It includes vases and statues and I'm scared the cupboard might collapse under the weight.

There's low key chatting, drinks being poured, I feel very grown up.

Maybe this is what being eighteen is about.

The only people I'm waiting on are Ty, Ollie and Tori and her boyfriend, who texted me to say they're running late.

The doorbell goes and I rush over, it must be Ty. Part of me is worried he's going to bail after our kiss. That he wouldn't want to face me. I'm not even sure I want to face him, but my desire for him to be here outweighs that.

I open the door, and Ollie smiles at me.

Thirty-Seven

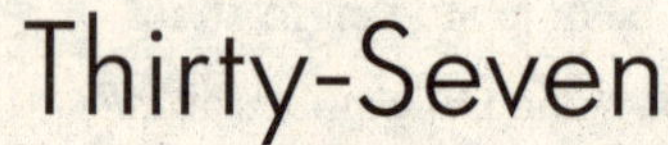

Don't hate me because I'll say what I think
Don't hate me because I'll write
your name in ink
Hate me because I hurt you

'Hate Me' from *Roses*

I STARE AT HIM in shock. I haven't seen him at my front door in months. Even though I expected him to be here, I can barely believe he is.

'You're here,' I say.

'Hey, you invited me,' he says, walking to me, arms outstretched. Then it hits me. The whole purpose of this party was to tell Ollie how I feel. With the work experience, and all the time I've been spending with Ty, I had lost track of that.

I hug him close. The shock eases into excitement.

'You're here,' I say, 'You're really home!'

'I guess I am,' he says, laughing into my hair.

'Look who's back from the dead,' says Kira, appearing at the door, crossing her arms.

'Ah, my favourite antagonist,' says Ollie. 'Hear you got into LSE, congratulations.'

'How's Oxford Law going?'

'Got my interview coming up,' says Ollie. 'I'm sure it'll all be fine.'

'Okay, no bickering tonight, it's my birthday,' I say, holding up my hands before Kira can get annoyed at Ollie's ease about university.

'If the birthday girl asks,' he says, swinging his arm around me and kissing the top of my forehead. 'I have to comply.'

I feel the kiss burn where his lips touched my forehead, my mouth suddenly dry.

Kira rolls her eyes and goes back into the kitchen.

The party starts to go at full force. Kira takes control of the music, blasting out a mix of pop bangers and dance music I've never heard before.

I talk to all my friends from school, feeling like this is about me, and everything is going right. Ollie and I take selfies in front of my bedroom door, a tradition we've done on every birthday since we've got mobile phones.

Around ten p.m., Tori shows up with her boyfriend, Michael, and three of his friends. I breathe out a sigh of relief when I see them. All in button up check shirts, awkwardly looking around. They looked like the type of guys to take DnD to a party rather than MD.

Tori hugs me as she comes in, dressed in an oversized fur coat. 'I've come Gatsby themed,' she says, taking off her coat and showing me her fringe dress. 'You know, since we're studying Gatsby.'

'That's fun,' I say, nodding. It's completely unnecessary, but Tori obviously wanted to dress up.

'We don't get invited to too many parties,' says Michael, sticking out his hand. I shake it and it feels rather formal.

'I'm glad you made it.'

'We've been drinking all day,' says one of the checked shirt boys, swaying slightly.

'But we'll be good,' says another one, looking very anxious.

'We've all been drinking,' I say smiling, trying to put them at ease. 'Come on in, there's some more drinks in the kitchen.'

A few moments later I'm standing around my kitchen island with my new friends, when Ollie pulls me over to the side.

'You looked like you needed rescuing,' he says, nodding over to Tori and the boys. They're passing around a bottle of vodka, taking little sips straight and then wincing.

'Ah they're okay,' I say, laughing. 'Kira's going to be mad at the lack of eligible bachelors. I don't think they're her type.'

'What *is* Kira's type?' says Ollie. 'Anyway, what did you do today, birthday girl?'

'Oh, today I went out with—' I look at Ollie and panic. I don't want him to think I was on a date with Ty. It was friendly. Mostly.

The doorbell rings.

'I'll grab that,' I say, using the excuse to duck away.

This time it has to be Ty. I look at my phone. It's nearly eleven. Why is he so late? A new thought: Ty and Ollie. In the same place. Why does that make me feel so uncomfortable?

I open the door. It is Ty. He's changed from what he was wearing before: he's now in a green shirt and jeans.

'You look good,' he says, hands in his pockets. It's such a casual statement, but it causes my heart to lift.

'So do you,' I say, meaning it. He does. The green picks up on his ever-changing eyes.

'What's going on?' says Ollie from behind me.

Ty's face changes as soon as he sees Ollie. It becomes cooler.

'I'm Ty,' he says, waving.

'The new neighbour,' says Ollie, smiling back. 'Well, I'm the original boy-next-door. And the best.' I wince, why does Ollie always have to big himself up like this?

'So this is the famous Ollie Pointer, in the flesh,' says Ty, stepping forwards, holding out his hand. Ollie grabs it and they do a handshake so tense I am surprised someone's arm doesn't snap off.

'And it's nice to see you in person too,' says Ollie. 'Surprised you've made a show. I hear you're a bit of an arse sometimes.'

'And I hear you're a bit flaky,' says Ty.

'How can I be flaky, I'm right here?' says Ollie, with a tight smile.

'Why don't you come inside, Ty?' I say, nodding towards the

party. Ty's still stood on the doorstep, Ollie almost blocking the entrance.

I see Ty hesitate, and I feel bad. Why is Ollie being so antagonistic? Is he . . . jealous?

In an alternate universe, maybe I would feel elated by Ollie's jealousy. But right now I feel stressed. I don't have time for male macho-ness – it's my birthday!

I turn around. 'Are you coming?' I say, over my shoulder. Ty shrugs, pushes past Ollie and follows me in.

Before we can reach the kitchen, Ollie grabs me and pulls me into the living room, instantly closing the door behind us. Tori's posse are the only people in here, playing a card drinking game that looks really complicated. They're so caught up in it, they barely look at us.

'What's he doing here?' he says.

'What does it matter?' I say, rolling my eyes. I have no time for this. I want to get back to my party.

'Because you guys seemed to be always fighting,' says Ollie. He's leaning against the door, his arms crossed, head tilted down towards me. I feel myself caught in his familiar gaze, I can smell his aftershave waft off him. It's distracting.

'He's fine now,' I mumble.

'How can he be fine now?' says Ollie, taking a step back and waving his arms around, clearly oblivious to what I'm feeling. 'I'm concerned about you.'

Of course it's concern, not anything more. I feel the sudden sharp sting of rejection all over again. Why do I keep getting my hopes up he might be feeling something more? Even though it's been over a month since we last saw each other, I still feel that pull towards him. But it's confusing, after the kiss with Ty.

'Look, it's fine,' I say. 'Let's go back to the party.'

I yank the door open, and Ollie grabs my shoulder. I turn to face him.

'What?' I say.

'I don't want this guy to replace me,' says Ollie, looking the most vulnerable I've ever seen him.

I soften. 'Ollie, how can anyone replace you? We've been friends since birth.'

'Okay,' says Ollie, nodding. 'I have a bad vibe from him, that's all.'

'Honestly, he's not as bad as you think.' And with that, I head back to the party.

In the kitchen, I see Ty standing outside the glass doors, a beer in hand, phone in the other.

'Looks like you're being sociable,' I say, grabbing a jumper I had left lying around and walking outside.

'You disappeared as soon as I came in,' he says. 'And I don't really know anyone else here.'

His straightforwardness sets me on edge.

'I'm sorry about that,' I say plainly.

'Where's Ollie?' he says, looking over my shoulder.

'We're not attached at the hip.' I'm feeling defensive.

'But wouldn't you like to be?'

'Does it really matter?' I say, getting fed up now.

He catches my eye. 'You're right. It's your birthday after all.' He taps his can against my plastic cup. 'Happy birthday.'

'This toast feels less fancy than earlier.'

'But more real,' he says, taking a sip of his beer.

I laugh, but the moment is short-lived as the loud yells of 'chug, chug, chug,' start from the garden. Ty and I look at each other, and head for the garden door. I battle my way through the small crowd to see Ollie and Tori's boyfriend necking bottles of wine.

Thirty-Eight

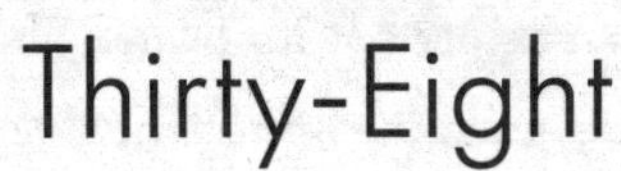

Swing sets and slides
I've always had you by my side
Sister, I've loved you since
The beginning of time

'Sister' from *Dreamers*

'WHAT ARE THEY doing?' I say to Faye, horrified. She and Kira are standing at the front of the crowd, Faye watching in pure horror, Kira with some level of amusement.

'They've got into some kind of drinking contest,' says Faye.

'Who can drink a bottle of wine the fastest,' says Kira. 'My money is on Ollie because the other guy looks kind of green already.'

'We have to stop this,' I say. 'They're going to poison themselves. What is Ollie thinking?'

'I am surprised he had it in him,' says Kira. 'But Ollie is

223

super competitive, and I think him and Michael were egging each other on . . . and well, now we're here.'

'I'm going up,' I say. But as I stride up to them, Ollie staggers away, holding up an empty bottle of wine. The crowd cheers.

'Come on,' I hiss, grabbing him by the shoulders and pulling him towards the door. We walk past Ty and I avoid his look. This is not what I planned, not what I wanted to happen.

'Selena, I did it,' he says, swaying, as we walk into the kitchen. 'Let's go upstairs,' says Ollie, grabbing me by the hands.

'I'm trying to keep the party strictly downstairs for everybody,' I say.

'Yeah, but I'm not *anybody*,' he says, rocking from one foot to the other on a step. For a moment he looks so devilish, he reminds me of the Ollie I know.

'Okay, let's go,' I say, grabbing his hand as he leads me upstairs. 'But you have to sit down up there.'

We go into my bedroom, and he lies down flat on the bed.

'Is it me or is the ceiling moving a bit?' he says.

'I think you're drunk,' I say, sitting down next to him. 'Which would make sense since you downed a bottle of wine. Why did you do that?'

Ollie shrugs. 'I did it before, a few weeks ago, and everyone was really impressed. So I thought I could impress everyone here with it too.'

'I think you could find better things about yourself to impress people with,' I say quietly.

Ollie props himself up on one hand, looking at me. 'The

thing is, Selena, I have learnt the best way of impressing people is by showing them you're on top. You're the best. And here, at Benson's, being the best at school impressed people. And in Manchester, being the best partier is what gets you far. So . . .'

I look at Ollie, digesting what he's said. This is not the person I thought I knew. Is he really just trying to impress people, no matter what? 'Do you really think you have to be the best?'

'Otherwise what's the point?' He's so drunk, he's being so sincere, it's almost funny. But this is the truth.

'The point is to go and do something you want to do, because you want to do it. Not because you're the best at it. Not to impress people.'

Ollie shakes his head. 'No success will ever be found that way. You know, Selena, I know exactly how my life will turn out. And it'll all be fine. So a few stupid things here and there to gain some . . . social currency. Does it matter?'

'What if it hurts you? What if it hurts others?'

He gives me a small smile. 'Do you know what Keeley and Scott and the others call that?'

'No,' I say, distaste starting to form in my mouth.

'Collateral damage. When people get hurt by what you do, even though you didn't mean it. I'm doing what I need to do, Selena. I'm not responsible for other people's feelings.'

Wow.

And that's when I realise. Someday I will become collateral damage to Ollie. Someday he will view me as unnecessary to him. A blocker to his goals. Because all that's ever mattered to Ollie has been winning.

And now that I see it, I can't unsee it. Our whole lives Ollie has been like this, boasting about his achievements in front of Kira, wanting nothing short of perfection, to be viewed as the best. I mistook it as a quirk, his cockiness part of his charm, but now I see it for what it really is. Selfishness and arrogance.

'Ollie, what do you think I want in life?' I ask him.

He looks thoughtful. 'I don't know, Selena, you've never struck me as the ambitious type, which is why I like you. You're the yin to my yang.'

That cuts deep. Everyone else in my life wants me to want more. Dream big. Kira, Ty, Mum, Ms Harkness – they have all been pushing me to realise I can do more with my life. And for the first time I've really started to think it's true.

'Maybe I needed someone to believe in me,' I say softly. 'And maybe you're not that person.'

'Selena,' says Ollie, putting his arm around me, so I'm now lying on the bed facing him.

The familiar brown eyes look at me. But maybe I've been misreading familiarity for knowledge. I don't think I really know Ollie, and he doesn't know me. He touches the side of my face. Normally this action, so romantic under the circumstances, would thrill me. But now, I don't feel anything.

'I think it's time to get back to the party,' I say softly. 'You can have a nap here if you want.'

Just then my door swings open.

I sit up abruptly, in time to see Ty shaking his head and leaving.

Shit, this must have looked bad.

Thirty-Nine

It's the red feeling
I can't explain
It's the boiling blood
In my veins

'That Red Feeling' from *Roses*

'TY, WAIT,' I say, running down the stairs after him.

'Selena, I'm really glad you got what you wanted, but I can't be here,' he says, opening the front door.

'It's not what you think,' I say, grabbing his arm.

'And I look forward to your explanation another time. But right now, I'm tired. Have a good rest of your birthday.'

And with that, he pulls his arm away and leaves.

I'm half tempted to run after him, when Kira grabs my arm.

'I think you need to let him go,' she says.

'What would you know?' I snap. I need to get my shoes and get going. I can probably catch him before he makes it inside.

'Woah, what's with the tone? He clearly doesn't want to talk to you right now.'

'I don't need any of your Kira advice right now.' I walk to the window, I can see Ty getting in his front door. Great, Kira's messed this up for me.

'And what would my "Kira advice" be?' she says, crossing her arms.

'You know, your opinions on stuff. "Don't chase after Ty. Don't be the Secret Sender." Even though you've been the one encouraging me to talk to Ty this whole time and you signed me up for the Secret Sender!'

'Ugh, Selena, we've talked about this a hundred times already. Just because I'm the reason you became the Secret Sender doesn't mean I agree with what's happened since that point. As for your Ty–Ollie drama, I am team Ty. Ollie's always been a bit of a narcissist. But obviously none of this will ever get resolved, because you hate confrontation.'

'So what if I hate confrontation? Is it such a bad thing to want people to get along?'

Kira and I are now standing face-to-face by the front door. Her arms are crossed, her lips tight, it's how she looks before she's about to take someone down in a debate.

'Selena, it's fine to not like confrontation, but it's morally questionable to be the anonymous judge, jury and executioner of everyone when you do hate it so much.'

'Is this about the Secret Sender again?' I roll my eyes. 'Kira, I don't want to talk about this any more.'

'You never want to talk about it! You never want to think too deeply about whether what you're doing is the right thing.'

'It's a small article,' I say, rolling my eyes. I hold my fingers in quotation marks as a I say, 'I am not "judge, jury and executioner".'

'Selena, the entire school cares deeply about what the Secret Sender says. People are changing what they do based on your opinions. Do you not think this kind of anonymous influence is bad?'

'You know what I think? I think you're jealous that for once I'm good at something. I'm on top of something. And you hate to see it.'

Pain flashes across Kira's face. 'That is totally not true. You know all I do is support you. It's why I got you into this mess in the first place! I didn't realise I would be creating a monster.'

'Kira, you're making this about you again. *You* created me? Those are my words everyone is reading!'

'You're not even standing behind your words! Because you know people would be mad at you if they knew it was you.'

'Just because you have unrealistic expectations of how your life is going to turn out, and you want your name attached to everything because of it, doesn't mean the rest of us should.'

Kira steps back. Now she looks furious.

'That's what you really think?' she says. 'My expectations are unrealistic? I'm jealous of you? I'm only doing this because I think it's my way or nothing?'

And because this night is already filled with terrible

outcomes – Ollie passed out on my bed upstairs, Ty storming out of my home – I say, 'Yes.'

'Right,' she says, shaking her head. 'I'm going. Have a good rest of your birthday, Selena. I didn't realise turning eighteen would make you such a dick.'

And with that, she walks out, slamming the door behind her.

Faye comes running up to me. 'Selena, we've got a problem.'

'How can anything get any worse?' I say.

'Michael was sitting down in the living room, playing a game with everyone, and he started to feel sick, so was looking for something, and he came across this cupboard . . .' She takes a deep breath. 'He's thrown up in your Mum's Greek vase.'

Fuck.

Forty

Standing at a crossroads

The compass knows

But I don't

Which way should I go

'Crossroads' from *Roses*

I PROMPTLY KICK EVERYONE out of the party. Faye and I start cleaning up. It's gone midnight, and I am exhausted.

'What happened to Kira?' says Faye, picking up bottles and cans and putting them in a bin bag, as I try and bleach the inside of Mum's vase.

This is a pretty disgusting job. Michael's vomit was nearly entirely red wine, and the smell of the wine mixed with sick is nearly making me retch.

'We had an argument,' I say. 'About the Secret Sender. And other things.'

In all honesty, I am starting to feel a bit bad about what I said to Kira. I don't think she's self-obsessed, and I know it's her way of looking out for me. But I don't think she sees things from my point of view at all.

'I see,' says Faye, tying up her second bin bag. 'I don't want to get involved. But I would say there's two sides to every argument. So just try and think about that.'

'How are you so even about everything?' I say.

'I don't mind saying difficult things sometimes, but I'll only do it if, one, it needs to be said, and two, I really believe it. I think both you and Kira say things you believe . . . but you probably hold them back too much, and sometimes Kira says too much.'

I stop scrubbing the vase and look at her. 'Wise words from Faye.'

Faye shrugs. 'Maybe I should have studied psychology after all.'

'Haha, no – the fashion world needs you.' I point at her dress, which is ethereally moving with her like water. Highly glamorous for the task at hand. 'How did you even make that?'

'A lot of time and patience. You know what my cranky teacher says?'

'The seamstress?'

'Yeah, she says, "what artists need to learn is you never get it right the first time". I think we artists can be a bit impatient.'

'"We artists"?' I say, smiling. I pick up the vase and look at the inside. It's a weird brownish colour, but I think that's because it's wet. It should be all right once it's dry.

'Well, you're a writer. That's a type of art.'

Writer. That's what Ty calls me. All at once my chest hurts.

'Are you okay?' says Faye.

'Fine, a bit tired. It's not how I imagined spending my eighteenth birthday.'

'Hey, as the cranky seamstress said to me when I complained about the trek to her workshop: growing up is dealing with the consequences of your actions.'

I exhale slowly, thinking about everything that's happened tonight. There are going to be a lot of consequences, for sure.

I sleep on the sofa while Ollie snores on my bed, fully passed out. It didn't feel right to sleep beside him, despite us doing it all the time as kids. As soon as we grew up a bit, there was never a need, because our houses were next door to each other. Now our bedrooms are hundreds of miles apart.

I wake up, my eyes stinging and dry, my mouth feeling rancid. I go upstairs to the bathroom, brush my teeth, splash some water on my face, take a few deep breaths and then head downstairs again.

Ollie is sitting at the kitchen table. Two mugs of coffee in front of him. I feel a rush of feelings when I see him. Annoyance mostly about last night, but also a bit of concern, considering the state he was in.

'Hey,' he says.

'How are you feeling?' I say, sitting opposite him. I take the coffee, not meeting his eyes.

'Like I've been hit over the head. And then run over by a truck.'

I shake my head, finally looking up at him. 'What's happened to you? You used to be so serious.'

He looks wryly out of the kitchen window, into the garden.

'I was, wasn't I? And I was a serious kid. I always made us follow every rule of the games we had.'

'Playing Monopoly with you as the banker was a nightmare!'

'That's because you tried to rob the bank.'

I shrug. 'I was low on money.' I know I sound distant, but honestly, I don't want to talk to him. I just want him to leave, and I can have my memories of my friend I used to have.

'Selena,' he says, hesitating. 'I shouldn't have said the things I said last night. I think I came across . . . more callous than I wanted. But you have to know, I think the world of you.' He touches my hand.

I look into his eyes, and I know he's not lying. He does love me, as a friend. But he doesn't know me. Not in the ways that really matter. And the way he sees me – well, I know that's not me.

I hesitate, but I have to say it. 'What you said last night, about me having no ambition? It was hurtful, Ollie.' I rush out my words, knowing once I say it, I can't take it back. I have never told anyone they've hurt me before. Let alone Ollie.

He looks at me and blinks. Then he says, 'I'm sorry, Selena.'

'It's okay,' I say, and I mean it. 'We see things differently too. More differently than I'd realised, maybe. I think we might have been changing for a while now and we've not really seen it. On both sides. I think there's a side to you I didn't see before, and there might be other sides to me you haven't seen either. It doesn't mean they're not there.' And as soon as I say it out loud, I realise it's true, and it's kind of a relief to admit it.

He looks thoughtful. 'I see what you mean. We've always been around each other, so it's easy to hold on to the people we were. And maybe that's not fair on either of us.' He gives me a smile, one that used to melt me, but now feels ordinary. 'I'm excited to see the person you become too.'

And although I'm sad for the Ollie I've lost, I feel relieved to have said what I think and be heard. 'Thanks, Ollie.'

He looks at his phone. 'I've got to get my train. Say hi to your mum for me?'

'And say hi to yours for me,' I say, opening my arms into a hug. He may not have been the person I thought he was, but he's still my friend.

And at the rate I'm currently losing them, I should hold on to that.

I feel quietly optimistic that I've erased every part of the party and Mum won't know what happened. Soon after Ollie leaves, she comes home in a good mood, all zen and relaxed after the spa.

I'm getting ready to go to lunch, when I hear her scream from downstairs, 'Selena!'

I don't think I've ever heard Mum yell. She's been short. She's definitely been angry. But I've never heard her raise her voice. Even as a child I don't remember a time when she yelled at me.

'Selena, why has the inside of my vase been bleached?'

Oh shit. She shows me the inside, and, yup, it's pretty discoloured. Then I see some bleach fingerprint marks on the outside of it. That's what must have given me away.

I'm silent. I don't know what to say. Tori's boyfriend chugged a bottle of wine and threw up in it? It may be true, but it doesn't sound good.

'Selena,' says Mum, now shaking. 'This is an *antique*. Not only that, this is something . . . something so important to me. It's a reminder of who I once was, of how far I've come. You know the story of this vase. So I'm asking you to explain to me truthfully – what happened?'

For a moment, I am frozen. But I know there's nothing to do but confess.

'I had a few more people over last night than I might have made out,' I tell her.

Mum's eyes narrow. 'How many?'

'Maybe fifteen . . . twenty?' I try to look nonchalant and it's not working. I feel like throwing up.

'And who out of the twenty to thirty people did this?'

'Well it was me, but via Tori's boyfriend. I tried to hide

everything valuable out of the way, but he found it and threw up in it, and then I tried to bleach it,' I say, my voice getting squeakier.

Mum looks like she wants to throw up.

'Tori's . . . boyfriend,' says Mum slowly. 'So not only did someone throw up in my vase, it was some random person you don't even know?'

I nod, wincing at the painful facts.

'Selena, do you know how irresponsible this is? You hosted a bunch of people, some you don't even know, in my house, without telling me. What were you thinking?'

'I wanted a proper party,' I say, quietly. 'To feel grown-up, I guess.' The words don't sound any better out loud.

'Why didn't you ask me?' says Mum. 'Because I would have said no?'

'Well . . . yeah,' I say, looking at my feet.

'I wouldn't have said no,' says Mum, so sternly it forces me to look back at her. 'You shouldn't assume things. If you had genuinely told me you wanted to host a bigger party, I would have said yes and supervised it.'

'But you love this house,' I say.

She raises her eyebrows. 'And I would have been concerned about it getting damaged? Yes, I would have been worried, but I would have helped you out. Because I trust you.' She shakes her head. 'But now, you've broken the trust.'

'I'm really sorry,' I say, the disappointment in her voice killing me.

'No, Selena, you're an adult now, this is not how it works. You can't say sorry and try to fix things. You need to sit with your mistakes, bear the consequences of your actions. It's time to grow up now.'

And with that, she leaves with the vase tucked under her arm.

The cranky seamstress was right about being an adult. And it sucks.

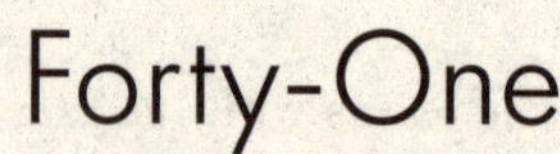

Forty-One

When it all burns down
I'll see through the embers
I'll be the one who remembers
What we had

'Burn' from *Dreamers*

SCHOOL IS PAINFUL. Kira is not talking to me. On Monday I eat lunch with random girls from my other classes because I feel like it's fairer if she gets Faye.

'I want to explain to her,' I say to Faye. It's our free period together, Kira has Economics. It's been one full day of the silent treatment now.

'You need to give her time,' says Faye., 'She's pretty cut up about it.'

'I know what I said was harsh, and honestly I didn't really mean it. I was having a terrible night.'

People start filing into the common room for lunch. I can

feel something is wrong. There're side eyes, hushed murmurs, whispers.

All angled at me.

I see Paula and try to catch her eye, but she looks away.

'What is going on?' I say to Faye. 'Has the whole school heard about our fall-out? Or the party? Neither of those is big news.'

Just then Tori storms in and beelines for us.

'I think we're about to find out,' says Faye.

'You,' says Tori, slamming down the latest issue of *The Common Room*. Which is weird as it's a Monday, not a Thursday. 'Your secret is finally out. I had to print it as soon as I heard it, and I can't believe I had to keep it to myself for a day, but I needed to see your face in person when it was in print.'

A sinking feeling starts in my stomach, as I take the paper from her and look at the front page.

★ THE COMMON ROOM ★

BREAKING NEWS:

SELENA PIA IS THE

SECRET SENDER

We've been following the words of the Secret Sender for a while. Clutching with anticipation to her every word. Well, today we can reveal that none other than Year 13 student Selena Pia is the mystery writer.

From her scalding comments on everything from attention seekers to Rose Conrad fans, the Secret Sender has had the final word.

Now the question is: what will she say now she's been unmasked . . .

I put the paper down, stunned.

'Anything to say for yourself?' says Tori, crossing her arms.

'I think this is the shortest article you've written,' I say finally.

Faye snorts besides me.

'I wanted to keep it in theme with the Secret Sender's style. Or, should I say, your style,' says Tori pointedly.

'Let me guess,' I say, looking down at the paper. 'Kira told you.' There is no way this was a brilliant feat of investigative journalism from Tori.

'I was getting close to figuring it out,' says Tori, as if she's a prime-time detective instead of a student newspaper editor. 'But yeah, Kira told me it was you. She showed me the email account. And why would she lie about it? She said something about how revealing you would be good for you.'

'Of course she did,' I say, shaking my head. 'She did what she thought was right.'

Tori shakes her head. 'I really didn't believe it at first. You've never expressed a controversial opinion in your life! You barely raise a hand in class.'

'I guess it was deep down inside after all,' I mumble. Tori's interrogation is making me uncomfortable. Like I've been pulled apart and laid bare for everyone to look at.

I'm overtly conscious of my surroundings. I can see more and more people start muttering around me. Suddenly Paula comes marching up towards us.

'Hey, Selena,' says Paula. 'I have to ask – what did you get out of it? Writing all those things? Putting people down?'

'I, er, wasn't trying to put people down,' I say. And it's true, it wasn't my intention.

'Bullshit,' says Paula, now looking very angry. 'At least own what you did. You had the whole school wrapped around your finger. Did you know Katy had this full-blown argument with me because of that salt-on-wounds thing? Told me the Secret Sender made her realise I was lording having a boyfriend over her. But it hadn't been an issue before, I thought she was happy for me. We didn't speak for a week!'

'I didn't know,' I say weakly.

'And now you stand here, unable to stand by what you wrote.' She shakes her head. 'Pathetic.'

She walks away, and the bell goes. It's time for English. Part of me wants to go home, but what did Mum say? Being an adult is about facing the consequences.

'This wasn't personal, you know,' says Tori, looking smug. 'I'm a journalist, it's within the public interest.'

Even though she says it sincerely, I can see something else in her eyes. Victory. It may not have been personal to her, but she's enjoying this.

And I am starting to have a sinking feeling that Kira was right about the Secret Sender all along.

— ⋆ —

I get to class moments behind Paula. It's completely full and the whispers rise as I walk in.

In truth, I'm really mad at Kira. How could she just out me like this without warning me? Maybe the silent treatment is a good thing, because I would have nothing good to say to her right now.

I sit down by my desk. Ms Harkness immediately starts class, handing out essays. I've got near full marks again, but I can't enjoy it. Not with the glares people are giving me. I sit in silence, noting down what Ms Harkness says, but barely taking it in.

The thing is, there's nothing to question. It's clear Kira did this to prove her point.

And it is clear people have found the Secret Sender controversial. Some don't like what she says. And now they have a face to pin that to, it's clear they don't like *me*.

I get handed a note during class.

It's easy to comment when nobody knows

I crumple the note. What's getting everyone the most is that it is *me* who is the Secret Sender. And it stings that to everyone, it's so unbelievable.

Ms Harkness comes by my desk at the end of the lesson. People are starting to pack up, slowly drifting out.

'How are you doing?' she says. 'Are people giving you a hard time?'

I think about it. 'No more than I probably deserve. I've been in the habit of falling out with people recently. It would make sense it's now the whole school.'

'You can talk to me, you know, if it gets too much.' She looks at me with a lot of concern.

'Didn't you tell me secrets weren't always good to keep?' I say.

'Doesn't mean you should be torn down for it.'

I shake my head. 'I'll be fine.'

'Getting some extra writing help?' quips Tori, looking at me and Ms Harkness. Ms Harkness sighs and backs away. 'Wouldn't think such an illustrious writer would need the support.'

It's a small jibe, but it really gets under my skin. Tori is doing it *because she can*. Because now I'm just Selena, the girl who doesn't fight back. Who doesn't confront.

But I'm also the Secret Sender. And it's time to own it.

'Illustrious writer is right, Tori,' I say sweetly. 'We all know the only reason anyone read *The Common Room* was for me.'

There's an 'ooooh' from all those still in the room.

Tori walks over with such intention in her step I can practically feel her coming towards me.

'You had the novelty factor,' she says.

'I think you'll find I had good writing,' I say, holding my ground.

'Your "articles",' she air quotes, 'were five lines long!'

'Some may say it's quality over quantity.'

Out of the corner of my eye I can see people's heads move between us, like they're watching a tennis match.

'Some may say it's not real journalism,' she says, and I can see she's getting riled by me. Good. I won't let her walk over me.

'Some may say you published me in the student newspaper. It's journalism.'

She rolls her eyes. 'What would you know about journalism?' she says.

'Well I got onto the *Croydon Post* work experience too,' I say. 'So I'm clearly equal to you there.'

'What?' says Tori, looking visibly disbelieving. 'You got onto the *Post*? By yourself?'

'Yes,' I say. 'With the help of the Secret Sender. I told them all about it.'

I look around the room, seeing everyone captured by me. And for once, I don't think there's any point shirking away.

The secret is out; I am not the person they thought I was.

'Oh, and I've been getting the highest marks in English,' I say, whacking down my paper in front of her. 'So I think I know something about writing.'

She looks at my paper, back at me, back down again, as if she can't believe what she's reading.

'Don't underestimate me,' I say, grabbing the paper off the desk and walk out of the class.

Yup, Kira was right. The truth needed to come out, and I needed to see what would happen, and to own my words. The question is, will she let me explain that to her?

Forty-Two

Hey it's me, calling up
To say I'm sorry
I've tried to get through
A hundred times

'A Hundred and One' from *Dreamers*

IT'S BEEN NEARLY a week since the day my life blew up. Or I turned eighteen. However you want to see it. Normally on a Thursday I would be excited to see the reaction to my article. But today there won't be one.

Kira is still not talking to me, despite me reaching out and trying to apologise to her. The Neapolitan group chat is a ghost town. I've told her I don't even mind that she outed me out as the Secret Sender. But I've got no reply.

I focus on showing Mum I'm sorry. She can't give me the silent treatment like Kira, but she's noticeably frosty. I don't remember her ever being this angry with me before.

'I'll forgive you eventually,' says Mum, as I scrub the hob. 'Seeing as you're my flesh and blood, which does mean more than material possessions.'

'Can we cut to forgiving me now?' I say, turning to face her, and I see a glimmer of a smile pass across her face.

'Patience is a virtue,' says Mum. 'Much like truthfulness.'

'And what does cleaning the hob come under?'

'Penance for your sins.'

'When did you get all religious?'

'When did you get all deceiving?'

'Point taken,' I say, returning to my scrubbing. Mum doesn't believe in enforced punishment, so I asked her what she would like me to do to make it up to her.

She came back with a very long list.

At least this way, she can see I'm sorry. I wish I could do the same to show Kira.

The next day, Faye hands me a note at school. It's my last day at school before I start work experience on Monday. I'm in the library, doing some revision. I didn't want to go to the common room and have people whisper around me like they've been doing all week. Faye perches at the end of the desk after she hands it over to me. The note is written on some lined paper, folded over in half.

'This is quite old school,' I say. 'Couldn't she have texted me?'

'She said looking at your old chat history made her upset.'

'Forget politics, maybe Kira should be the one writing stories,' I say.

But I'm glad to hear from her. I open the note.

I have not forgiven you.

'Good start,' I say, after reading out loud the first line to Faye.

I am still feeling very hurt, but I heard about how you stood up to Tori in English. Good for you, girl. It's a shame this is how we had to get here. I know you're sorry, and you didn't mean what you said, but I'm not ready to forgive what you said. You cut me deep, Selena. I valued our friendship more than anything. I don't think you did.

I'm sorry I blew your Secret Sender cover like that, but I'm glad you realise it had to be done. No good comes from secrets. Say what you think, say it with pride. I need a friend who is willing to stand up for me, the way I would stand up for them.

Kira

I look up at Faye. 'This sucks,' I say.

'It does,' she agrees.

'Not because Kira's mad at me, which does suck. But it mostly sucks because she's right.'

Faye nods. 'I think she'll come around, but you know that though.'

I slump down onto the desk. 'In my heart, I didn't think this would ever catch up to me, which is why I kept pushing my articles further and further. In the moment I did believe in what I was writing, but now I've seen everyone's reaction, maybe I should have kept my thoughts to myself.'

Faye touches my shoulder. 'No, Selena, you should say what you think, you need to own what you're saying. That's why Kira was impressed when she heard how you stood up to Tori. You said what you thought and you stood by it.'

Say what you think and stand by it.

Maybe Kira isn't ready to hear from me yet, but there's one person I've not tried that out with yet.

I knock on the front door and Daze opens it.

'Selena?' he says, confused.

'I need to talk to Ty,' I say.

Daze sighs. 'He doesn't want to talk to you. What went down between the two of you anyway?'

'Can I come in at least?' I say. 'It's freezing out here.'

'Yeah, yeah, this country is wild, man. How do you cope with this cold? I'm always wearing about five layers.'

'Doesn't it get cold in San Francisco?'

'No,' says Daze. 'It's always kind of the same weather. Cool, breezy, and a bit foggy all year round.'

'That's a bit bleak, isn't it,' I say. 'Don't you want seasons?'

'I like it,' says Ty, appearing at the top of the stairs. 'It's nice to know what you're going to get. The UK is . . . unpredictable.'

I look up at him, he has a cool look on his face. I fight the urge to flee. It's time to stand up for what I think.

Ty walks downstairs.

'Sooooo . . .' says Daze, drawing out the word. 'What's going on here? It feels like we've gone back in time.'

'I think Selena has made her feelings clear,' says Ty.

'Can we talk alone?' I say. 'Please.'

Ty looks at Daze, raises his eyebrows.

'I'm going to go and chill somewhere else,' says Daze. He looks between us. 'But you guys need to sort this out. I don't like picking sides, especially when I have a brotherly duty to pick Ty's side.'

Ty rolls his eyes and pushes him.

'Come on,' he says, nodding his head upstairs.

All this time, I've only been into the hallway of the Browns' house. And it feels bizarre, as I knew it for so long as the Pointer house. Different but the same. The family photographs have morphed into tasteful art. New plants have sprung up. Daze has stuck a sign to his bedroom door.

We get to Ty's room, and it feels like I'm going into Mr Pointer's study, a room which for so long had been forbidden.

'What?' says Ty, seeing me hesitate.

'This room used to be off limits,' I say, turning the handle. 'But I guess things are different now.'

Ty's room is more artistic than I would have given him credit for. Huge black and white photographs hang on the wall, a record player and vinyl collection is stacked in the corner, where Mr Pointer's desk used to be. It's spotlessly clean. Unlike Ollie's room, which always had some mess lurking in it.

'So,' says Ty, sitting down on his desk chair. 'Why are you here? I've not heard from you all week.'

'I've been struggling to know what to say to you,' I confess, sitting down on the edge of his bed. 'For once I've run out of words. And there's been so much crap that's been happening, and all I wanted was to tell *you* about it, but that would require addressing what's been going on with me. What's been going on with us.'

He crosses his arms. 'And what has been going on with us?'

'You're important to me,' I say, trying to look him in the eye. *Say what you think and stand by it.*

I take a deep breath, try to ground myself in what is real and true, and decide to tell him the truth, instead of running from it.

'I liked Ollie,' I say, and it hurts me to see how his face falls. 'But I think I liked the Ollie I thought I knew, not the Ollie who actually exists. And it would have been a perfect ending, if we got together, and I got too wrapped up in the story. I wasn't looking at what was right in front of me,' I say.

I meet his eyes and they burn into me. I have to say it. I have to say what I think.

'I like you, Ty.'

Ty shakes his head. 'Then what about you and Ollie at your party?'

I rub my face. 'It's really not what you thought. At that moment, I had a revelation about how Ollie isn't the person I thought he was. And I'm not the person he thinks I am too. You're the person I told about Secret Sender, not him. You're the one I've been talking to about my university applications, not him. He thinks I'm some wallflower, and you . . . you've never made me feel like that.'

'Because you're not.'

'And there's so much stuff that's happened this week that I've wanted to talk to you about. Kira's not speaking to me because I said some awful things at my party. Everyone knows I'm the Secret Sender. I had a face-off with Tori—'

'Woah, woah, woah,' says Ty. 'What? All that's happened in a week?'

'Turning eighteen has been fairly eventful,' I say.

Ty sits down next to me. 'It's really sucked not speaking to you this week too,' he says. 'I was so mad at you. And I didn't feel I had any right to be, but it made me not want to talk to you. But you're my only real friend here, and it was so . . . lonely.'

'So where do we go from here?' I say, turning to him. I feel that invisible string tugging me towards him. It feels impossible to fight it now.

'Let's go back to where we were,' he says, and my heart soars. 'As friends.'

My heart crashes down like a kid's kite in a park.

'Friends,' I repeat. Not sure if I'm saying a question or a statement.

Ty runs his hands through his hair. 'I think it's less messy this way. I don't want to fall out again. Plus at the end of the summer we'll go our separate ways, and . . . well, my dad still wants me to go back to the US.'

I feel hurt. I thought we had something and he felt the same way. But maybe after everything he doesn't like me like that any more. And I don't want to ruin things between us any further.

So, even if deep down I don't want to, I say, 'Okay.'

Forty-Three

Lights, camera, action
Can you feel the attraction?
I'm addicted to the fame
Addicted to the game

'Addiction' from *The In-Between*

KIRA IS STILL ignoring me. This is the longest I've gone without speaking to her ever. Faye has been splitting her time between us all weekend, and it feels like she's a child of divorce, the way she's had to trek from house to house.

But in big news, I've now sent off my UCAS form! Applying to study English Literature with English Language, all with London universities. And I'm waiting to hear back. Ty tells me he's starting to be accepted both into UK and US universities. He's still not told his dad how he feels.

Today is the first day of my work experience at the Croydon Post. Everyone else will be starting their final week of winter term. Tori and I have got permission to miss it for this. Despite Mum's best effort in trying to get me to dress 'smart', even though the email clearly says the dress code is 'casual', I turn up in a carefully selected jeans and plaid shirt. What do journalists wear? This feels a bit businessy, but artsy enough to be a professional writer. If I'm overthinking the outfit this much, god knows how much else I'll overthink.

Ty texts me good luck, as does Ollie. Ollie and I aren't talking as much any more, but we still check in now and then. We share the big stuff. It's a good way of honouring our friendship without creating any pressure. Last time I heard from him, he'd started going out with Keeley.

I arrive at the office and check in. I'm taken to get my photo done, a scenario I'm unprepared for, and handed a badge with my face printed on it. Great, if I had known this I would have worn something plainer than plaid!

Tori, of course, is already here, tapping away at a laptop she must have brought in with her. We've not even formally started the day yet.

I sit down next to her, and opposite a boy I assume to be the third intern, who's tall and lanky with a smattering of acne on his left cheek. Horrifically, he's also in a plaid shirt and jeans.

'I'm Doug,' he says, nodding at me.

'Selena,' I say back.

'Tori,' says Tori, waving her hand without taking her eyes off her laptop.

'What are you even doing?' I say. 'They've not given us

anything to do yet.'

'Yeah, you're making us look bad,' jokes Doug.

'Overworking is her thing,' I say. 'You'll get used to it.' I see the confusion on his face. 'We go to school together.'

'Same English class and everything,' says Tori, not making eye contact. 'I'm writing up the headlines of the different news outlets from this morning,' she says. 'In case it comes up.'

'Are you guys on the same student newspaper?' says Doug. 'I'm the editor of mine.'

To be fair to Doug, this is an innocuous question, given the circumstances. He does not realise the minefield it is for us.

'I'm the editor too,' says Tori, sweetly. 'And Selena somewhat contributes.'

Doug looks between the two of us, obviously sensing the tension.

'It's a long story,' I say. 'I'll tell you later.'

'Morning, interns,' says a man walking over to us. He's in a checked shirt, not plaid – there is a difference – with glasses and a short grey beard. 'Welcome, welcome. I'm Gareth and I'll be supervising you here for the next week at the Post.'

Tori immediately snaps her laptop shut.

'Now, you'll be shadowing a lot of our staff writers here,' continues Gareth. 'Helping them out on day-to-day tasks and hopefully getting a feel for local journalism.' Gareth goes on to explain different journalists we'll be assigned to, events that are going on during the week, and admin like when to take lunch.

He continues, 'Lastly, you'll be gearing up to write your own article. We have found it's a good way for you to put everything you've learnt into practice, as well as getting some healthy competition going. So, we'd like you to interview a local person and write it up for us. The best interview will be published in the *Post* in print and online, getting you your first official byline. We know you only have a few days to do it, but such is the pressure of journalism.'

We all look at each other excitedly. Tori looks smug, no doubt she thinks she has this in the bag.

'But not only that,' says Gareth. 'This year we have an additional prize. Do any of you know of Rose Conrad?'

We all gape at him. Me especially. Where is this going?

'Yes!' I say.

'My girlfriend loves her,' says Doug.

'Good news,' says Gareth. 'We've got two tickets to cover the concert in Central London this weekend, as it's a big event happening in the city. We thought we'd give them to the winner of this – you're her target audience and can write a more authentic review. Pull in some younger readers. So if you win, you'll get two bylines! One is your published interview, one is the review of the concert in a few weeks.'

We're all stunned. Forget the byline, those tickets are like gold dust! Extremely expensive gold dust on resell sites. And this is my chance to get them and go.

Tori turns to me, a cold and calculated look in her eyes. 'Those bylines are mine,' she says. 'You may think you're better than me, but I'll prove it by winning here.'

Okay, it may not be a good chance to get them, but there's still a chance.

— ★ —

My evening is spent calling local business owners to see if they'd be interested in talking to me. I get some outright no's, a few maybe's, and a couple of yeses. But deep down my heart isn't in it. I could interview Annie Bannanie of ice cream fame, but for some reason, it doesn't feel right. Having spent five minutes on the phone with her, I can tell Annie is a creative woman with a mind for wild ice cream flavours, but there's no story there. But I guess it's better than nothing.

'I don't see how I can win,' I say, pacing Ty's living room. I'm exhausted. 'Tori has spent all day mentioning all the local celebrities her mum knows and how she is going to get a great interview. Somehow her mum knows every person from the mayor to that guy who ate all those jelly babies and made national news!'

'Let's work through it,' says Ty. 'Who else do you know?'

'You. Mum. Faye. Ki— My friends from school. And Mum's got no useful connections, unless I want to interview someone about planning permission from the council. I don't even know what planning permission is! I hear Mum complain about it.'

I sit on the sofa, with a sinking feeling of disappointment.

'This is our chance to go,' I say to Ty. 'Those Rose Conrad tickets are within my reach! I've been holding on to this spark of hope that there would be some kind of magical coincidence and I'd be able to go. Like Cinderella and the ball. And now the fairy godmother has turned up in the form of Gareth, and Tori is about to turn my tickets into a pumpkin!'

'What a metaphor,' says Ty, shaking his head. 'And you would take me to the concert? Are you sure?'

'You or Kira are the next biggest fans I know, but Kira isn't exactly speaking to me.'

In this moment, I really miss Kira. She would know exactly what to do or say. She would tell me that I could do it, that I could win against Tori. And no doubt she would come up with a hundred ideas of how I could try.

Kira was more than my friend, she was my champion. She's always backed me to be a writer, it's why she submitted me to *The Common Room* in the first place. And I really took her for granted.

'I have to go,' I say, standing up. 'I have an idea.'

'What? About who to interview?'

'No,' I say, running out of the door, 'Something more important.'

I get home and run upstairs to my laptop. Words are all I've ever had. And even if I can't use them to beat Tori, maybe I can use them to fix this.

I start drafting an email to Ms Harkness, hoping I can make it in time.

Forty-Four

That girl, she grew up to be an
Actress with blonde curls
Always pretending, started forgetting
Until the part hit her too hard

'The Part' from *Dreamers*

THIS IS ONLY the second day at the *Croydon Post*, but I love it! I'm sad it's going to be over soon. Even though we're not exactly covering breaking news, there's something exciting about working on live stories, watching the writers plan and pitch articles. I mostly observe, trying to be as helpful as possible, and I get this huge rush of satisfaction when someone thanks me.

Disaster has struck in the form of my interview though. I was meant to interview Annie yesterday, but she has a family emergency in Scotland and will be gone for the rest of the week. So now I'm back to square one.

'Who do you think I should interview?' I ask Gareth. We're sitting together, going through some library archives on the history of the city. Gareth is doing an article of strange laws that are still in existence today, and we're trying to cross-reference.

'Ah, I am the judge of the competition, Selena. I don't think it's fair to hand out advice,' he says.

'A fair judge,' I say teasingly. 'Can you at least give me an idea of the criteria? I don't really have any connections, and I want to be in with a shot of winning. My first proper byline. And I'm a huge Rose Conrad fan.'

'You do have a shot of winning,' says Gareth. 'And no part of the criteria is about how famous a celebrity you interview. I would focus on the story you're telling. And a good story can come from anyone.'

'Okay . . .' I say, finding his advice more mysterious than helpful. I've still no clue who to interview.

At lunch, I meet Tori and Doug.

I've been getting along much better with Tori over the past two days. I think it's abundantly clear she is not top dog in these circumstances, and the levelling of the field has made her more approachable. She even asked me for help yesterday on how to navigate a database I had used the day before.

But I know Tori, and she still wants to win.

'I overheard you talking to Gareth earlier,' she says, as I sit down. 'It's a small office. I know you care a lot about Rose Conrad, Selena . . . but I want the bylines. I want to prove myself as a writer.'

I look at her and realise, 'So do I. It's not about winning the tickets for me. I want to prove to myself that I'm good at this. And of course win the tickets.'

'Well then, let the best woman win,' she says.

'Or man,' says Doug. 'My girlfriend really wants to go to the concert.'

I laugh. 'Fair enough. Some healthy competition will be good. I've already lost out on tickets once, it's not going to kill me to lose them a second time.'

We start talking about the projects we're working on, when mine and Tori's phones vibrate.

My hands start to tingle, a nervous feeling spreading through me. I think I know what this is.

Tori opens her phone. 'It's an email: *The Common Room: festive edition*,' she reads out loud, slowly and confused. 'But I haven't created a festive edition of *The Common Room*. It's also a Tuesday, not a Thursday. We decided not to release anything on the last week of term, as I'm here.'

I tap on the email on my phone and open it up, although I know exactly what it says.

★ THE COMMON ROOM ★

**A FESTIVE MESSAGE FROM
THE NOT-SO-SECRET SENDER**

As the year draws to a close, I realise I owe a lot of people an apology. Firstly you, the reader. What started out as a harmless way of voicing my opinions derailed into harmful opinions. Ones with no consequences for me, as I could hide in my anonymity. You all took what I said as truth, without anyone being able to hold me accountable. Like Santa is also Saint Nicholas, the Secret Sender is also Selena. It's time to ditch the mask.

That's not good journalism, and I apologise for it. I am sorry if my opinions harmed you or your friendships; if you felt attacked and had no way to respond. I excused myself by pretending to be above it all, but I was taking out my feelings on others through quips and jibes.

So, to the whole school, I am sorry.

Also, Ms Harkness, you were right. Secrets get you nowhere.

There's another very public apology I must make.

Kira Ganyo, I am sorry.

I am sorry for taking your support for granted. I am sorry for calling you interfering, when all you were doing was trying to help me. I am sorry for being so self-conscious I accused you of jealousy.

These are all very embarrassing things to admit, but Kira, I am not embarrassed about how much I love you.

And in the season of giving, I am giving you this very public apology. With my own name attached.

Please forgive me, because I need you to be my friend.

From the person who used to be known as the Secret Sender.

Selena Pia

'Wow,' says Tori, finishing reading it. 'How did you get this published?'

'That's all you have to say about the article?' I say, shaking my head.

'It's not my opinion that counts here, is it? Do you think Kira has read it yet?'

Forty-Five

And I'm sorry that I
Didn't pick up the phone
That I left you alone
That I wasn't there

'A Hundred and One' from *Dreamers*

MEET KIRA AT a coffee shop the next day, after work. I left a bit early, but I don't think anyone noticed. I said it was for my interview.

'Why did you agree to see me?' I say after we get our drinks.

Kira shrugs. 'It was a very over-the-top way to get my attention. It deserved a response.'

'How's the end of term going?' I say.

'All good, everyone's starting to take it easy you know.' She shrugs, takes a sip of her coffee. 'Honestly, it's been quite shit without the three of us hanging out. How about you? You're doing the work experience, right?'

'It's so good,' I say. 'I'm really enjoying it. I like doing this stuff! Even the boring bits.'

'How about hanging out with Tori all day?'

'She's not so bad. I mean, we're both doing this competition, but I think . . . I think she respects me now. Since I stood up to her that time.'

'I wish I could have seen it,' says Kira.

'I was definitely inspired by you,' I say. I think about it. 'And I was inspired by me. It was time I started saying what I thought.'

'Well, the letter in *The Common Room* really sounded like that.' Kira smiles.

'Did you like it?' I say.

Kira rubs her chin. 'I liked seeing you speak out publicly as yourself, you know. To Faye and I in private, yeah, you say what you think. But to everyone else, you've always been afraid. So I was impressed to see you less afraid.' She pauses. 'And the public apology was nice.'

I take a deep breath. 'I am sorry, Kira. I'm sorry I said you were interfering, you were jealous of me and your expectations of life are unrealistic,' I say, trying to remember everything I said on my birthday.

'That cut me deep, you know?' she says. 'Like, I know they're sky-high ambitions. I know wanting to be, not even Prime Minister, but wanting to be *someone*, is unrealistic. But what hurts is I thought you would have believed in me.'

'I do believe in you,' I say urgently. 'If there's one thing I believe in it is your ability to crush it. If anything, I'm the jealous one. I've always been jealous of your focus.'

She shakes her head. 'Let's cut jealousy out of this.' She reaches over the table and takes my hand. 'I forgive you, Selena. It's going to take a lot more than a fight to break our friendship.'

I smile at her. 'I'm glad. I realised how much I needed you.' I look at her slyly. 'But you will never guess what I did by myself.'

'What?' she says, leaning forwards.

'I sent off my UCAS.'

'No!' she says, banging her hand on the table. 'Really?'

'Yup,' I say, leaning back, happy to have told her. 'And you know when I did it, the main person I wanted to tell was you!'

'I'm pleased for you. What did you apply for?'

'English Literature and Language. Keep my options open. And only London universities.' I feel a tension in my chest. 'I still don't like the idea of leaving home, but I thought I should just send in the applications and figure it out later if I get accepted.'

'Yes, Selena!' says Kira, hitting the table. 'I'm glad you've worked out how to do it your way. That's all that matters. We're all different, and that's okay!'

'I'm just so glad I can tell you about it. I really needed to start reversing the list of people I pissed off.'

'Who else have you pissed off?' she says, laughing. 'Faye told me about your mum and the vase, which is really bad . . . but you got to admit, Tori's boyfriend throwing up in it is an image.'

I shake my head. 'The list was you, Mum and Ty,' I say. I then fill her in on everything that happened with him and Ollie. 'So then he said he thought we should be friends because he might be moving away in the summer, and he doesn't want us to fall out again.'

'And you kissed on your birthday?'

'Yeah.'

'And you told him you liked him?'

'Yeah.'

She leans back. 'Well, girl, that really is something.'

'I was hoping for some advice!'

'Well, it sounds like he likes you, and you like him, and you both told each other you like each other, so I'm not really sure what else you can do here.'

'Well, he's never explicitly said he likes me.'

'He kissed you back, I would say it's implicit.'

'So what do I do?' I say, sitting forwards. 'What would you do?'

'I would walk up to that man and tell him he's being ridiculous and kiss him.'

I bury my head in my hands. 'You make it sound so easy.'

'You asked me what I would do. In all seriousness, I would tell him this is stupid. None of us really know what's going to happen in the future. Why be stopped by possibilities?'

'Even you, who knows exactly how your life is going to turn out?'

'That's the point – I know how I want my life to turn out, I don't know how it actually will. Sometimes you've just got to do what you want to do in the present.'

'So I should try and convince him.'

'If you don't try, you'll never know. Think about the Secret Sender. Yeah, there were a lot of bad things that happened, and yeah you got completely carried away with it – but if you had never put yourself out there, you wouldn't have realised you liked writing so much. Not doing anything at all would have been way worse.'

'Have I told you enough yet that you were right about that?'

'You wrote it all in the school newspaper, but I won't get enough of being told I'm right.'

'I think I forgot how annoying you were during this silent treatment.'

Kira flicks her hair with her hand. 'Well, I'm back. So you better get used to it again.'

Forty-Six

And when we kiss, we touch
Oh its a hard rush
It feels, it feels … electric
I hope I don't regret it

'Electric' from *The In-Between*

AFTER I GET home from meeting Kira, I sit in the kitchen, staring at my laptop. It's the evening, and Mum is out for dinner with Gina, so I'm eating alone. There's two tabs open. One, a crossed-through list of potential people to interview. Two, my empty UCAS status screen. Both are disheartening.

A tap at the kitchen-door window. I look around and nearly jump out of my skin.

There is Ty, waving at me.

I open the door and he's standing on the step in a white jacket and jeans. He looks almost angelic in the garden lights.

For a split second we stare at each other, and the air feels heavy, pulsing between us. I think about what Kira said, how she would kiss him if she was me. I can't do that, can I? But now she's said it, I can't get the idea out of my head.

Ty pulls me outside. It's good I'm wearing thick slippers, it's freezing out here!

'What are you doing?' I say.

'I was feeling . . . warm,' he says hoarsely. 'The fresh air is good.'

There it is again. The undercurrent of something more.

'So warm that you're making me stand in the freezing cold? It's basically the middle of the night,' I say, taking a step closer to him, so I can feel the warmth radiating off him. 'Why did you come over?'

'Selena, it's seven p.m. I wanted to hang out,' he says. 'See how your interview was going?'

'Not well,' I confess. 'I still don't have a person to interview. I feel I've now called up half the town. I did make up with Kira though.'

'How did that go?' he says.

The cold bites me. *Remember what Kira said.*

'She forgave me.' I pause. 'And she said, "Sometimes you've got to do what you want to do." It was good advice.'

'And what do you want to do?' he says. There's a glint in his eyes.

'Right now? Be inside.' But I have to ask. 'Why did you bring me out here?'

Ty sucks in his cheeks. 'Why is it that I can't get you out from under my skin, Selena?' he says hoarsely.

'What are you talking about?' I say. 'You're the one who wanted to be friends.'

Could it be that he's changed his mind?

He steps forwards, and I step back, so I'm standing on the doorstep to the kitchen.

'All day, all I can think about is you,' he says. 'All I want to do is spend time with you.'

'I want the same thing,' I say, softly. 'But you said we were friends.'

Ty's face twists, and he takes another step closer to me. 'I know I said that.' He's so close to me, I can see the flecks of brown in his eyes. Maybe this is how they look, like they're shifting colour all the time.

'Because you might be moving,' I say.

'Because I might be moving,' he repeats, his gaze dropping to my mouth.

'I've been clear with what I want,' I say softly. 'This is me, putting myself out there.' My heart feels like it's about to burst out of my chest.

'Why are you doing this?' he says, putting his hands on either side of my head, so I'm pinned between him and the wall. I don't mind it at all.

'Because it's the truth. Why are you fighting this?' I say. 'You don't know what's going to happen, neither do I. You're torturing both of us. Unless you *want* to leave.'

The last word chokes out of me, like it's been wanting to escape from me this whole time. That's the fact. I am afraid Ty deep down wants to go. That's why he's been avoiding getting close to me.

We stare at each other for a few seconds, the air feeling even heavier than it did before, like it is about to suffocate us.

He shakes his head, and pushes himself away, spinning around to head back to his garden.

Without thinking what I'm doing, I run after him, grabbing his shoulder.

He turns around, grabs my wrist, pushes me back against the wall of the house. I feel the winter sun on my face, the chill in the air, and all I see are Ty's brown-green eyes.

And then he kisses me. Or I kiss him. I'm not sure what happens, but we collide.

I've been kissed before, hell, I've been kissed by Ty before, but I've never been kissed like this.

Ty kisses me like he's been waiting his whole life for this. It's hungry and raw, and I'm pulling him closer and closer, as if I can crawl into this kiss. It's somehow angry and tender at the same time. I've never felt more alive.

When we finally pull away for air, he rests his forehead on mine, and for a few seconds there's this peace between us, like it this is the way it's meant to be.

Then he steps back. And everything snaps back to where it was before.

He rubs his face.

'I'm sorry, Selena, I shouldn't have done that.' He turns and heads back to his house.

— ★ —

After the kiss, I head upstairs and lie on my bed, my head spinning. I'm emotionally exhausted.

What was that about?

Why was he sorry?

He never said he didn't want to leave.

The last realisation punches me in the gut. Does he really want to go? He's been saying for ages he wants to stay here, but what if he's changed his mind?

Ty is a chivalrous guy. And if he thinks he's moving back to the US . . .

But I still haven't told him how I really feel. I told him I want to be with him, but I haven't told him why. I asked him if deep down he wanted to leave, but he never answered. And if I'm honest with myself, I'm afraid of the rejection.

Maybe he got caught up in the moment. What if he doesn't really like me that way, and feels bad about kissing me? What if I was wrong about everything?

Ugh. I roll on my bed, and sink my face into my pillow, as if I can suffocate the thoughts.

I resurface to text the Neapolitan group chat: *SOS.*

Forty-Seven

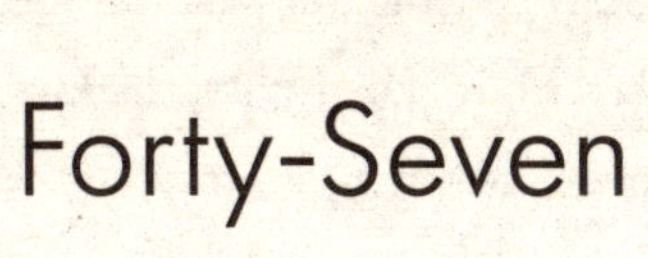

It's reckless, the way we're doing this
It's a mess, I can't lose you another time

'Reckless' from *Roses*

IT FEELS GOOD to have Kira pacing my room again. She and Faye immediately drove over, despite it getting late now. Luckily Mum isn't home yet, otherwise she would have kicked them out because it's a school night.

'Okay, so why did you call us here?' she says.

'Take this as calmly as possible, but Ty kissed me. Or I kissed Ty. I'm not entirely sure.'

'WHAT?' they both chorus. Kira immediately stops and turns to face me, jaw slack. Faye sits up and stares at me.

'Okay, okay,' I say. 'Just don't … don't get overexcited. I took your advice, Kira.'

'One, I'm excited you took my advice. Two, how can we not get overexcited at Ty kissing you? Or you kissing him? Which is a detail we are going to need,' says Kira.

'Yeah, tell us everything,' says Faye, more simply.

I exhale, and start spilling out what has been going through my head for the last hour. The fights, the kiss, the apology, the walk away, and now me sitting on my bed with no idea what happened.

'Sounds romantic,' says Kira.

'Are you joking?' I say.

'You had a wild, passionate kiss at the side of your house – I would say it was romantic,' says Kira.

'And then he left abruptly. After apologising for the whole thing. What part is romantic?' I say.

'Well, he clearly likes you,' says Faye.

'I'm not sure that's clear,' I say. 'He said he wanted us to be friends.'

'Yeah but then he kissed you. Mixed messages,' says Kira.

'I think that's the problem,' I say.

'He probably has a reason for what he said,' says Kira. 'The only way you're going to find out is if you talk to him.'

I groan. 'I'm going to have to, aren't I?'

'Yes,' chorus Faye and Kira.

'And I'm not going to like it.'

'Yes,' they say again.

'And I won't know what he's going to say.'

'Yes,' they say back.

'You know, Selena, I think deep down you know what you have to do even before you call us over here,' says Kira.

I throw a pillow at her. 'Therapy is over now. I will talk to him. I need to think about what I want to say.'

'And what do you want to say?' says Faye.

I look out of the window. 'I need to tell him why he's important to me. That this means something more to me. That no boy has made me feel so seen or heard before. That when I'm around him, it's not just that I'm attracted to him, but I appreciate him. We can't just be friends.'

'But first you need to hear Ty's side too,' says Faye.

'Yes, I do, and I don't have a good feeling about it.'

'Selena?' says Kira.

'Yes?'

'Can you try and be a romantic for once?'

I still have no idea what to write my essay on, the guy I like is avoiding me, and it feels like I'm running out of time on all accounts.

So before work the next day, I turn up at his house. It feels a safer bet than having my texts ignored.

He opens the door and sighs. Not a good sign.

'It's eight a.m.,' he says.

'We need to talk,' I say. 'Can I come in?'

He nods and leads me to the living room and flops onto a sofa.

'I wanted to come talk to you,' he says, 'but every time I

thought about it, I . . .'

'Chickened out?' I say, sitting in the armchair opposite him.

'Well, you're not easy to understand. I was trying to gather my thoughts,' he says.

'*I'm* not easy to understand? You're the one who kissed me and ran away!'

Ty shakes his head, leans back in his seat. 'The difference is I know why I do things and how I feel.'

'And I don't?'

'Not historically, no. Based on the whole Ollie thing.' He looks at me sadly. 'How do I know you're not confused about me in the same way you were about Ollie?'

I chew my lip. 'Okay, I understand why you think that. But you have to believe my feelings for you are different. And I know I've not been the most . . . straightforward.'

'Selena, I think you might be the most confusing thing that's ever happened to me. And I sat through AP Algebra.'

'Did not understand the reference, but beside the point,' I say, looking out of the window and not at him. I take a deep breath. 'And if you want me to tell you how I really feel, I'll tell you. I still like you. I like you more than I ever cared to admit, well, because you're annoying. But I think that's why I like you. I can be myself around you. You're the person who picks me up when I'm down, cheers me on when I need it. And I'm not going to change my mind. This is more real to me than anything else. I've been fighting it, and it's still so real to me.' I pause and wait.

Ty's face is blank, and I feel a rush of rejection. This is so much worse than what happened with Ollie.

'I should go,' I say, standing up.

'No,' says Ty, also standing up. 'Sorry, I'm . . . I'm also confused.'

'That's becoming clear,' I say.

Ty smacks his hands onto his face, exasperated. 'Selena, you know I like you.'

'Do I?' I say. 'In what way?'

'I like you in the way that everything about you consumes my every thought so much that I realised this is what falling for another person is.'

'Then why are you making this so hard?'

'Because we can't be together!' he finally exclaims, the words leaving him in a half-strangled scream.

'Because you're going to go to America?'

'Yes.'

'But you don't even want to go back.'

'This isn't about what I want.'

'Everything is about what you want! It should be about what *you* want. It's your life, as much as my life is my life.'

'Selena, it doesn't matter.' He sighs. He looks a bit defeated. 'Don't you think this is a bit cliched? Star-crossed lovers?'

'I wouldn't call us enemies by fate. More by the circumstance of you being a prick.'

He laughs, and I feel the tension release.

'I forget you're an English student. I meant how you will

be in London and I will be in the US.' He looks away, rakes a hand over his head. 'Which is why I shouldn't have kissed you. Mentally, I'm not in a good place right now. Yesterday? I had literally had an argument with my dad beforehand. He's insistent I go to Berkeley.'

I cross my arms. 'But what has that got to do with me?'

'Because you make this place feel like home, and I know that it isn't.' He raises his voice for the first time. I flinch. He shakes his head. 'Sorry, it's that every time I'm with you I feel at ease, I guess. You're the person I want to run to when everything is going wrong. You're the person who makes me feel myself. But I don't have a future here. And I'm deluding myself I do.'

I want to argue with him, ask him if I'm not worth it. But then I realise, it's not about me. It's about him. And there's nothing I can do about that.

Failure crashes over me. Because I had really hoped I would turn up here, and it would be like a movie or a song. That we'd get our happy ending.

It turns out life isn't straightforward.

'You're right, you shouldn't have kissed me.' I stand up, trying to hold in the tears. 'I'll see you around.'

Forty-Eight

I'm still figuring it out
I might look like I have it together
I just want this to last forever

'Figuring It Out' from
The Brink of Teenage Freedom

MY FIRST UNIVERSITY acceptance arrives later that day. A small one in London.

I gasp as I see the email in my inbox. I immediately tell Faye and Kira and we agree to meet up to celebrate after my work day. I don't tell Ty. I haven't spoken to him since yesterday.

In a few hours we're in the coffee shop, clinking cups together.

'To Selena Pia figuring it out,' says Kira.

'Well, there's a lot of things I haven't figured out,' I say.

'Would that be a certain next-door neighbour?' says Faye.

'I can't believe I've tried and failed with two next-door neighbours in the space of a month,' I say.

'Maybe you should try boys who live more than a few metres away from you,' suggests Kira. 'Try one road over next time.'

'At least we can make jokes about my sadness,' I say, rolling my eyes.

'Hey, if you can't laugh, you're going to cry,' says Kira. 'It's better this way.'

'Also, doesn't it feel like a lifetime since Ollie?' I say. 'I can't believe how much I liked him, considering how terrible he was!'

'He was not always terrible,' says Faye.

'Beg to differ,' mutters Kira.

'He was always an arse to you, but he did love Selena. At least once upon a time he did,' says Faye. 'You could see it. He just changed, we all have. I think that's what being eighteen is about.'

'Well, my grown-up choice is I've decided to let Ty go,' I say firmly.

'What does that mean?'

'It means Ty feels he has to go, and who am I to stop him. If he's determined, I've got to let him go.'

Faye is shaking her head. 'He likes you, you like him – why are you both making this so complicated?'

'Because his dad is insisting he goes!'

'Is that the whole of it?' says Faye, looking at me pointedly.

I crumble. Damn, she's good.

'What if it doesn't work out?' I mumble into my coffee.

'What?' says Kira.

'With Ollie, I thought he would be the one, and he clearly isn't. What if it doesn't work with Ty either?'

'Selena, you are smart and beautiful and have everything going for you,' says Kira, taking my hands. 'And Ty is one of the good ones. You can't put yourself down like this.' She pauses, thinking. 'But maybe this is one of those things not in your control. You've got to have hope.'

'Sure, I'll also hope I'll win this interview competition, then everything will work out fine,' I say, semi-sarcastically.

'And why won't you win the competition?' says Kira.

'Because the deadline is tonight at midnight and I've not interviewed anyone! Forget winning the competition, I'm not even going to enter it.'

'Selena,' says Kira, leaning forwards. 'You cannot not enter. It's fine if you don't win, but you have to try.'

'I've been trying! I've been calling up places. I nearly had Annie Banannie, but she had a family emergency. But I don't know anyone good enough to interview!'

'Well, if you really can't find anyone, you can interview me,' says Kira sitting back. 'And don't tell me I'm not good enough to interview. They'd be pulling it from the archives in twenty years' time, when I'm running the country.'

I laugh and shake my head. Kira always has a plan.

'But I'm sure there's the perfect interviewee out there,' Kira says. And Faye nods.

'You know what?' I say, looking at them both.

'What?' they chorus.

'I really hate it when you're both right.'

Forty-Nine

And every day that goes by
I have had you by my side
The woman I aspire to be
Mama, you made me

'Mama' from *Roses*

'HOW'S MY SOON-TO-BE university student?' Mum says, patting the spot next to her on the sofa. She pulls me in for a hug. 'Congratulations, Selena.'

'I can't believe I've got in somewhere,' I say. 'I'll actually be going next year.'

She squeezes me tightly. 'I'm going to miss you. What will I do without you?'

There it is. The thing I'm most afraid about. 'I don't have to go if you don't want me to. Or I can stay at home and commute in.'

Mum's head turns so sharply I didn't realise it was possible for her to move that fast.

'What are you talking about?' she says.

'What will you do without me?' I say. 'It's what you said. And . . . I don't know. That's why I don't need to go if you think I should stay.'

'Selena,' says Mum, moving so she's now sat fully facing me. I pivot so I'm sat cross legged on the sofa. 'There is no way on the planet I would let you miss out on university to stay here with me.'

'But what about your arthritis? Your cane . . .'

'Look,' says Mum, touching my hand. 'I have been looking after myself a long time, and I'll be able to do it for a time longer. You don't need to worry about me.'

'But who else will worry about you? I'm all you have.'

'You're the most important person I have in my life, that is true. But I am not alone, and I will be fine without you. You should go, experience university properly.'

'You don't really talk to Nani and Papa,' I whisper. 'And you're sick.'

'Oh Selena, you've really been feeling the brunt of this.' Mum looks visibly upset. 'Is this why you took so long to apply?'

All at once the immense pressure feels like it's going to explode in me. All this time, worrying and deciding and putting things off. It's too much. And I start crying.

'There doesn't seem like a good option,' I say, my voice shaking with the sobs. 'I want to go. But I don't want to leave you, or home. I'm so scared about the future. And it's just the two of us. So I have to be around for you.'

Mum pulls me into a hug. 'Selena, I wish you'd said something earlier. Because I would have told you, it's going to be fine.'

'But how do I know you're not just saying that so I go?'

'Well, you don't know, but you're going to have to believe me. I've always had a strong support network, even if you don't see it. Nani and Papa do support me, though we don't see each other often. I raised you by myself, but I've had people to lean on. Like you have your friends, I have mine too.'

'Who do you think I called after that outrageous house party you threw? Gina. And she made me feel better and was there for me, like she has been all these years.' She grips my shoulders. 'I will not be the person to hold you back. You have to live the biggest life you want to. That's all I want for you.'

I nod, wiping my tears. 'I don't want to let you down,' I say.

'As long as you try your best, you cannot let me down. I've had so many adventures in my life, but my biggest one has been raising you. And I can't wait to see what you do next.'

Adventures. I look at Mum, and I realise there's so little I know about her, except the big brushstrokes of her life. This house is littered with all the places she's been, everything she's seen, but there's still so much I don't know, because I've been too afraid to ask.

'Mum,' I say.

'Yes?'

'Please can I ask you to do something for me? And be honest about it.'

KAJAL PIA
"WHAT IS A GOOD LIFE?"

An interview by Selena Pia

I met Kajal at birth. As in, she gave birth to me. Kajal is my mother, if I'm not being clear enough. So, safe to say, I've known her my whole life. I'm taking this interview in the house I've grown up in, in Croydon.

'I moved here a year after you were born,' she tells me. 'I got pregnant unexpectedly, and went back to live with my parents. And it turns out moving back in with them wasn't the best idea.'

To unravel this thread, we need to go back much further in time. To long before I was even born.

Kajal Pia was the only daughter of Des and Naveena Pia, who had immigrated to London in the eighties. Born and bred in East London, Kajal was a creative and precocious child.

As her daughter, I can say she's a creative and precocious adult too. Once neither of us had any idea what to make for my science project, and she managed to convince my science teacher that our illustration of astrological signs somehow counted as an entry. It didn't, but she made a compelling argument, plus helped me create the poster.

'I was always getting into trouble, much to my parents' annoyance,' she says, not quite meeting my eye. 'But I was very good at school, even though I was a troublemaker.'

Des and Naveena had ambitions that Kajal was going to live out their immigrant parents' dreams, become super successful as either a doctor or an engineer. They had sacrificed so much for her, the least she could do for them was to get a good job, find a good husband and live a 'good' life.

'But what is a good life?' says Kajal, a mischievous flicker in her eye. 'I think we had very different views on that.'

Kajal told her parents she didn't want to go to university straight away. She was going to take a gap year. It was 2001, and gap years were the new norm. Kids were flying all over the world, lured by cheaper flights and promises of personal growth. Naturally, Des and Naveena were not keen on this.

'But it didn't matter to me,' says Kajal. 'I deferred my entry to study Law, packed a bag and went to Greece. It was the cheapest flight out of London I could get. In hindsight, was it crazy for a young, solo female traveller to pack up and leave? Yes. Now I have a daughter, do I realise why they flipped out so much when I called them from Athens? Yes. Would I do it again? Also yes.' There's that flicker of mischief again.

In Athens, Kajal got a job working in a museum cafe. 'A lot of tourists spoke English, so it was useful to have someone who could speak it fluently. In a sign of my naivety when I left home, I hadn't even considered the language barrier!'

Between making coffees and waiting tables, Kajal developed a strong interest in the ancient world.

'To me, it was so much more interesting than science and maths. It was the stories of humanity. How we got here.' She was taken under the wing of a leading female curator and was soon offered a job as her assistant.

Kajal was meant to be there for a year before continuing her studies, but she never turned back.

'I was learning more there than I ever would at university. Something which my parents couldn't wrap their heads around.'

She travelled the world, becoming a professional curator, working in China, Vietnam, before arriving in the place of her ethnic origin, India.

'I hadn't expected to fall in love with India the way I did,' she muses. I'm always reminded it's not only where she came from, but also where I'm from too. 'It was this faraway place when I was growing up, and my parents taught me some of the language, culture and traditions, but I never could really imagine what it was like until I went. And it was beautiful.'

Kajal started working in a museum there, where she fell in love with a fellow curator. 'It felt like pure magic at the time. In this beautiful country, with this beautiful man who promised me the world,' she says wryly. 'But I was still so young.'

Kajal fell pregnant. My origin story was always shrouded in mystery, much like a poorly written superhero. And now I can't believe I'm about to find out the details.

'The man's family didn't take to it too well,' she says. At this point she pats my knee. 'Which is why I never told you this. I didn't want you to think it was your fault, because it's entirely theirs. His family threatened to disown him for having a child out of wedlock. So he gave me a plane ticket and some cash, to go back to London. And because I had nothing else, I did. I never spoke to him again.'

Now, this is the first time we've really spoken about my aforementioned father. I've spent years wondering who he was. A pilot? A movie star? A spy?

But he was a man. A man who for some time my mum loved. A man who made me. Their story didn't last, but it shaped both of our lives.

I'm okay with that.

Kajal moved back in with her parents in East London.

'It was fine, but they were clearly disappointed in how my life had turned out,' she says, looking out of the window. 'But for me, my life had been brilliant. And the most brilliant moment of it all was when I had you.'

But Des and Naveen didn't want Kajal to return to museum life.

'They wanted me to stay local, get a small job somewhere, dream smaller now I was a mother. But I thought: why can't I have you and the life I want for us? Well, one argument led to another, and because I'm so stupidly independent, I left for a second time.'

She moved to the cheapest place she could afford to buy a house, Croydon, commuting in long hours to work at city museums, sometimes with a baby in tow.

'I had two good pieces of luck,' she tells me. 'One was that I made friends with my next-door neighbour, Meredith, who had a son a similar age and could watch you while I was at work if you couldn't go to nursery for some reason. The other was my friend Gina, who I met a work and who kept me together.'

Kajal climbed the museum ladder, becoming a member of boards and a well-respected voice in her field. She travelled a lot less, but displayed her treasures in her home. She lived her full life without regrets.

And she is an amazing mum. She's been there my whole life, for every essay I struggled to write, to twisting my ankle from cross-country. Every scrape, both physically and emotionally, my mum has been there for me.

Which is why when she got diagnosed with rheumatoid arthritis a few years ago, I promised I would be there for her. Despite the arthritis taking over her joints, it didn't stop her from pushing forwards with her life.

Kajal is now the Programme Director at the Croydon Museum, putting on local events for kids and adults. Her favourite events are the ones about the ancient world.

'There's nothing I would change and nothing

I am disappointed by,' she says. 'Even now my knees have gone, I am still happy to have the life I lead. I'm proud to make a difference to my community. And I'm so proud of the daughter I've raised.'

So what is a good life? After talking to Kajal, I've realised it's a life we live in the way we want to live it. It's what good looks like to us. It's having a mother that loves you and stands by you. It's not being afraid of what other people think, and reaching for your best.

It's something I hope I can honour her with throughout my life.

Fifty

'Winter' from *Dreamers*

'AND THE WINNER of the best interview is … Selena Pia,' says Gareth.

On Friday afternoon, we're at a writing staff meeting, with all of us standing up in a tiny conference room. Everyone immediately starts clapping for me. I feel shocked. I knew my article was good, but I didn't know if it was good enough. We read each other's articles earlier today. Tori interviewed a firefighter who had saved fifteen people from a beloved shop that had burnt down, and Doug had interviewed a local business owner who was going viral on TikTok.

Both were interesting, funny and moving, and I didn't know

what chance I had to beat them. I've been nervous all day. But it doesn't matter. Because I won!

I catch Tori's eye as I walk to the front. She gives me a nod.

'Your article was really good,' she whispers. 'I accept defeat.' I double take. That might be the nicest thing Tori has ever said to me.

'Selena, your interview impressed us not only for the great quality of writing and storytelling, but also for its heart. It showed it's really the ordinary people who make up this town, and how everyone's stories are unique,' says Gareth. 'Your prize is that it'll be published in tomorrow's paper, and you'll be covering the Rose Conrad concert for us.'

He hands me a frame, which has the printed newspaper version of my article in it. Inserted is a picture of me and Mum that I had submitted.

'Thank you, I don't know what to say.'

'You've got a bright future,' says Gareth, shaking my hand. 'I think your article was one of the best interviews I've ever read on this programme. I nearly cried at the end. Thank your mum for being so honest and sharing her story.'

'I will,' I say. 'She's going to be so pleased.'

'And I'm sure you are pleased with your Rose Conrad tickets! I know you're quite the fan.'

It's true, but for me, the real prize was finding out so much about Mum. About the father I never knew, and still don't really mind not knowing about. How our home came about. How we came about. And how, because Mum at her heart is such a survivor, she'll be fine without me.

It's time to go have some of my own adventures.

After telling Mum, I have to tell Kira and Faye.

'Your girl has got two Rose Conrad tickets,' I scream at the FaceTime to them. I'm lying on my bed, still in my work clothes.

'I can't believe you're going to go,' says Faye.

'After all that stress of not getting tickets! And how much you bitched and moaned about it,' says Kira.

'You even wrote a Secret Sender article about it,' says Faye.

'Okay, okay, no need to bring up the past,' I say. 'The point is, I have the tickets now. For this weekend.' I pause. 'I think the hard question is, who am I going to take?'

'Oh that's obvious,' says Kira.

'Totally,' says Faye.

I feel a sense of relief. 'You guys have already decided between you? That's good.'

'Yeah,' says Kira. 'You've got to take Ty.'

'Wait, what?' I say. 'You guys don't want to go? Ty isn't even speaking to me.'

'We discussed it,' says Faye, 'and we thought, number one, if only one of us went it would be unfair to the other, plus we couldn't decide between us, and two, you need to take Ty and tell him how you really feel. He loves Rose Conrad.'

'And three, you will owe us big time for this!' says Kira.

I would love to take Ty. But it feels like a betrayal to both of them.

'Are you sure?'

'Yes. Now stop asking us, otherwise we'll change our minds and Faye and I will have to Hunger Games to the death for the second ticket! Trust me, it's better this way,' says Kira.

Once again, it didn't feel right to tell Ty the news over text. It had to be in person. Which is easier said than done when your neighbour is a hermit who's avoiding you. But the concert is tomorrow. I have to tell him today. And as I arrive home from my final day at the *Croydon Post*, I see him outside, photographing the garden pond in the sunset.

I pull on my coat and race downstairs.

'Ty!' I yell, running up to the fence.

'What's happened?' he says, worry on his face as he runs over to meet me.

Okay, in hindsight, legging it out of my house screaming his name might cause some worry.

'I won,' I say, grinning at him over the fence. 'I won the competition.'

'Holy shit,' he says. 'Who did you interview?'

'Mum,' I say simply. 'And I discovered she's even more badass than I thought.'

'In that case, I need to read the article, because your mom

already seemed like a badass!' He smiles. 'Well done, Selena.'
He scuffs his shoe on the ground. 'I was afraid you wouldn't want to talk to me any more, after what we said a few days ago.'

'After you said you couldn't be with me.'

'Well yeah, that.'

I inhale, feeling the cool air fill my lungs. 'Ty, I want you to come and see Rose Conrad with me.'

He looks at me with shock. 'I was not expecting that,' he says.

'You've been on this journey with me since the start. You're the one who encouraged me to keep writing as the Secret Sender. And you're the one I want to be with all the time. And I need to get that off my chest. I like you so much more than a friend. And it might not work out in multiple ways, but it's what I want. I want to be with you.'

He meets my eyes, and I can't tell how he's feeling.

'Okay,' he says.

'Okay, what? Okay, I've heard you or okay, I'll come with you to see Rose Conrad?'

'I've heard you and yes to Rose Conrad.' He grabs my hand over the fence and squeezes. 'Thank you, Selena. And well done, Writer. I knew you could do it.'

Damn this boy can make my heart melt. Even when it's zero degrees outside.

Fifty-One

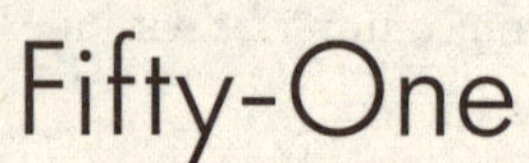

It'll be a while, but it'll be the best of times
Take a chance, take a shot
On this moment of time
For we might not have it again

'The Best of Times' from
The Brink of Teenage Freedom

THE MORNING OF the concert, I'm a mess. It feels like my entire life has been working up to this moment.

My mind is going into hyperdrive. What if I am near the front and someone from Rose Conrad's team spots how big a fan I am and invites me backstage? What if she sees me from the stage and clocks how I know the words to every song? What if I run into her on the way home, as she's dressed undercover but I know exactly what she looks like? All of these possibilities have a near-zero chance of happening – but you never know.

Kira and Faye arrive at lunchtime to help me get ready.

'I'm really sad you both can't come,' I say, as Faye braids glittery strands into my hair and Kira paints my fingernails.

'Me too, girl,' says Kira.

'But we're glad you can go,' says Faye.

'Yeah, you were the OG Rose Conrad fan,' says Kira. 'If anyone deserves to go, it's you.'

'And we'll be watching the livestream, for sure,' says Faye.

'It's the reason we're all friends,' I say, looking over to my school bag, where my Rose pin glints.

'It's the reason we all became friends,' says Kira. 'We're friends for so much more than that.'

'Also despite it,' says Faye. 'Do you remember in Year 9 when you sang 'Torn' twenty-four-seven?'

My chest seizes up and a strange choking sound comes from me.

'What's up?' says Faye. 'Did I pull too hard on your hair?'

'No,' I say, and I can hear my voice choke up too. 'It's just – who's going to remember these things about me when I go to uni?'

Faye pats my head soothingly. 'We're not going anywhere. We'll still be friends.'

'Yeah, and you'll get so many new firsts with your new uni friends too,' says Kira.

'Like what?'

'I don't know yet, but I don't think all your firsts happen before you're eighteen,' says Kira. 'And even then, you'll still have us, like Faye said.'

'Do you think we'll be friends forever?' I say.

To my surprise, it's Faye who responds, 'No.'

I laugh. 'I thought Kira would say that.'

'I'm not trying to be negative,' says Faye. 'I don't think we know the future. And that's okay. Maybe we'll be friends when we're fifty, maybe we'll be distant memories to each other. But what matters is right now, in the present, we're here for each other.'

'When did you become so wise?' I say, turning around to face her.

'When did we all start growing up?' she says, with a small smile.

'Are you excited for your apprenticeship next year?' I say.

'I'm excited to stop studying, honestly,' she says. 'And do something.'

'I'm excited to see what you become,' I say.

'*It'll be a while, but it'll be the best of times*,' sings Faye to me.

'Speaking of which, I should get going,' I say, looking at the time. 'Oh crap, I'm already late.'

'Didn't you set the time?' says Kira.

'Yes, but I lost track of it!' I say, stuffing on my shoes.

I pull them both into a group hug. 'Thanks for always being by my side,' I say.

'Go get 'em,' says Kira. 'Or I should rather say, "go get him".'

I roll my eyes. 'None of that will be happening tonight,' I say. 'I think he's made his feelings clear.'

'You don't know,' says Faye.

'You're both right, I don't know. Maybe he'll profess his undying love on the tube. While queuing for drinks. As the opening act comes on. So many opportunities.'

'Hey, you're the writer,' says Kira. 'You never know where the moment will take you. Be open minded.'

'I have to be open minded,' I say, opening my bedroom door and walking out. 'I've been waiting for this night for so long.' I turn back to them. 'You guys can get out yourselves, right?'

'Selena,' says Kira. 'Your mum gave me a key years ago.'

'I know, I know,' I say. 'See you both later. Love you!'

And with that, I run outside into the day, unable to believe this is the night I see Rose Conrad live.

— ★ —

I stand outside our houses and Ty is nowhere to be seen. Weird – if there's one thing I've learnt about him in the past few months is that for a teenage boy, he's strangely punctual. Where is he?

I look at my phone, no texts. I'm getting impatient. There's a reason I wanted to go this early. What if we miss a chance to get a prime spot?

I'm also freezing. I'm stood outside dressed in gauzy blue-green fabric that snakes around me, with the thickest coat I could find thrown on top. I'm going as the sea-green eyes from 'I Loved You Like That'.

Just when I am about to go and bang on his front door, Ty swings it open and slams it shut behind him.

He looks slightly erratic as he approaches me, with this weird energy.

'What's going on?' I say.

'Let's go,' he says, grabbing my hand and pulling me forwards. 'We've got a show to get to.'

We barely speak as we navigate into London, and I can tell he's twitchy but he won't talk about why.

'What's going on?' I ask again.

'We can talk in the queue. We've got a long wait,' he says. 'I want to make sure we get there first.'

We sit in tubes full of girls in tulle and lace, smiling and laughing, and all I can think about is how I'm going to have to beat them to the front of the line.

I take off my jacket, sling it over my arm. I know my outfit is ridiculous for normal wear, but on this tube, anything goes.

Ty makes a noise.

'What?' I say. He blinks, double takes.

'You look . . .' He pauses, breaks off. 'Well, you look—'

'Like a five-year-old dressed me?' I say. Do I look like a clown?

'Incredible,' he says, and in that moment time stands still. He waves his free hand up and down, struggling with words. 'Just, wow, Selena. You've always been the brightest thing in the room to me. But you look, just, wow.'

He's so devastatingly earnest I don't know what to do with it. I nod dumbly, my throat feels dry. I feel like I could cry or laugh at any second.

'That feels like a stupidly nice thing to say on the tube,' I say.

'I think any time is a good time to say a stupidly nice thing,' he says with a smile.

'You look nice too,' I say, smiling at him. Even though he's wearing a T-shirt and jeans.

'Don't lie,' he says, reaching into his pocket and pulling out a tube of glitter. 'I know I'm underdressed, I'm waiting until we get there to glitter up.'

'Well, I'm glad you're prepared.' I laugh.

'I'm taking this very seriously,' he says. He thinks about it, 'But maybe not as seriously as you.'

Fifty-Two

I exit stage left

My guitar's taken off at my right

My feet tired and sore

But the magic of the night keeps me alight

It's the end of the show

But it's not the end of us

'The End' from *The In-Between*

'OKAY, THERE MAY have been other people who have taken this seriously,' says Ty as we arrive at Wembley.

'There's too many people here!'

'How do you know?' says Ty. 'You said you've not been to Wembley before. This stadium is very big.'

'Look at the amount of people already queuing,' I hiss. And there in front of us, is a large queue of people in various costumes of floaty materials. There must be enough material here to drape Buckingham Palace. Rose Conrad is famous for her love of everything bohemian, and the fans have got the memo.

'Oh good, the queue is moving,' says Ty. 'I still don't understand why you British people love to queue so much.'

I stand there, watching the volume of people mass and move.

'Come on,' says Ty, grabbing my hand and pulling me forwards.

I feel Ty pull me through the crowd and up the stairs to the stadium. I see the back of his head, feel my hand in his. And I don't want to let go. Instead I keep hold of him, as he leads us to the back of the queue for the entrance we need to go through.

The queue is moving forwards slowly, people chatting to each other eagerly. I see girls dressed as different songs: strings of stars for 'Under the Night Sky', feathered dresses referencing the cover of 'Jungle', where Rose Conrad was dressed as a parrot. Then there's some memes, white T-shirts scribbled with her SNL sketch quotes. And I feel this deep sense of belonging. These are my people; I am meant to be here.

And I'm still holding Ty's hand.

I don't drop it as we start moving slowly forwards. And there's no reason to keep holding it either; we both aren't going to get separated from each other in this queue moving at a snail's pace.

But he keeps holding my hand too.

I feel the electricity sing and spark between us. I wonder if he feels it too. There's no denying, as much as I've tried denying, the connection between us.

I lean into him. He tenses briefly, then lets go of my hand. I start to pull myself away, but he swings his arm around my shoulder, pulling me in closer.

For a split second, I see us through other people's eyes, looking like an ordinary couple standing here. This version of Ty and Selena. The ones who are happy and content and queuing to see their favourite artist. And maybe for one day, this is what we can be.

For a few minutes, we don't say a word to each other, and I'm caught in this being the moment, and the worry it will disappear if we do or say anything else. But then Ty leans down to me and points at a girl two rows up with a giant feather headdress and says, 'If she's stood in front of us I will have to rip that thing off her head.'

I snort. 'Not very considerate, is it? Plus, how many birds do you think died for it?'

'I don't think birds die when they lose feathers,' says Ty, with a wry smile.

'With the amount of feathers on that headdress, I wouldn't be so sure!'

He laughs, and I'm looking up at him and laughing too, and his arm is still around me.

We chat our way through the queue, and my annoyance at the number of people ahead of us starts to disappear. The number of people is the reason Ty and I can spend time like this together.

At the front of the line, we break apart. I go and scan our tickets, and then after a security check, we are in.

'Are you ready to get a prime spot?' says Ty.

I roll my eyes. 'I'll take a good spot. Clearly I'm not as much of a superfan as I thought I was.'

He nudges me with his shoulder. 'Hey, you deserve to be here. How many people here can say they got their tickets through talent and grit?'

We end up nowhere near the front, but we get a spot that I can still see the stage from. As people continue to pile in, I look around, at all of the people in tiny seats in the sky, and I feel very present here. Like I'm part of a mass, but I'm still at the centre of it all.

'Okay,' I say, looking at him. 'We're in, we've got time to kill. Will you now tell me what's going on?'

'I read your interview with your mum,' he says, looking down at me.

'And that's what you're being so weird about? My writing?'

'No!' he says. 'It was great. One of the best interviews I've read. Writer, you can write.' He bites his lip. 'No, what happened was, I read your article about your mum, and so much clicked for me when I read it. Your mum was brave, Selena. She did what she wanted to, because it was the right thing for her. She didn't let anyone tell her what to do or not to do. And yeah, it made life harder, but it was clearly worth it.'

I see the nervousness in his eyes. 'It really struck a nerve with you,' I say softly.

'It did. I've been telling you to go put yourself out there, and you have with your writing. Meanwhile, I've been refusing to stand up to my dad because I was afraid. But your article showed me it's worth doing the scary thing if it's the right thing. And after you told me you wanted to be with me, well the truth is I want that too and I don't want to fight it any more. So I did what had to be done.'

My heart is in my mouth.

'So what did you do?'

'I told Dad I wasn't going back to the US, whether he liked it or not. That I've been accepted into some great universities here and I want to stay near Mum and Daze. There's nothing left for me in the States.' His hand grazes my cheek. 'But there're things for me here.'

'What are you saying?' I whisper.

'Selena Pia,' he says, touching a strand of my hair. 'I think you're brilliant, funny, smart, but yet have the ability to do some dumb things sometimes. I think you're one of the most human people I've ever met. And I think it's time to stop overthinking things.' He leans down and I look up at him, and it feels totally right.

I don't know how this will turn out. But if there's one thing I've learnt, it's that we can't be scared of doing things because we don't know what will happen next.

'We've got to try, right?'

He smiles at me, and in that moment all I see is those green-brown eyes before he closes the gap between us with a kiss.

We stand there for what feels like forever, until the crowd goes silent around us. We break away, turn towards the stage.

The lights go up. The show begins.

And the best night of my life so far starts.

But I know there might be better ones in the future.

Acknowledgements

Thank you to Hazel, Becky and the Fox & Ink team for the support of *say what you think*, and giving me the space so I could move to San Francisco. Ty and his world are better off for it. Tilda – thank you for seeing the vision and pushing me editorially, I am better off for it.

I'm forever grateful to my agent Lauren and the team at Bell Lomax Moreton for championing my work.

Ysabelle – you were the first reader of this, and my first ever reader since we were Ty and Selena's age. Thank you for your wise words and feedback. And here's to reading about more people who look like us in YA fiction!

I wrote this entire novel having just moved to San Francisco, in a whirlwind time of my life. Shoutout to the *Shut Up and Write!* Richmond district writing group, whose support, camaraderie and motivation fuelled a lot of this writing. And shoutout to the bagels of Cafe Enchante, which also fuelled a lot of this work.

Rose Conrad was inspired by my unashamed love of Taylor

Swift, who I've been a fan of since I was Selena's age. I saw The Eras Tour three times the year before I wrote this, and the lore of her eras inspired my own lore for Rose.

To my family, Mum, Dad, Aaron and Sophia, for the endless support of all my writing. I was born and raised in Croydon, and am proud to represent it here.

My friends – on both sides of the world, you all inspire me.

Finally, thank you, Lawrence. My eternal reader, even though I know you'd rather be reading science fiction, and constant cheerleader. Your support makes all of this possible.

I**T'S ONE THING TO HAVE AN UNFLATTERING PHOTO** of yourself on @BirdsHillHotOrNot, it's another to have a humiliating video of you there too – which Candice posted last night after our biology run-in yesterday.

The problem with the account is that it's private but it's followed by everyone in the school, making it completely public and also completely unaccountable at the same time.

'I can't believe she wiped a heart on your face?! A heart! Your face!' Lucie says. 'She knows no bounds.'

We're heading to the arts block, a building on the fringes that is home to the art, music and drama studios. It's currently peppered with sign-up flyers for the school musical production of *We Will Rock You*.

Today, Lucie is wearing black skinny trousers, a floaty black shirt and a black wide-brimmed hat. Complete with black sunglasses, of course. I am again rocking my school receptionist outfit, with a beige suit this time.

'It's over, Lucie. I'll get my time after Birds Hill. Candice is going to peak at life now; she can have all the power she wants. I'm playing the long game.'

'You're missing the point here. She basically assaulted you with an internal organ!'

I look Lucie in the eye. 'We both know there's no point in going up against Candice. She runs this school, and her parents run the governors' board. I'm being the bigger woman.'

'You're not being the bigger woman; you're being a coward.'

'Snitches get stitches, Lucie. It's a tale as old as time. We'll be telling it to our grandkids.'

I take this as a good moment to change the subject.

'You know it's February? Are you wearing sunglasses inside too?' I say as we walk in.

'Of course I am. I'm going for A-list-celebrity-on-the-run vibes today.'

'I'm no expert, but I think the shades might get in the way of seeing your lunch?'

She whips off the sunglasses, her blue eyes blinking in the school's fluorescent light. 'You are correct – I cannot see a damn thing. What would I do without you, oh practical one?'

'Lead a more interesting life?'

She puts her sunglasses on me, making the world shaded. 'A life without Maya would be like a life wearing sunglasses constantly: incredibly dull.'

'But more stylish?' I laugh and tug off the shades as we head into the rehearsal room, which I get unlimited access to as an

A level Music student. Granted, I think I'm meant to use it for violin practice rather than hiding and eating lunch.

'This Hot or Not account is the worst,' I say, biting into my cheese and chilli chutney sandwich after we sit down and take out our phones.

'It feels like Candice has ripped it off from an old movie or TV show,' says Lucie.

'The girl has never had an original thought in her life,' I reply, opening up Instagram. 'So it's not surprising she's a rip-off.'

'What's new on it?' says Lucie. Candice has posted three posts since yesterday, alternating between hot and not. Not great for whoever they are about, but at least the new posts have pushed us to the bottom of the pile.

'What's so annoying is that reading it is so addictive,' I say. 'Why does her opinion have this control?'

'Because we allow her to,' says Lucie, snatching my phone. 'Oh, it's a hot post!'

'Who is it this time?' I ask.

'To be fair, it is someone who is hot, rather than just her friends,' says Lucie, and starts reading out loud in a sing-song voice. 'Hot: Harry Wu caught stepping out of the drama studio. Musical theatre may normally be for dorks, but no doubt this leading man has won our hearts.'

I take my phone back and glance at the photo.

Harry has a bone structure gifted to him by the gods. At eighteen, no one is meant to be this good-looking. He has a chiselled jaw, a slim frame that would be too lanky on anyone but him, and a captivating smile. The standard sixth-form uniform actually suits him. Unlike half the school, Harry doesn't need to alter his clothing to stand out. With a face like that, no one's looking at your clothes. And when he's on a stage, you can barely take your eyes off him.

'It's so unfair he photographs so well,' I say.

'That's what you get for being hot. Also, she's expanding to other year groups. Harry's in the year above, right?'

'I hope she gets bored of doing this soon. Candice deciding the fates of every person is getting to be a bit much.'

I scroll down the feed to a photo of Candice. Obviously, she's posted herself up. It's a candid photo of her with a coffee cup near the school gates. I bet she staged a full photoshoot to pull off such a carefree shot.

HOT: Candice Riley getting her morning caffeine shot. How does this lush girl manage to stay on top of her grades, friends and social life, while looking so put together? The secret is a skinny flat white every morning, she tells Hot or Not with a coy smile.

'I can't believe she writes this stuff about herself. Did you see that the coffee shop by the school had a queue outside it this morning?' I say.

'The myth of Candice Riley never ceases to amaze,' says Lucie, rolling her eyes.

I swipe off Instagram and notice the time.

'Crap, I need to grab my violin before the end of lunch,' I say, standing up and brushing crumbs off me. I notice some chilli chutney has escaped onto my white shirt. Great. 'I'll see you later.'

'You're helping me babysit tonight, remember?' Lucie calls out to me.

'Wouldn't miss the terrible twins for anything!'

A minute later, I walk into the storage room looking for my violin. People love to move things around in here. It's filled with discarded posters for old recitals, amps with hazardous electrical leads poking out and drum kits that are missing a piece. Finally, there are everyone's instruments: zipped up like they're in body bags, waiting for breath and movement to bring them to life. I find my violin tucked next to a forlorn oboe and take it out of its case to give it a quick tune.

The wood has a familiar weight to it, as I rest it on the crook of my elbow, positioning it under my jaw, as if in a caress. Let's be fair, it's the closest to a real caress I'm ever going to get.

I tighten my bow in preparation, and get ready to tune. People normally need a piano, but I have the eerie ability to know what each note sounds like in my head. I'm pitch perfect.

I close my eyes, and tweak and turn the pegs to get the notes crystal clear. An out-of-tune violin is like a dagger to the heart.

Heart. I shudder. Bile rises in me as I remember the cool flesh against my skin.

Then I do what I know best. I feel the shame, transfer it into a minor key, sad and sorrowful, a sonata for the moment. Then it dissolves into anger and my arm is flying over the violin. Staccato notes, major key, an angry and deep vibrato. I end feeling exhausted but rejuvenated.

And then I hear the boy singing.

'How do I know?

Where to begin?

How do I find the person within?'

The voice is full of sorrow, with a rich tonality that makes me hold on to every word. But it's not just the singing that makes me pause. He's playing the piano too. A slightly clunky chord progression, as if he is thinking about what would fit best with his words. Together it is achingly raw.

I realise the sound is coming from the music studio that is adjacent to the storage room. A sliver of light escapes from the door. It is ajar. A massive security breach for everyone's instruments, but a door to the mystery boy's voice.

Without really realising my feet are moving, I walk towards the door.

'How do I piece together a mind

That I thought I knew

That I thought I could find?'

Lyrics are always something I struggle with. And this is impressive. He sounds haunted, really living the words. Part of me wants to open the door and see who it is, but the other part wants to wait and listen. Who knows what I'd find on the other side of the door.

He pauses, hits a few keys on the piano. I know what he's doing; searching for a cadence he can't find. I lean in closer to the door.

It feels so wrong, standing here. Like I'm reading someone's diary. Getting an intimate glimpse into someone's mind without their knowledge.

He starts again, tweaks the key.

'How do I know? . . .'

And with the first chord of the piano, it overcomes me. I pick up my violin and start to play, in sync with his chorus. I match his chords and add a couple of motifs, making it sound distinct.

I'm reminded of how amazing music is. Just pressing and pulling objects in certain ways creates soundwaves that travel to our ears and fire neurons to our brain, which fits it all together to make meaning. Two people standing with a wall between them, able to work together just through sound.

He stops.

There's a beat of silence. Has he realised that I'm playing with him?

He starts again, from the top, and I overlay on his lyrics. His voice is stronger now, like my music is carrying it too. The piano is more volatile, a few slides and slips of emotion.

I wonder what he's singing about. Is it about a girl? Or maybe a boy? Or maybe he's singing about himself, finding out who he is? I'm welling up, but I know that tears on the fingerboard can really hamper your movements.

He stops. I stop.

There is silence.

I'm about to leave when he says, 'You can come through if you want?'

I'm silent. There's no way actually seeing me is going to improve this moment. Better if we both just call it a day.

'I promise, I don't bite. It is the music studio, I wouldn't say the people who hang out here are the most threatening,' he says. As if reading my mind.

I briefly wonder who the voice belongs too. He's not in my year – I would have recognised it. There's something vaguely familiar about it though – so he's either the year above or below. Which is good, because it would be embarrassing if this was a deep-voiced Year 8 I'd just improvised with.

'This is the point where I find out you left ten minutes ago and I've been talking to myself the whole time.' He sighs out loud.

I take a deep breath, hold on to my violin and walk through the door.

Also available from Fox & Ink Books